THE PRISM FILES BOOK ONE

THE FRACTURED PRISM

BRENDAN NOBLE

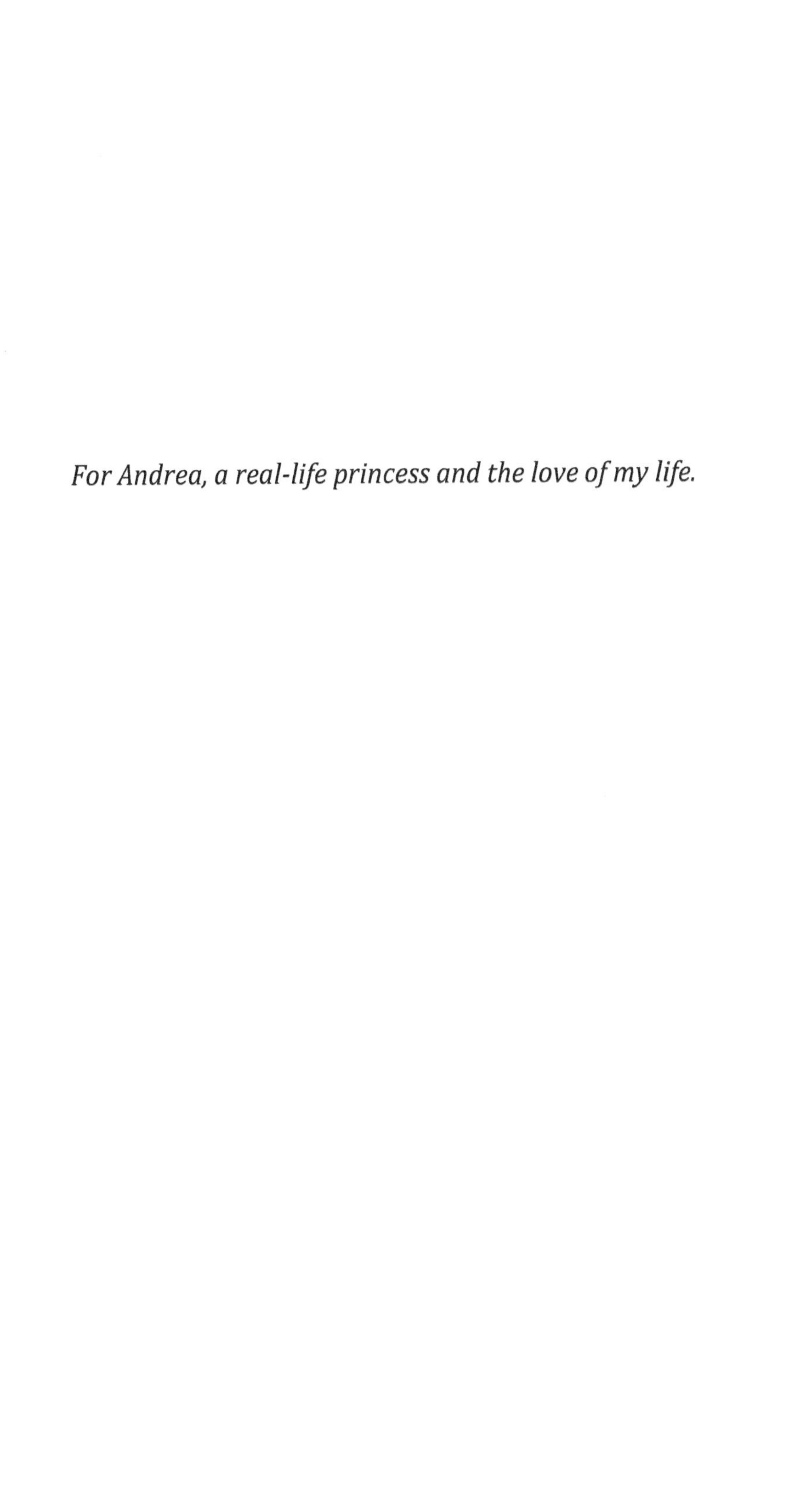

For Andrea, a real-life princess and the love of my life.

CRIMSON
REIGNS
BRENDAN NOBLE

Contents

Chapter 1

Two windows on the south wall allowed the tiniest slice of moonlight to creep into the otherwise dark room. The stairs creaked outside for a moment before complete silence.

We were motionless, barely even breathing. The silence was deafening. The seconds seemed like an eternity, and my heartbeat felt like a drum inside of my chest. Delaware peaked her head into view, her red dog tag earring glimmering in the moonlight. We're doomed.

She ducked back into hiding just as they blew the door off its hinges, and the light from the hall flooded the room. The intruders slammed furniture against the walls, and a wave of shouting hit me like a brick as they searched the room. "I thought I saw something over here," one of them yelled as he approached the ashy brick fireplace. A harsh flashlight beam scanned the hearth, then searched up the first few feet of the chimney.

No, no, no. They're going to find Delaware. Do I sit back and hope, or do I distract them?

Wiggling in the crawl space above the bookshelf in the corner, I grabbed a small combat knife from my pocket and tossed it onto the wood floor behind the secret police. The resulting *thud* prompted them to divert their attention from the chimney as the knife skidded across the floor. *She better be thankful. I liked that knife.*

A stern voice near the door barked across the room: "Find them now! We can't let these terrorists get away again! I know the two downstairs weren't the only ones here."

"Damn it," I muttered, prompting a flashlight in my general direction. We couldn't afford to lose Southpaw and Bobcat, but it was too late for them now. They would be tortured before being killed... a terrible way to die and exactly what we signed up for when we joined the Militia. I didn't have time to dwell on it now, though. We needed to survive if we wanted to worry about grieving.

Drawing in a forced breath, I hoped the crack between the ceiling and the shelf was deep enough to avoid the flashlight's beam, or at least that the intruders couldn't see me from eye level. The beam scanned through the crack before hitting me in the back and hovering for a second. *Crap!* I winced and waited for the shout, but it never came. The light moved away. "Must have come from outside." I released a raspy breath. *Too close.*

At least Razor is well hidden. He was under the trap door covered by the trunk in the opposite corner. They had searched the trunk itself but hadn't considered moving it, which left the barely visible gap between the two boards hidden for now.

As if reading my mind, one Blue Tag intruder slowly moved towards the trunk, tugged at it, and then began pulling. I watched in fear as the chest screeched away from the corner and had nearly uncovered the trap door when the intruder that seemed to be in charge fired a bullet into the ceiling, causing my ears to ring as the noise echoed in the small space.

"Well boys, I guess they made it out." I saw her pace around for a second, taking one last look through the room. "Burn the place down, just in case."

That was met with laughter from a few of the intruders, and the smell of gasoline slowly filled the room as the footsteps left. We waited a few moments before exiting our hiding spots. The small room was trashed, but we were unharmed, for now.

Delaware coughed to get the ash out of her lungs and flicked a brown tuft of hair from her eyes. "We need to get out of here, *now*. Any ideas?"

Razor was dazed, his narrow green eyes lost in some other world. His black tag earring smacked his face as he shook his head sharply. "I... I don't know." He was breathing hard and looked disoriented. "They got them, they got Bobcat and Southpaw. We're so screwed."

I grabbed his shoulders intently as his thick black hair fell over his face. "Pull yourself together man." Turning sharply towards Delaware, I pointed towards the door. "We need to get to the roof before they set this place ablaze."

Her eyes were wild. "They will see us!"

"Listen, Del. If we go out the window, we will fall right on top of them, and we obviously can't go out the front door. If you don't have a better idea grab Razor and let's go." She shook her head. I walked towards the door and cautiously looked outside before waving to them and whispering, "C'mon, we don't have time."

She rolled her eyes and reluctantly grabbed Razor, following quickly into the hall before looking up at me. "Coyote, what are you doing?"

I was hanging from one arm holding a small handle on the ceiling in the hall. "The latch is stuck, one second." I curled up my body before pushing down with my momentum, breaking open the door. The ladder slid to the floor just as I felt the heat.

Chapter 2

"Get up the ladder. Go!" I grabbed Delaware and pushed her up. Razor was lean but slowing her down significantly, and the fire had already reached the second floor. Delaware's small frame may have earned her codename, but it sure wasn't helping her half-carry Razor.

As the flames approached, she was almost to the roof but making far too slow of progress. Behind her I groaned, trying not to scream as the smoke filled my lungs. The heat was unbearable, and the smell of charred wood burned my lungs. I coughed and looked up the ladder to see Delaware slipping. *Dang it Razor.* I sighed. *Now or never.* Taking a three-step run-up, I put my foot on the bottom rung before throwing myself up into Delaware, knocking her and Razor out into the open air and ricocheting me back down the ladder.

In the resulting scramble to return to my feet, my left arm slammed into a burning floor board, searing through my jacket and sending a setting my nerves ablaze. I groaned in agony as my whole body coiled on the floor from the pain and my eyes watered from the smoke. *You need to live. Go!* Struggling to my feet, I stumbled towards the ladder and pulled myself up with my right arm as the other hung, useless, at my side. Each step felt like a mile as my lungs screamed, calling for air.

Smoke poured out behind me as I reached the top and pulled

myself onto the roof, coughing and wiping away the tears that were running down my face. Pulling myself to my feet, I muttered to the others, "Let's go, now. We don't have time to rest. The fire will reach us soon." I stumbled over to Razor. "You almost got all of us killed! We got you out of the house, but Delaware can't make that jump for you. Look at me, Razorblade!" My voice shook with adrenaline. "*Look* at me Razor! I don't want to leave you behind. We've made it this far. Don't give in now."

Razor grabbed my arms and eased them away. "I... I will try."

"Good enough." I sputtered, then coughed again and stumbled over to the southern edge of the small building, looking over it and calling back to them. "It's a two-story drop down into the bushes. It'll hurt but you'll be fine. Delaware, you go first and make sure Razor gets down safe after you. I'll be right behind him."

Delaware smiled, her big red cheeks full of anticipation, matching her tag. She tightened her brunette ponytail, took four quick steps towards the ledge, and jumped, flying past the bushes and rolling as she hit the ground, absorbing the impact well. Although she would never become a gymnast, she sure knew how to fly like one.

Razor then stumbled to the edge and fell more than jumped. He landed in the bushes on his shoulder, which did not make a friendly noise as he lacked much of anything, fat or muscle, to break the fall. I quietly called down, "You alright?"

His young raspy voice responded weakly, "Screw this." *Guess he's alive at least.*

I looked back towards the door to the roof. Even without the fire, there was no way to go back for Southpaw and Bobcat. They were gone, and that was on me. *Live first, mourn later.* I sighed, tucked in my injured arm, and threw myself over the edge. Luckily, for me at least, the bush provided a decent enough cushion, though my arm still felt the impact and stabbed in pain. I pulled myself to my feet and looked at Razor's dislocated shoulder. "I thought the bushes would be enough. Sorry. We need to go. Delaware can fix it when we're clear."

Razor groaned and looked up at the burning house longingly. Delaware and I turned to leave. Razor didn't budge.

I grabbed his arm. "Razor... Razor! We need to go. We lost them, and I hate it, but if we stay here they'll get us too, so *come* on!"

He nodded solemnly and his sharp green eyes focused before he followed me, holding his arm while Delaware took the rear. We shuffled across the backyard and the one behind it, through to the opposite neighborhood street.

The world was dark except for the moonlight and the eerie flickering of the fire, which emitted an aura around the surrounding area. A few Yellow and Orange Tag residents of the area were outside, wondering what was going on. In this part of town, no one would question us running around, though. We were just another group running from the secret police of the United People's Front, aka the UPF. It was 2020, and Red Tags fleeing from death had been an everyday occurrence in St. Paul for decades.

The three of us moved slowly through the side streets, heading south, towards the Mississippi River's northward bend. The Summit Hill safehouse had been an important one for our operations in St. Paul, but it was lost now. The mission had taken its toll in lives and resources. *I just hope this stupid flash drive is worth it.*

As we crossed West 7th Street and approached the riverfront, I looked back at the heart of St. Paul. I could just see the remnants of the old Minnesota Capitol building, now the headquarters of the St. Paul branch of the UPF, less than two miles from the safe zone. Even from this distance, we could see its intimidating white dome stabbing into the night. The red and gold Northern Mississippi flag hung below. Delaware noticed my gaze. "I wonder what it was like to look at that building and not feel fear."

I kept staring. "I'm not sure it was ever like that. One government rises from another's ashes, but they're all the same." After a moment, I turned to look the other direction and could smell the river just across the road. "We're almost there. Let's go."

We began crossing the High Bridge over the Mississippi, entering the Riverview safe zone, which we called "The Enclave." In reality, it was nothing but the worst of the slums. Nobody but the Reds and a few rebellious Oranges lived there, in addition to their Black Tag children, for good reason. Ever since they bombed the hell out of it during the Third American Civil War, the place was a disaster. You lived in a wreckage of a building, if you had a building to live in. It made a perfect home base for the Militia: no cameras, no slave owners, no UPF goons.

The old High Bridge was in rough shape. Chunks of the cement siding had fallen off, leaving gaping holes. The rusty metal that supported it creaked, and you could just hear the calm flow of the Mississippi splashing into its supports nearly fifty meters below. The view from the bridge was amazing, and despite the mental and physical pain I was in, I couldn't help but look in awe. To the east, the lights of downtown St. Paul cut through the night sky. I could hear sirens echoing from downtown - likely the fire crews responding far too slowly to the fire at the safe house. To the west, there was almost nothing but nature in sight as the trees and hills along the river's sides covered the view of Minneapolis. Only its lights were apparent in the distance, like a halo above the trees.

Sometimes I liked to come and sit along the side of the bridge, when I wasn't running a mission or working late, and would just watch in the night. It was peaceful and some nights I needed the time to sit and think. Tonight was not one of those nights.

I sighed and continued down the bridge. *How am I going to tell Zeus I lost two of his agents?*

We reached the southern end of the bridge and entered the Enclave. Delaware and I pulled our smoky bandanas from our faces now that we were away from the cameras. Razor had lost his in the fall and we just had to hope the night covered his identity well enough. I looked down at mine: the crimson emblem of a coyote stared back at me from the black fabric. It was hard to know if Coyote was just a part of me or if he was me.

Facial recognition was everywhere, except the Enclave, and it was one of the only things that worked in the People's Democratic Republic of Northern Mississippi. Despite the cameras being often ineffective in the dark, we used the bandanas, hoods, and (during the day) sunglasses to protect our identities during missions. If the UPF figured out who you were, you were never heard from again. They mostly kept out of the Enclave, though, to avoid being shot at from every corner and because the area was too desolate to be worth retaking. Not everyone there was a Militia member, but enough were that it was a risk for them to come anywhere near it. Besides, thee UPF had enough on their hands controlling the Twin Cities, Milwaukee, Des Moines, and the other actually useful areas under their control. After ninety-nine years of reigning over Northern Mississippi, they'd become ineffective and complacent beyond those centers.

We zig-zagged through the disorganized dirt and crumbled cement paths until we reached an old bombed out apartment building. Nothing but the first floor and parts of the second floor had survived, but it had a massive basement, where we made our base.

Poseidon, my mentor and another Red Tag, was leaned back against the wall as we approached. He ran his hand through his early graying beard. "How'd it go?" After scanning Razor's shoulder, my burned arm, and noticing only three of us made it back, he sighed. "Shit. What happened?"

I looked at Delaware. "Take Razor down to the med-bay, I'll be down in a second." The two of them shuffled through the rickety door. I looked into the dirt, uncomfortable with my failure, and kicked it restlessly. "Someone ratted us out. They knew the exchange was taking place and where the safe house was. We lost Southpaw and Bobcat." I sighed. "Do you think..."

He gave a deep sigh, understanding where I was going. "I'll talk to Zeus for you. He won't be happy."

Poseidon was one of the other Militia lieutenants, and one of Zeus's older brothers. Both had previously served as Captain of the Militia before El Capitan, but they preferred to stay as lieutenants. It was weird to be in the same position as them, with the twenty-five year or so age gap, but they didn't let age factor into making decisions, and Poseidon never held his mentorship of me over my head.

I looked up at him. "Thanks, Poseidon. I really appreciate it."

He crossed his arms and laid his head against the wall, looking up into the night sky. "You get the drive at least?"

I looked aimlessly around at the ruined buildings around us. "Luckily. I hope we can actually make use of it."

"Me too, Coyote. Speaking of. El Capitan is waiting for you. You should go see him."

I nodded. "Talk later."

I walked down the creaky wooden stairs to the third of the five floors in the basement and entered our sad excuse for a medical bay. The little energy we got from the solar panels around the building was barely enough to keep the lights on, and the flickering wasn't enough to distract you from the obvious makeshift style of the place. Old folding tables were used as medical beds, blood stains were everywhere, and we lacked pretty much any equipment that a real hospital would have.

Delaware was working on Razor's shoulder at the nearest table when I arrived. While she wasn't a medic, she had picked up a few tricks from watching the doctors. She gave me a slight smile as I passed.

I waved down one of the Orange Tag doctors. "You got anything for this?" I showed him my arm and the burn that was showing through the hole in my white jacket's sleeve.

"One second." He grabbed a knife, gripped my arm, and cut off the sleeve from above the burn. *No worries, I didn't like that jacket anyway.* He applied some type of ointment that stung but was nothing compared to the searing pain from the burn itself, and then wrapped my arm in gauze. "Obviously using this arm is going to hurt for a while, and it will probably have some serious scarring. Keep the wound clean and please don't get in any fights for a while, Coyote."

"Keep it clean and use my right arm more in fights. Gotcha, thanks doc." He shook his head as I jumped off the medical table, gave a mini salute, and marched back over to Delaware and Razor, the latter of which was complaining about something, as per the usual.

"...on two. You said on three, damn it!"

Delaware looked at me, gave a wry smile, and rolled her eyes before directing her attention back to Razor. "You would have moved if I did it on three and then your shoulder would be even worse." Razor grunted something under his breath that I'm sure involved a few four-letter words.

I stepped in. "Now, if you guys are done with arithmetic, we need to see the boss." I looked to the side and took a breath. "I'm not looking forward to this."

Chapter 3

We reached the bottom floor of the basement, also known as the war room. Dozens of Reds sat with headphones on along the edges of the room, corresponding via radio with agents and patrols across the region and tracking their positions on the computers. In the center of the room was an old pool table that we had turned into a strategic map; markers of all colors and shapes were spread across it, indicating important buildings, agent locations, and more. A strong aroma of cigarette smoke wafted through the room, mixing with the ashy smell from decades of disrepair. *He is definitely here.*

El Capitan was in his usual position: hunched over the map when he wasn't barking orders at someone. With his red hair and beard the guy looked like he belonged in the old Irish Republican Army, not the Northern Mississippi Militia. Even his tag was red. He liked to say he was born with brown hair, but he killed so many tyrants that it stained him red. You didn't mess with El Capitan.

I smiled as we approached, hoping to lighten the mood a little and avoid death by an angry El Capitan. Stopping at the table, I slapped my hands against its sides and exclaimed, "Oh captain, my captain!"

He didn't look up from the map and spoke with a Milwaukee

accent, "Cut the crap Coyote. What part of 'without being detected' didn't you understand."

I paused for a second and crossed my arms defensively. "Something went wrong. They knew where we'd be."

El Capitan looked up at me, still leaning on the table, his sunken eyes like daggers. "I've heard reports of *both* Southpaw and Bobcat being captured as well as one of our safehouses burning down. What happened?"

Sighing, I paced along the table, looking at nothing in particular on the map. "Well. The initial meet-up went well. The five of us got the camera locations from them and were about to leave when the UPF goons swarmed the place. One of those bastards must have leaked the location for the transfer to make some side money. We barely made it out but couldn't shake them. The safehouse seemed like a reasonable spot to lay low until they gave up looking, but apparently, they knew about that too. Bobcat and Southpaw were downstairs when they broke in..." I lowered my head. "I doubt they even had a chance to hide."

His cold glare continued as he paced around the table, ending up right in front of me. "Please tell me you have the flash drive."

I reached into my bag and pulled out the small black drive. *So much lost for such a little thing.*

He snatched it eagerly from my hands, hesitated, and then spoke again, softer, "I'm glad you're okay. I can't afford to lose another lieutenant and a friend. Though I'm sure Zeus will not be happy you lost two of his people."

Biting my cheek and scanning the room, I struggled to find a response. "No, he won't. How did they know we were coming and where the safehouse was?"

His brow furrowed as he scanned the room. "I'll look into it. There's a chance we have a mole. Keep an eye out among your people too. There are only so many people that knew about this mission." He put his hands on his hips and sighed. "Even with the losses and trouble, this," he held up the flash drive, "this will change everything. With the details of their cameras, we can map out their coverage zones and what holes we can exploit. Plus, now that we have their system data, we can finally start the last phase of preparations for Operation Blackout." He looked over to Razor. "Not bad for your, what, third mission?"

Razor gave a tentative half-smile back. "Yeah, but..."

"No 'but.' You did good. What happened to Southpaw and Bobcat is awful, and we'll get to the bottom if it, but their sacrifice will save so many more lives. We might finally be able to make a difference."

I thought for a second before responding, "Razor, you did everything you could. Don't worry about what you can't control." I turned back to El Capitan. "Let me know if you need anything. I'm going to take these two home before running an errand."

He turned his attention back to the map. "Tell Aaron I say hi."

Chapter 4

Razor was one of the few Militia members who lived with his family, or even had a family, though he was technically adopted into his just a few years ago. Most of us with Red parents had lost them to slavery or a tragic death a long time ago and were left to fend for ourselves. Few Reds were provided housing by the government or their owners, and we weren't paid beyond our measly rations, so we scavenged what we could just to survive. That's what we got for failing the Prism Test.

Razor was one of our youngest recruits, just a few months away from his sixteenth birthday, when he would pass through the Prism, lose his black tag, and earn his colored one. I gave him his name because he was just starting to grow a few patches of facial hair when he was assigned to me four months before. The kid could fight with a knife like nobody else and was a sneaky one, though he was sloppy with a gun. I liked him. He was my favorite agent besides Delaware, but because of his anxiety and clumsiness in any situation that didn't involve hiding from people, I could tell he would need special help too.

His adopted family was rough. His dad was addicted to anything that could make him forget the pain of the life he was forced into. He never did what his previous owner demanded and was sold to the state for dirt cheap. When you're owned by the state and don't work, you're punished; it was only a matter of time until they found his dad and dragged him off somewhere to be killed for his "insults to the people."

Razor's mom raised kids while stuck working at least twelve hours a day in the chemical factory. She had seen one of her kids taken to work in Minneapolis while the other two were able to work in St. Paul and live in the Enclave. Razor, meanwhile, did the classic work of being a janitor at a coffee shop for the Purple, Blue, Green, and Yellow Tags. He didn't enjoy it, but it was lighter work than most.

We reached his home on the west side of the Enclave; it was nothing more than some ragged green tarps thrown over what used to be a house. I stopped him before he went in. "Hey, Delaware, give me a second to talk with Razor."

She nodded understandingly and kept going.

I held onto his arm, speaking softly. "You alright? I know today was rough, but you did everything we needed from you, what *I* needed from you. Bobcat and Southpaw, that's not your fault."

He solemnly nodded, keeping his head down.

"This life... this life is not easy man. It's not easy being from a Red family, but actually standing up for something and risking everything, that's brave. I'm proud of you, Razor. You came to me younger than most other recruits and trained as an agent faster than I've seen in a long time. Most Reds don't get to really see what we do in the field. It's easier to give the occasional tip here and there. What's hard is what you're doing, fighting for something even before you face the Prism. You understand that?"

He nodded again, still avoiding eye contact.

I patted his upper arm. "We'll have a full debrief later. Go be with your family."

He walked solemnly towards the house.

"And Razorblade. I don't give everyone such a badass name. You earned it today." He turned back to look at me, and I handed him a few dollars, most of what I had. I was not well off, no Red was, even as a lieutenant, but he needed the money way more than I did.

He looked up at me with his youthful eyes in a battle to avoid showing emotion. We met in a brotherly hug; he didn't need to say anything.

He let go and walked in before turning around at the last second and quietly saying, "Thank you, Coyote."

I smiled and nodded, then ran back towards Delaware. "Sorry about the wait Del."

She had been gazing at the stars, her brown monolid eyes full of wonder. "Someone's gotta help the new kid."

I laughed. Delaware was eighteen, three years younger than me and sassy as hell. When she was assigned to me four years ago, after I had pulled her out of a tough situation and into the Militia, I knew we would be having some good battles of wit. The girl knew how to talk shit and could take it right back, a rare quality for a 5-foot-4 scrawny wannabe gymnast. She was the closest thing I had to a best friend. Both of our families had been killed when we were little, probably why we had both developed such independent streaks. Neither of us took orders well, but luckily, she had learned to trust me at my word, though I could count on her to tell me when my ideas were useless. I also knew that on a night like that, if anyone could help me feel better about what happened, it was her. "So, on our list of adventures, where did today rank on us almost getting killed?"

She pondered as we walked. "It's pretty near the top. I mean, there was the time with the grenade on one of my first missions."

"Oh yeah... Dang, that feels like centuries ago at this point. Lucky, I grabbed you before that thing went off." I gave a slight smile and laughed. "I had a burn on my butt so bad that I couldn't sit down for a week after that."

She laughed. "You saved me there, didn't you?"

"I had to. No one else on my team is going to tell me when I'm full of crap." I sighed, still shaken from the night. "Shit. This sucks."

She noticed my shift in tone. "We'll figure out who told them."

I shook my head. "Doesn't fix it."

"Can anything?"

"I guess not." *Losing people sucks.* "I don't know what I would have done if I lost two of you guys. Zeus has been around so long and has seen too many people come and go, but this stuff is still new to me."

"Yeah. Without me and Razor you'd be lost. Penn, especially, is a pushover, and Snapback and Blitzkrieg would just encourage you to run in guns blazing and get more people killed." She shrugged, either too jaded to care about tossing around the possibility of death or too scared to address it without a laugh. I secretly worried that I was no different.

"It just wouldn't be the same. Blitz doesn't tend to have his head on straight, and Snapback would be lost without his crush on you."

She blushed and sighed, embarrassed. "Oh, Snap…"

"I'm your lieutenant, not your relationship counselor. I will say no more." I raised up my hands in surrender.

She was intent. "We're *not* a couple."

"In his head you are! Ha!" *Well, I guess that lightened the mood at least.* She punched me in the shoulder. *I deserved that.* "This is workplace violence and it will not be tolerated."

We both laughed and took a breath before walking in silence for a bit. We needed a good laugh after such a crappy night, but it felt wrong. Any one of us could have been on the first floor when they came in, and we were lucky to be alive. That was too often the feeling as a Red. I felt numb to it and just added it to the jar of things that had gone wrong.

We had reached her house: a one room red brick building that she shared with Pennsylvania, who I lazily named because she was taller than Delaware. I gave her a hug. "Sleep well."

"Night, Ivan. Don't blame yourself for this. Don't." She gave me a stern look and then lightened up. "Tell Aaron to run a story on my suggestion for once."

"Okay. Debriefing tomorrow night."

Now for my errand…

Chapter 5

Everyone knew that my "errand" was visiting Aaron at the St. Paul Free Press, our underground paper and the only one not run by the government. Aaron was a stressed-out upper thirty-something Yellow Tag who needed me to annoy him every now and then. On a night like tonight, I needed the fresh air to clear my head and a good chat with an old friend. Aaron was also one of the few people who I could trust with both my real name, Ivan, and my Militia codename, Coyote.

I knocked on the door to his house in downtown St. Paul with the code: three quick knocks, hesitate, one, and then two more. He was careful for good reasons. Being an underground printer would get him killed if he was discovered. The Ministry of Information didn't like competition.

He popped open the door and I was met by his gravelly voice. "Oh, hey Ivan. Come on in."

I followed him through the house and down into the print shop he had in the basement, hidden beneath a trap door in the back corner of the living room. The overwhelming smell of paper and ink smacked into me the second I was beyond the trap door. The machines were hard at work and making a lot of noise while they were at it. Aaron looked at them with a sense of pride.

I hopped up onto one of the printers, just to annoy him. "Man, it has been a *crappy* day."

He glared at me for violating his precious printer but didn't interject. "What happened?"

"We had a trade set up with some underpaid UPF bureaucrats who got us the information on all of their camera systems, but someone sold us out."

"So, you didn't get it?"

"We got it, but the police found our safe house. They caught two of our agents, Bobcat and Southpaw, and burned the place down."

He ran his brown hands through his basically non-existent hair. "Dang."

"Yeah."

"But at least you got the information, right?"

"Yes, but I lost two of our people." Emotion surged into me and I slammed my hand against the printer in frustration. "Damn it!"

Aaron rubbed his hand across the printer like it was a wounded child. "Hey, Ivan. I understand you're mad, but let's not destroy more stuff in the process."

I sighed and jumped off the printer. "Sorry, I just hate this crap. Every time I think we're going to make progress, something bad happens along the way."

"That's not your fault."

What if it is? I walked over to one of the finished papers and grabbed one, eager to change the subject. "So... am I on the front page?"

He looked skeptical of my change of topics but complied. "No, sorry. The cover story is about the Anglo-Nordic Coalition's coup in Denmark. The Fifth International is pissed."

"Huh. So, the last two capitalist countries in Europe finally decided to push back against the socialists. Took them long enough."

He shrugged. "We'll see if it works. Rumor has it, they're looking at the Netherlands next. Who knows what the USSR will do in response?"

I spun my finger in a sarcastic circle. "Yay, World War III."

"Oh, I hope not." He sighed. "Anyway, you are mentioned in an op-ed's critique of the Front making Coyote one of their main targets."

"Why are they criticizing the government for moving me up the rankings? I'm finally getting the credit I deserve for my mischief." I grinned maniacally.

He shrugged. "She said that they should focus on investigating the fraud in the state-owned enterprises instead of a freedom fighter."

"Well, she is right. Sounds like I have a fan." I started flipping through the paper. "What's her name?"

"You know full well that everyone's articles are anonymous or by codenames, *Coyote*."

"I'm going to ignore you using my awesome codename in a sarcastic manner. You're not going to tell me who my ardent admirer is? C'mon, I just told you I'm having a rough day. You can't help a guy out?"

"No, Ivan, I've told you this a thousand times. Anyway, you've got more important things to worry about than the girls fawning over you." He mimicked a fainting motion. "'Oh, Coyote!'"

I laughed. "So that's why everybody was falling down on the

streets yesterday. I thought it hitting eighty in St. Paul had every-one getting a heat stroke."

He shook his head. "Did you have a reason for visiting?"

I smirked. "Do I ever?"

He scoffed. "No."

I sighed and set down the paper. "Just needed to vent and up-date you on our progress, so nothing else really... Actually! Wait. Delaware says you should publish her article idea about how the community has managed to bond together over the solar energy innovations that keep..."

He pretended to fall asleep.

"It's actually pretty cool. I mean, we have lights now in the En-clave. We didn't a few years ago."

He blinked at me.

I raised my arms in a sarcastic surrender. "Fine, I promised her I'd tell you. Peace, Aaron. And make sure you publish a good mug-shot of me when the police finally get me. They're going to give you a bad picture. Just make sure my good side shows up."

"Oh, I would... if you had one. Night, Ivan."

I laughed and stepped out into the cool late Summer evening. I felt better. Losing Southpaw and Bobcat still hung over me, but I couldn't let it slow me down too much. That was the eternal struggle: trying to move forward without losing our humanity.

Fall was coming. *Good.* I always enjoyed the cooler weather of old Minnesota. The bell from the Cathedral of St. Paul rang across the town. *Ten o'clock and the night is still young.* It was ironic that the bell still rang, reminding us of the cathedral's presence, de-spite the UPF's near complete elimination of religion over the past century. Those that still practiced were either royals, Reds, or killed. *When you worship a god, you can't worship the government.*

The wind whipped through the trees as I wound through the side streets to avoid the police and cameras on my way back to the Enclave. The city was quiet past curfew and all I could hear beyond the wind was the birds and the crickets. *I love the night.* It was mysterious, I didn't have to deal with people, and the world felt like mine. I was wanted for way more than breaking some stupid curfew law. This was my time.

My quiet stroll was abruptly interrupted, though, by what sounded like a scuffle around a corner near Smith Avenue. I crept to a tree at the corner and peaked around it. Two middle-aged men were arguing with a woman who they had pushed up against an abandoned brewery warehouse. An expensive handbag hung from her gloved hand and she wore fancy ice-blue neck-wrap peacoat: she wasn't from around here, though I couldn't see the color of her tag through her hair. *Tonight just got even more interesting...*

From behind the tree I analyzed the two men: one Orange and one Yellow. Their ripped, muted jackets and tattered jeans hung loosely on their bodies. Muggings weren't uncommon among the Reds and Oranges, but with the levels of starvation spiking over recent years, the Yellows were getting desperate too. A rich girl like that was too easy of a target.

Yellow Tag had her arm and hissed. "Come nice and quiet and we won't slit your throat." His partner pulled a knife.

She looked around, searching for a way out, her eyes full of fear and her voice smooth but panicked. "What do you want? Money?"

Well if this isn't the classic Damsel in distress. Obviously, a rich girl, but that doesn't mean she deserves this. Maybe I can do something good tonight. I snuck around the corner while the attackers bickered with her.

The girl noticed my approach, and I put a finger to my lips as her narrow eyes screamed for help. When I was about three meters away, I spoke sarcastically, "Excuse me, good sirs. Isn't it a little past your bedtime?"

The one with the knife turned to me, his voice like gravel. "Turn your ass around and go home. She's ours."

"That's not a nice way to talk around a lady." His hand shook as I stepped closer. *Wimp.* Swiftly, I drew two of my knives from my pockets and charged him, knocking him over with my shoulder and the knife flew out of his hands. As he stumbled back, he grabbed my burned arm and I yelped, falling on top off him. While I knocked him out with a few swift head punches in the resulting struggle, his partner scrambled for the knife, still gripping the girl's forearm. I lunged at him and cut his forearm, forcing him to scream in pain and release her. He grabbed the knife as I drove my own blade into the side of his neck, and crimson blood spurted from his neck as he gasped and fell. I collapsed next to him. I didn't want to kill him, but I'd learned the hard way not to wait and see what the other guy would do with a weapon in his hand.

Exhausted, but triumphant, I struggled to my feet. The girl was gaping at my stomach, and I looked down to see what she was staring at. *Well, shit.* My abdomen was bleeding, a lot. I reached down and felt the knife as a sharp pain shot through my side. "Ack!" It was in deep and pulling it out without a doctor was just going to make things worse. I looked up at the girl and reached out my non-bloodied hand, speaking weakly, "Ivan, pleased to make your acquaintance m'lady."

She just stared at my hand before looking back at me in shock. *Do rich women not like handshakes? Or maybe it's the blood...* "You need a hospital!"

"Was, ahh, was that a question? Because yes, yes I do." My hood dropped as I said that, revealing my red dog tag earring.

Her ice-blue eyes filled with surprise. "Oh, you're a Red."

"And you're obviously not. So, are you going to help me out or not?" *Where is her tag?*

Shaking her head sharply, she broke out of her shock. "Oh, yeah." She made a call on her cellphone, giving directions to someone. "My driver is coming to pick us up." *Oh, she's "my driver" rich.*

Once she was finished, she put my arm over her shoulder to support my weight, and we made our way towards the main road. Once we were under the light from the street lamps, I could see her heart shaped pale face, and she failed to hide her discomfort as some of my blood dripped onto her fancy jacket. *She looks familiar. Or am I just that woozy?* I could have sworn I recognized her, but from where?

The world was spinning in my head as we waited, and I could feel my mind slipping. *Stay awake.* I muttered to her, "Keep me talking or I'm going to pass out."

Shock was plastered over her face, but she pulled herself out of it, feeling my urgency. "Thank you... thank you for helping me. I'm not sure what I would have done."

"No, ack... uh, no problem. What was someone like you doing out in St. Paul at this time of night?"

She hesitated and blushed, embarrassed. "I was at a party with some friends and was planning to meet my driver a few blocks away. I didn't want him telling my parents where I was."

"Ah, well, I'm not sure if you're naïve or just stupid, but a young, attractive girl like you walking through dark alleys in the west end of St. Paul is not the greatest decision you've made in your life."

"No, no it isn't." She pondered for a second before responding with a bit of insistency, "Why are you out here? A Red past curfew is really risking it with the UPF."

I groaned in pain. "None of your business."

She insisted. "Well, I told you my secret. You have to tell me yours."

I shook my head weakly. "I promise you, a secret that gets you yelled at by your parents is nothing close to what I've got."

"Well, you..." She was cut off by a fancy black SUV pulling up. A Green Tag man rushed out, opened the door and pulled me into the back seat. The girl climbed in the other side and helped me sit up.

The car screamed rich, with authentic wood paneling, an engine that didn't shutter every few seconds, and leather seats that punched me in the face with their aroma. *Wow, this is a nice car. I hope they like red seats...* I was feeling increasingly light headed and couldn't sit up, even with her help, and my vision slowly faded to black.

Chapter 6

Bright light burst into my eyes as the smell of antiseptics knocked me awake. *Where the hell am I?* Panic surged through my chest as I saw the tubes attached to me. I was a few seconds from tearing out my IV and throwing a few people against the wall, but the stitches stabbed into my side as I tried to stand. I pushed back against the large arms trying to hold me down, but they injected me with a serum that knocked me back out.

Did I overreact? Probably, yes. But imagine being in a high-class hospital with all sorts of fancy stuff you haven't ever actually seen in person before. The Reds didn't get special medical care; we were replaceable.

When I awoke the second time, it was slow. The straps they had added rubbed abrasively against my arms, and I couldn't move. A Blue nurse, female this time, was watching nearby. Her upturned eyes were wide with a bit of fear, though shrouded in exhaustion. She was sharp in getting to her feet, though, and would have been ready if I had actually tried to put up a fight.

I coughed weakly. "What time is it?"

She looked relieved that I wasn't feeling violent. "Four in the afternoon. You're lucky that they got you here as fast as they did. You could have died, especially if you had pulled the knife out. How did you know not to?"

I tried to sit up but was held down by the straps. "Ack! Well, when you live in the slums, you've dealt with enough people being stabbed that you figure out what works and what kills you. You know, because we aren't allowed to visit an actual doctor."

"That makes sense…" Her voice almost held a bit of guilt. "Since almost all the royals' servants are Blue or Green, you're the first Red that we've ever treated here."

Royal servants? Holy crap… I'm in THAT hospital? "Wait, this is the Royal Hospital?"

She looked confused why I didn't know. "Yes? Princess Julia brought you here." She wiped a strand of black hair away from her face. *Princess? I saved a Princess? That explains the lack of a tag. Screw this. I'm out.* I started fighting against the straps. "Please don't do that."

I insisted and continued struggling against the straps. "I need to leave, *now.*"

She grabbed my arm and gave a disapproving look. Even when you didn't grow up with parents, you know what a mom glare looks like, and it was frightening. "You need more time to rest. Besides, you can't leave yet. The King has requested your presence once you're ready to walk." *This must be a weird dream…*

"You must have given me the good stuff, because I thought I heard you say the King wants to see me."

"That's correct. We washed your clothes. They are on the table when you're ready. Press the button if you need anything." She removed my IV and the straps, striking another glare at me.

"Uh… thanks." *What is going on?*

She left, and after a while I struggled to my feet to put my clothes on. It was almost a relief to put on the white tattered jacket and ripped jeans, grounding me back into reality. I stumbled into the bathroom and grabbed the edges of the sink. *Holy crap.* I looked at myself in the mirror and tried to straighten the black mess on my head. *How did I get here? In what world does a Militia lieutenant save a princess and get to meet the King? And man, I look awful.* I touched my tag hanging from my right ear. Blood red. It felt appropriate now. *Ivan 181375.* I spat into the sink. "Shit."

A few minutes later, a man called for me from the hallway. "We need to be on our way."

I didn't respond and splashed the cool water on my face before looking at myself one last time, my upturned dark blue eyes sinking ever deeper into my pale narrow face. *I look exhausted.* Grasping my side, I slowly shuffled towards the door. Waiting for me in the hallway was a short, bald Blue man who didn't seem to know what a gym was.

He raised his eyebrows. "Ready to go?"

No. I nodded.

"Good, follow me." I shuffled weakly along behind him as he waddled out of the hospital and directed me into the back of a black sedan that was waiting for us.

Chapter 7

I had not been in many cars. Red and Orange Tags couldn't afford them - beyond the few beaters the Militia had hidden away - and there weren't many Purples, Blues, Greens, or richer Yellows, let alone royalty, willing to have one of us in the backseat. Then again, even the cars most people drove were from the state-owned factories, and those were awful. This one, though, was the kind of car that reminded you constantly how many cows were needed for its seats and was entirely meant to tell other people, "You can't afford this."

The drive was short and quiet. I got the feeling he didn't want to talk to me any more than I wanted to talk to him. We approached the golden gates that sheltered the palace from the rest of the world. They glided opened as the guards on duty nodded to the chauffeur.

I stared out the window at the beautiful and serene royal grounds, trying to compare it to the Enclave in my head, not that a comparison was really even possible. Trees stretched across the grassy yards: oak, maple, elm, you name it. It was the closest thing possible to a forest without quite being one, and yet its planned layout seemed to flow naturally. Beyond the trees stretched an open lawn as if nature had left room for the palace itself out of respect. The palace's white marble shone in the sun, somehow extravagant and meshing into the surroundings at the same time. *What have I gotten myself into?*

We pulled around in the circle drive and he put the car in park. "Before you go in, I need to give you some instructions."

Here we go.

He continued facing forward. "Do not speak unless asked a question. You go where you are told to go and will not wander around the Royal Household. You will refer to all your superiors as 'sir' or 'm'lady,' and will refer to the King as 'your highness' or 'my lord.' When you enter the throne room you will kneel before him until he tells you to stand. Do you understand?"

"Yes, uh, sir."

He signaled to a Blue butler, and they opened his door for him. I waited for a second, then opened my own door, clutching my side as I stood. This wound was going to take a while to heal - more time than I had to spare.

The palace felt menacing now as it towered in front of me. It looked like something from a different age. Located on the western edge of Minneapolis in the Calhoun Isles, the Royal Household was the obvious contrast to the rougher parts of St. Paul and the Enclave. With its wide-reaching grounds extending to Cedar Lake, it was an impressive sight, and quite disgusting when I thought about how so many of us struggled to survive. While the royal family lived here, the surrounding areas were inhabited by many of the other, minor royals. The royals' influence was much weaker than before the Third Civil War, but they still flaunted what they had.

I slowly moved towards the grand marble staircase that led to the massive main doors before the chauffeur stopped me. "You are to go through the servants' entrance."

Bullshit. I nodded. "Yes, sir."

He showed me towards the servants' entrance and unlocked the simple wooden door.

Before entering, I stopped him. "I, uh. I forgot to ask your name... sir."

"Phillip, but you can call me 'sir.'"

"Of course... um, sir."

We entered into what appeared to be the hallway for the servants' chambers. Small rooms were scattered along the narrow, grey stone hallway. Phillip showed me the way through, each step echoing through the halls. Eventually, we entered a much larger and fancier room, the Great Hall. A warm aroma, whose source I could not identify, filled the air, with soft pouring through the windows along the sides of the domed ceiling. A Blue Tag royal guardsman, dressed in the traditional blue military uniform, approached us. Each of his footsteps sounded like an army as they echoed throughout the marble room. "Ivan 181375?"

"Yes." Phillip shot a glare. "I mean... yes, sir."

The guard grabbed my tag and held a scanner to it. "Multiple items of contraband were found on your person following your encounter with the princess. They will be stored until the King says otherwise. As a precautionary measure I also need to search you, thoroughly."

I hesitated before managing a nod. *Bastards.* I felt naked without my knives and radio, but that wasn't as bad as being strip searched down to my underwear in the middle of a giant room with multiple guardsmen and a few servants watching. I was determined not to show any embarrassment despite my awareness of the stares, so I stood still and just looked ahead at the mole on the guard's left check, focusing on it until they were finished. The servants may have been only servants, but they were Blues and Greens still; a Red in the palace was abnormal. I was sure they enjoyed watching me be degraded.

He finished his search. "Thank you, Phillip. I will show him the rest of the way." He escorted me past the other Blue guards and through a few more marble hallways until we reached two large doors with an elaborate ice-blue lion stretched across their face. "I assume he told you the instructions for how to approach the King?"

I nodded. "Yes, sir."

He narrowed his sharp eyes at me skeptically before responding, "Good." He nodded to a stout Blue man standing by the doors.

The man entered through the doors and stayed there for a minute before returning. Upon his return, he spoke in a high, nasally voice. "His highness King Timothy will see you now."

Chapter 8

King Timothy Hughes III was the third king of the People's Democratic Republic of Northern Mississippi. The Third Civil War had split the Kingdom of America into multiple parts following the socialist uprisings, and what had been known as Minnesota, Wisconsin, and Iowa joined into Northern Mississippi following the war. The remnants of the American monarchy ended up with varying amounts of power throughout the multiple newly created countries, despite losing the war overall.

In Northern Mississippi, the official story was that the "enlightened" socialist movement united with the monarchy to end the fighting and build a "better world together." In reality, King Timothy III's grandfather, Duke Timothy Hughes I, gave up almost all real power to the socialists. He agreed to allow the United People's Front to create the Prism Test and Tagged System, named for the ugly dog tag earrings they forced upon us. In return, the UPF allowed Timothy I to symbolically crown himself King of Northern Mississippi and exempted the royal families from the test.

Under the Tagged System, all non-royals were given a black tag from birth, marking that they had yet to "pass through the Prism." In theory, the Prism Test was meant to determine how "beneficial to the collective" you were through a series of physical, oral, and written examinations. After you took the test on your sixteenth birthday, you were filtered into one of six colored tiers based on your results: Purple, Blue, Green, Yellow, Orange, or Red, with Purple as the top tier and Red as the bottom. Your color determined rations, priority of work you received via the planning committee, and how many privileges you had. The range between top and bottom was extreme. Purples and Blues lived in relative luxury, while the Reds were stripped of our last names and enslaved: owned by the government, a Purple, or a Blue, as we were deemed damaging to the collective. Meanwhile, due to their agreement with the UPF, the royals avoided the test and lived in luxury only matched by the richest of Purples. The royal exemption created what we called the Fractured Prism, as the royals passed through the fracture in the Prism unfiltered, earning their nickname: the "Whites."

The UPF claimed that the Prism was a fair and equal evaluation of a person's worth to the collective as everyone started as a Black Tag, yet they had manipulated the test over the past century to consolidate the number of Purple Tags into a small group of the most loyal and elite. Over three-quarters of the post-Prism population were Yellows, Oranges, or Reds, and unlike the UPF's claims, your family and loyalty to the government had the largest impact on your color. It was easy to move down colors from your parents while extremely difficult to ever move up. I was born at the bottom with no last name and had not done myself many favors to gain ground, not that it would have mattered. *Born Red, always Red.*

The monarchy was not the focus of the Militia's missions, but we did not forget what the royals would do when given the choice between status and protecting freedom. They were the lesser of two evils, nothing more.

The throne room was decorated with the ornate ice-blue shade of the Hughes family. A carpet stretched from the entrance of the room up to the throne, with the color extending onto the throne itself. The large stone room was obviously meant to look like the throne room of a medieval king. *Wannabes.* Small sitting and standing areas were also scattered throughout the room, where I assumed members of the court would meet to conspire about some useless and unimportant plans.

I shuffled slowly down the carpet, taking it all in. Before me sat King Timothy III himself, leaning back as his large frame filled the throne, dressed in some stupid royal garb with the icy-blue colors matching his eyes. Like all royals, he was untagged, instead marked by his royal family ring: a platinum band accented with his family's colors. He studied me with interest as I approached. I knelt when I felt I was near enough, but not too close.

He said nothing for a while. His forehead wrinkled with his furrowed brow. *Should I speak? But wasn't I supposed to wait for him to speak first? Ugh, I hate this.* Eventually, he broke the silence, his deep voice filling the room, "Stand, and let me look at you."

I did, groaning a little too loudly in pain.

"I was told you had incurred an injury. How is the wound?"

I hesitated.

"Go on."

I struggled to maintain eye contact. "Deep enough to hurt like he… to hurt a lot, your highness. Thank you for asking."

He nodded with what little neck he had. "Well, I am pleased to hear that those criminals did not kill you. One of them is in our custody, though, I am told you were more… effective… with your blade when it came to the other."

I didn't respond and stared at the ground.

"It is alright. You were protecting my daughter, were you not?"

"Yes, your highness."

"What possessed you to believe you could fight two men on your own?"

I glanced up at him. "Two thugs were threatening someone with no means to defend themselves. Not that your daughter is weak or anything…" I caught myself before continuing. "Didn't matter what I thought I could do… uh, your highness."

His cold eyes narrowed. "Still, that is a lot of *prohibited* weaponry for a Red Tag to possess on top of breaking curfew." He waited for me to reply, I didn't. "What were you doing out that late at night?"

"Meeting a friend, your highness. I, um, I had not seen him for a while as I have been busy with my work."

"I see." He paused for a moment, his brows furrowed. "Where is your work assignment? Who is your owner?"

My assignment is to make the UPF's lives living hell. "The eastern St. Paul steel mill, your highness. I am owned by the government."

His eyes narrowed, his voice questioning. "Ah, I see. So, you work near that place you Red Tags call the Enclave."

"Correct."

"Do you live in the Enclave?"

"Yes, your highness."

"What do you know about the Militia?"

I sighed. "I don't know much. About as much as any Red I guess. They're a bunch of rogue Reds and Oranges fighting against the Prism."

He stood with some effort and approached me slowly, his eyes studying me. "Terrorists, Ivan. They are terrorists threatening our fragile peace. Do you happen to know the names of anyone in this 'Militia?'" He finished uncomfortably close to me, his eyes like daggers.

I kept looking him in the eye, trying to equal his intensity. "No, I do not."

He pushed harder. "Are you, yourself in The Militia?"

"No, your highness."

His glare continued, not accepting my denial. My attempt at a solid look in response broke as the doors opened behind me. I looked back to see Julia, flaunting a knee-length coral dress and gliding down the aisleway. Her blonde hair flowed behind her as her heels clicked against the marble floor. "Father, why are you interrogating him?" She stopped a few feet behind me. I turned so I was out of the way of their glaring match. As her eyes met her father's, I swear that the temperature in the room dropped a few degrees. *Her turn to save me...*

"Julia, I am just ensuring that he is not dangerous, and you know that. With the amount of knives he was carrying, who knows what kind of nefarious activities he participates in?"

Julia released a heavy sigh of disapproval and pursed her thin lips. *He has a point and she knows it.* She looked at me for half a second, her gaze softer, before snapping back and continuing the glaring match. Frustrated, she flung her arm towards me. "Ivan saved my life, dad. Who cares if he is a Red?" *She is bold for a twenty-one-year-old third born.*

The King made an exaggerated motion to the sky as if he were looking for godly support. "You might not care, my daughter, but I do. You cannot trust people like him. You should not have been out there in the first place and neither should he! We will talk about your punishment later, Julia. Go. I will speak to you when I'm finished here." He pointed with his large arm towards the door. The platinum and ice-blue ring on his finger sparkled in the light.

She gave me a helpless look that held a wish to stay and a million different questions at once. I nodded to let her know it was okay to go. Wherever this conversation was heading, I needed to do it myself. She pounded out of the room, each footstep cracking like thunder through the chambers.

The King turned to me again. "Regardless of my skepticism, Ivan, I am thankful for what you did. My hands are tied, though, due to your... condition. Julia has expressed interest in having you act as one of her servants, but I cannot trust you in a position that could bring harm to my daughter. Unless I say otherwise, you are to not go near her, understand?"

"I, uh..." I cleared my throat. "Yes, your highness."

"Your presence will make many uncomfortable. Therefore, you will work out of sight in the theater, assisting the technical crew in preparation for the next show."

Theater? Weird, but whatever. "Yes, your highness."

"You will be employed by us, and you will be given a room in the servants' wing. We will provide you food and a room as well as any other items you might need to complete your work. You will be watched closely, though. Do not fail or you will regret it. Understood?"

I was overjoyed and my eyes watered. *I must be dreaming. It'll be difficult to coordinate with the Militia, but a job with the royals, my own room, and my food provided for? Wow! Though, I would like to see Julia again.* I dropped back to a kneeling position. "Yes. Thank you, your highness."

"Good. Now, Phillip will drive you to wherever you live so that you may pick up your things. You may have your radio back, but not your knives. You need to prove to me that you deserve my trust. Now, get up and go."

"Thank you, your highness." I left the room in a daze. *Today is strange.*

Chapter 9

"Coyote to Delaware. Come in Delaware."
"Hey Coyote. You alright? El Capitan…"
"Rendezvous point. 45 minutes. Out."

Chapter 10

It wasn't hard to convince Phillip to leave the car on the north end of the bridge and let me go into the Enclave alone. The guy would have stuck out like a sore thumb in an area where being an unathletic Blue was dangerous. Plus, he would have gotten in my way.

"You have half-an-hour, or I tell the King you fled."

It was risky to meet with Delaware on such a time crunch, but talking with her was more important than forgetting some crap at home. I opened the cellar door in the abandoned house we had set up as our rendezvous point years ago and went down the stairs. The room smelled of a thousand fires long past, but the soot had remained.

She was waiting for me. Her anxious look turned to worry when she saw me grasping my side. "What happened? Where were you?"

I grabbed an old chair and threw myself onto it before explaining what happened as quickly as I could without leaving out any important details.

Her look changed slowly to confused amazement. "I… I don't know if I believe you or if you just got hit way too hard in the head."

I painfully stood and put my hands on her shoulders. "Listen, Del. I don't have much time. This is a lot to take in, but I need you to do something for me."

Her eyes were curious. "Anything."

"I need you to be my leader here, as acting lieutenant. I will do what I can, but I need you to help execute the plans. I'll be available via radio occasionally, but you'll be making a lot of decisions. El Capitan will tell you more."

"Coyote, I..."

"You're ready. I wouldn't put you in this position if I didn't believe that. I'm not going to be gone, just a bit further away, and I think we can gain something from me being closer to the royals."

With tears in her brown determined eyes, she hugged me. I groaned in pain but hugged her back gently.

"Now, I need to go before Phillip leaves without me. Go talk to El Capitan. We have a lot of work to do."

She let go and looked up at me, her round face full of intent. "I won't let you down, but I'll miss you."

"Same... uh... keep in touch." I held up the radio. There was so much more I wanted to say but couldn't in such a short time. We shared a heavy moment of silence before I shuffled towards the door.

My so-called house was not far. It was an old bombed out brick ranch that still had one usable room. The rickety wooden door creaked as I entered and looked around the dull blackened room, met by the familiar smell of rotting wood and an excessive amount of dust. I was never one for decorating, so the space lacked any real personal touches. *Charred wood and soot, classy.*

Shuffling over to the cheap, water-stained wooden dresser I'd recovered from one of the other abandoned houses years ago, I quickly collected a few pieces of clothing. I left some spare clothes and my weapons, since they would search my bag upon my return. I also left my Coyote bandana and black jacket, not willing to risk anyone finding something to connect me to him. Nothing else was worth taking, so I opened the door, took one last look at the place that had been my home for so many years, smiled, and headed back to see Phillip.

Phillip wasn't happy. He glanced at his watch. "It took you 37 minutes to grab one bag?"

I shuffled up before throwing the bag over my shoulder and onto the ground. "Traffic was awful."

He rolled his eyes and searched through the bag. "You're lucky the King doesn't hate you, yet." He pointed to the bag and then the car when he was finished. "Pick that up so we can return. I don't want to miss the party tonight."

I slowly and painfully reached down and grabbed the bag. "What kind of party?"

Climbing into the front seat, he looked back. "The kind that Reds aren't invited to. Come on." He slammed the door. *Isn't that every party?*

I climbed into the back with my bag. "Not even a classy Red?"

He looked at me in the rearview mirror as he started the car and began the trip back. "You need to stick to the rules I taught you already, kid, if you want to make it a week."

I saluted sarcastically. "Yes, sir."

He just shook his head.

It was getting late as we arrived at the Royal Household. Phillip pulled the car up through a side ramp I hadn't seen earlier in the day. "The party has already started. I'll take you to your room. You are to stay there and not interact with anyone, including the servants, unless told otherwise. Understand?"

"Yes, sir."

We entered through the same servants' entrance that we had earlier in the day. He guided me down a few hallways before opening a creaky wooden door on the right. "There you are. Get settled in. You start work tomorrow. Don't be late."

I stood in the doorway and investigated the room, if you could call it a room. It appeared that they had repurposed the broom closet and squeezed a shoddy wooden twin-sized bed and a night stand into it. I sighed.

"What? Never had a room to yourself before? Congratulations, you're living the high life, Mr. Hero. Now, if you'll excuse me I have a party you've made me late for."

I watched him walk away before calling after him. "Phillip!"

He stopped, visibly frustrated, and glared back.

"Thank you for everything, sir."

He nodded sharply, before continuing on his way.

I threw my bag on the stone floor and shut the door behind me. It popped open. I tried shutting it again. It popped open. *What did you expect? The King's Suite?* I slammed it one last time, pulling the door towards the latch, *click*, and smiled to myself, content with the little victory.

The room had nothing but a night stand and a box under my bed for clothes. I looked at my bag, then at the night stand, then back at my clothes. *Screw it.* I plopped onto the bed. These two days had felt like the longest in my life, and tomorrow would be bringing a whole new set of challenges, but for today, I was exhausted, physically and mentally. *New adventures, broadening my horizons, yay.*

Eventually, I found the energy to change out of yesterday's clothes and into some clothes to sleep in. It was nearly the start of Fall, and the stone walls and floor filled the room with an isolating chill. I curled up in the thin blanket they had provided. It was neither comfortable nor warm, but I was exhausted and faded to sleep.

Sometime later I awoke to my door creaking open. My instincts kicked into gear - not effective in a small, dark room when I was injured. Effectively, this meant that I fell out of bed and hit my head on the night stand as the single light bulb hanging from the ceiling illuminated my humiliation.

A young Blue royal guardsman, no older than me, was standing in the doorway, looking puzzled. "Uh, Ivan 181375, right?"

I rubbed my head where it had hit the nightstand and slowly pulled myself to my feet. "At your service, sir."

He chuckled. "Are you alright?"

"Wonderful. What can I do for you?"

He smiled genuinely and reached out his hand. "I wanted to introduce myself. Jonah. I tend to patrol the southern part of the palace. We'll probably be seeing a lot of each other, and I thought you might need a friendly face."

I shook his hand, confused. *Dang, guy has a grip.* "Thank you, uh, Jonah. Nice to meet you. Um, are you supposed to be talking to me? Phillip said I shouldn't talk to anyone."

He chuckled and shrugged his thin shoulders. "What are they going to do, report me to the guard? Listen, I know you're a Red Tag, but not all of us are pretentious snobs. Let me know if anyone gives you trouble. I'll try to help. Around here, everyone needs someone watching their back. Especially a Red."

I smiled. "Thank you. You don't know how much that means to me. I'm just trying to figure this all out. And I will return the favor however I can."

He nodded. "Well if you ever have any questions, let me know. Most people around here won't be so accommodating, and it can take a while to figure out how the social spheres around here operate." He turned his head as he heard a noise in the hallway. "I need to get back to my patrol. Too many important guests to be gone for long. See you around."

Chapter 11

Sleep came quickly that night; it ended quickly in the morning as well. I awoke to light flooding into the room and a curly haired Green Englishman yelling at me. I understood little of what he said in my sleepy stupor but did grasp that he wanted me to follow him to the theater. *So much for a shower. Would they even let me use it anyway?*

I rubbed my eyes and sat up. "Yes, sir. Did I, uh, did I miss your name?"

He looked proud, his English accent in full force. "Archibald, master of the fine arts and technical director of the Royal Theater. Now get ready, we have work to do."

As he waited outside, I quickly changed into some shoddy work clothes. Granted, all of my clothes were shoddy. I still felt a bit shell-shocked from the day before, but I had a feeling that the high and mighty Archibald wouldn't be showing me any pity.

When I was finished, he was leaning casually against the wall, waiting for me in the hallway. His long jet-black hair covered part of his eye. I wondered if the royals only let him wear it like that because he worked away from sight: backstage in the theater. He guided me out the servants' entrance and through the yard to the theater, an impressive sight with a pillared marble entrance that made it seem like we were entering another palace.

Entertainment was what the royals valued most, and it

showed. They had obviously spared no expense in the theater's creation. Its dome ceiling was painted like a sky, creating a feeling that you were in a new world instead of just a theater.

Archibald caught me gawking. "The ceiling is painted entirely new for every show. The country's greatest artists, or what's left of the country's greatest artists, are brought in to work on it. It's quite spectacular, isn't it? We are preparing now for Chekhov's *The Cherry Orchard*; opening night is at the end of next week."

I nodded as if I knew what he was saying. Chekhov sounded Russian to me. Of course they would put on a Russian play. The People's Front and the royals each had their obsessions with Russia: the UPF with the USSR and the royals with the old Russian monarchy. I found the latter's obsession ironic, considering how the monarchy came to an... abrupt... end in Russia slightly before the American one did, though the Queen herself was from Russia.

He continued going over technical details of the theater as we went backstage. "I've been told you have no experience with theater work, correct?" I nodded. "Unfortunate. The last thing I need is to show a new guy the ropes so close to opening night. Hope you learn quick. Before we start, let me introduce you to the part of the crew that is here."

I shook hands with the dozen or so Green Tags on the crew as he explained each of their roles. None of them looked too fond of working with me. I couldn't blame them. On top of being a Red, I looked like a mess because of the morning rush. *Solid first impression.*

Much of the rest of the day consisted of various tasks involving physical labor and a healthy dose of sarcastic comments from the crew. Despite the mocking, I was actually glad to be working with them. They may have been Greens, but they were hard workers and ruthlessly efficient. Unfortunately, I was a bit slow with the pain in my side, but I clenched my teeth, determined to impress them.

When the lunch break came, I filled in for those who were eating or on other high priority tasks. It wasn't like I had a lunch to eat anyway. I had been told the royals would be providing food for me, but they didn't tell me how that would work yet.

One of the crewmen threw a piece of half eaten bread at my feet and laughed. "Don't starve, Red. We need you to do our jobs." Hunger was no stranger to me, so I wasn't desperate enough to fall for the joke. I rubbed my heel into the bread, which received some sarcastic *oohs* from some other crew members. *Assholes.*

Later, I was leaning over the railing in the catwalks above the theater, analyzing Archibald's designs before, suddenly, I felt a force from behind throw me forward. Gripping the bar, I kicked out behind me, groaning a bit with the pain in my side. My foot made solid contact on something... well, someone. I spun swiftly, trying to make sense of the situation. One of the Green crewmen had been messing around, and I had hit him pretty solidly in the chest, knocking the wind out of him and causing quite a lot of noise as he fell against the railing on the other side of the narrow catwalk. He weakly coughed, "Screw you, Red," and tried to stand back up.

Enraged, I grabbed his arm, pulling him to his feet and face to face with me. "Do you want to die? Because I'm pretty sure that's how you die up here," I growled.

He pushed me off him. "A Red Tag with no sense of humor. Great."

Archibald had heard the commotion and was on the balcony outside the light booth. "Knock it off up there! Ivan, I swear, if you're causing trouble already I will not hesitate to throw you out of here and back to the dump you came from."

I glared at Rick, the crewman, before calling back to Archibald, "There's no problem."

Archibald flicked the rogue hairs from in front of his eye and crossed his arms, skeptical. "Fine. Last set of lights before we get out of here for the night."

Chapter 12

Following work, I took a detour on my way back from the theater, doing a quick tour of the massive gardens that spanned the distance between the Royal Household itself and Cedar Lake. It was a maze. Rumor had it that the Queen maintained the gardens herself (alongside her army of gardeners).

A sea of aromas filled the air from all types of flowers I had never seen before. Servants and minor royals were scattered throughout the gardens - working, gossiping, and scheming - different people in very different roles, but they all gave me the same disapproving look. *Everyone's got that in common at least.* For many of the royals, I was probably one of the few Red Tags they'd ever seen. They considered themselves above the slavery of the Reds, so we *never* served them. I was an outlier. *Whites hate outliers.*

As I approached the palace, a middle-aged Blue butler approached me in an extremely formal fashion. *How do they have that good of posture?* His voice was as pompous as his looks, overemphasizing each and every vowel. "Your presence is requested in the small parlor immediately."

"Oh, ok. I could change into some more appropriate clothes first, if that's okay, sir."

The butler made an uncomfortable face and awkwardly replied, "If you have an attire that would be appropriate, then yes, you may."

"Well, uh, no I don't really, but I have slightly better than this." I gestured at myself in a sweeping motion.

He scrunched his nose. "Of course. Though…" He sighed. "Never mind. You may change into your more *appropriate* attire and then I shall escort you."

We walked towards the servants' wing. He deliberately stayed a step or two ahead of me at all times. Curious, I asked, "Who requested the audience, sir?"

He opened the door to my room and gestured for me to enter, his narrow eyes judging me. "The Queen and Princess Alexandria."

The Queen and her second oldest daughter. What could they want? I rummaged through my bag, grabbing the one button up shirt and pair of slacks that I owned. Both were worn out and quite obviously not tailored, but I figured it was better than my raggedy jeans and T-shirt from work. I met the butler in the hallway. "Ta-da."

He did not look amused and sighed. "Well, it is a marginal improvement. Follow me and please do not talk to anyone. There are important dignitaries around and I do not want you embarrassing the royal family."

"Yes, sir."

He guided me on a similar path to the one we had taken to the throne room and then went farther, into the north-wing of the palace. We approached a door on the right and he gestured for me to wait as he entered. He emerged moments later and rocked his head to the side, silently telling me to follow. As I entered behind him into the cozy parlor, he spoke, "May I introduce Queen Vera Hughes and Princess Alexandria Hughes."

I bowed. "Your highnesses."

The Queen and Princess Alexandria looked like an odd pair: the mother in a formal white dress and her daughter in a blue T-shirt and sweatpants. *I didn't know royals knew how to be casual.* The Queen spoke first, her eyes narrowly observing me. "Please, sit." She made a sweeping motion with an open hand to the chair next to me.

I slowly sat across from their red velvet couch and analyzed the room. To their right was a fireplace, warming the small stone room and making it feel homier than the rest of the palace that I had seen. The Queen looked towards the butler. "Michael, please wait for Ivan in the hall."

The butler bowed. "Yes, your highness."

I squirmed a bit. While the chair was comfortable, I felt out of place and was outnumbered by royalty, which was intimidating. My fight or flight instincts were mass producing escape plans in my mind. *She isn't going to kill you, idiot. They have people to do that for them.*

The Queen sat back and continued. Her voice had a touch of a Russian accent, likely smoothed over with time and practice. "I am sure you are wondering why you are here." I nodded. "While my husband had the opportunity to thank you for saving my daughter, I have not. You cannot grasp how grateful I am for what you did, risking your life for hers." I nodded again. She smiled and laughed a little. "You are allowed to speak, even if you are a Red

Tag. As far as I'm concerned, we owe you a massive debt."

I shook my head. "I am incredibly honored to be here, your highness. You owe me nothing."

She waved her hand dismissively. "Nonsense. You were almost killed protecting my daughter during one of her silly trips into the city unguarded, which is exactly why I brought you here." She looked at Alexandria to her left. "My daughters are all I treasure in the world, and while my middle two daughters, Alexandria and Julia, are less willing to accept protection, it is becoming all the more apparent that it is needed." Alexandria responded with a disapproving look, her eyes ice cold like Julia's. "My husband does not trust you yet, but I believe Julia does. I believe you can help me keep my daughters safe, especially her." *Does she want to make me a guard?*

Confused, I shook my head. "The King expressly forbade me from seeing Julia, I mean Princess Julia."

Alexandria gave a bit of a rebellious snort, laughing to herself. Her mother shot her a look before returning her attention to me. She thought for a second. "I am aware of his decision. It is why she, and he, are not here right now, but I believe that we can help each other. I realize that I just said we owe you and am now making a request, but I hope you see that we can make things better for you if you help me... help us."

I considered responding but simply nodded slowly instead. *Where is she going with this?*

Alexandria spoke for the first time, her voice deeper than Julia's and her tone much more casual and less refined. "A few little things can go a long way in this family. Now, I need help, and my dad will appreciate it as well…" She looked nervously to her mother, spinning her own platinum and ice-blue ring around her finger as she thought. "I have a, uh, *friend* who has gotten himself into some trouble."

I cocked my head to the side, curious. "If you don't mind me asking, what kind of trouble?"

"That isn't your business." She scolded. The comment was out of line and I received the same glare from both mother and daughter. In that moment, I realized that Alexandria looked like a younger version of the Queen. They had nearly the same heart-shaped face and the family's bleach-blonde hair. The only difference was that Alexandria had her father's eyes.

Alexandria remained firm, but her casual tone returned. "His connections to me could cause a bit of a fiasco for our family if he isn't released before the papers catch wind of it. I would… appreciate… if you could deliver this letter to the police station where they are holding him with as much discretion as possible." It sounded physically painful for her to say that. "I would send a courier, but that would draw too much attention. A Red walking into a police station would not. He was arrested a few hours ago, and we need to get him out by morning. Can you help?"

"A piece of paper, huh. That's all it takes to get one of you out of jail?"

Alexandria scowled, and she pursed her thin lips, just like her sister. "Ack. Are you going to do it or not?"

The Queen put her hand on her daughter's shoulder. "Shh Alex."

I thought for a second. "Fine, I'll do it, m'lady." *If I want to get any important intel, I need to get closer to the family.* "A Red Tag walked into a police station. Sounds like the start of a bad joke."

Alexandria ignored that last part and held out the letter, making me stand up to get it. "You're looking for Officer McBart. Just go in, give her the letter, and get out. Don't talk to anyone, don't draw attention to yourself, and don't say anything about us. Think you can do that, Red?"

She was almost daring me to do it. While Alexandria looked a lot like her sister, her mannerisms were much sharper and less diplomatic. "I will do my best m'lady."

She nodded, then looked at her mother, who finished. "Thank you, Ivan."

I grabbed the door handle and began to turn it before Alexandria stopped me. "And Ivan." I turned to look back at her. "Don't open the letter. I'll know if you do." I looked down, nodded, and headed into the hall.

Quickly returning to my room, I changed into a more casual outfit, fitting the average Red Tag: a black T-shirt, ragged jeans, and my jacket, then grabbed my messenger bag, threw in the letter and my radio, and went on my way.

Chapter 13

I t was getting dark. It wasn't past curfew yet, but I would have to hurry if I didn't want to be caught out too late. Unlike in St. Paul, the police closely monitored the Calhoun Isles. Luckily, though, the police station was only a mile from the Royal Household. I received some curious looks from the guards at the palace gate, but they let me pass along with a cold glare.

A sprinkle began as I left the palace grounds and the wonderful smell of rain on the pavement filled the air. I held out my hand to feel it, cool against my skin. A rainy night made me feel at home. While people were scattering inside, I ruled the night. With the dark, the rain, and my hood, it was the only time that people couldn't immediately tell I was a Red, and I treasured that.

When I reached the station, I was greeted by a chubbier Yellow Tag officer sitting behind the front desk, a donut in one hand. *Classic.* He gave me a look up and down quickly, drawing the obvious conclusion before returning his attention to his donut. "If you have a complaint against your owner or manager, you can fill out this form, but it won't do anything."

I shook my head. "No, I'm here to see Officer McBart."

He sighed, rolled his eyes, and looked back at me. "Why?"

I didn't respond and glared intently.

He mumbled something under his breath before picking up the

phone. "Yeah, McBart, this is Oliver. Some Red kid is up here asking for you. You want me to send him away? No? Oh. Okay then." He hung up, shook his head, and pointed lazily to his left. "Her desk is that way. Don't cause any problems. I have enough reports to do already."

I huffed as he grabbed his donut. *Looks like it.* I shuffled around, looking for a McBart name plate on a desk. The place was pretty empty besides a few officers on the night shift, so I figured finding McBart wouldn't be too hard. My assumption was wrong, though, and I walked around the station for a few minutes without any luck. Finally, as I approached the back of the office, a woman called from across the section of the station, "Hey, Red, over here."

The smell of old coffee smacked me in the face as I approached her desk. A short, skinny Green woman sat at the desk. The look on her face told me she was more of a force than she initially appeared. "What do you want? I'm not exactly happy to be on night duty here, and I don't have time for your problems, so this better be good."

Without speaking, I reached into my bag and tossed the letter onto the desk with a flick of my wrist.

As it slid across her desk, she snatched it skeptically with a glare and examined the seal. She looked up at me skeptically and then back at the letter. Her voice became hushed. "They're sending Reds as couriers now, huh." She quickly skimmed the contents of the letter, looking up at me occasionally. "You can tell our mutual acquaintance that he will be released immediately, and the charges will be dropped. Anything else you have for me?"

"That's it. Thank you, officer." *That was easy.*

She nodded. "Watch yourself with that family, kid. They have a million secrets, and they'll do anything to protect them."

I hesitated, nodded, and left the station, doing a mini-salute to Oliver at the front desk on the way out and receiving another head shake in response.

On my way back, I sent a report to Delaware over my radio. She needed to know how things were evolving, and I wasn't sure how often I would get to check in.

When I returned to the palace, Michael was standing like a statue outside my room. "Did all go well?"

I smiled. "The cat is in the bag."

His brow furrowed. "What?"

"The turtle is in its shell."

He scoffed. "Excuse me?"

I rolled my eyes. "The sword is in its sheathe."

"So it is done."

"Yes."

He glared. "You could have just said that."

I chuckled. "Yeah, but what's the fun in that?"

He sighed. "You've forgotten the basics already. You will not last long here, Ivan." *But I'll have fun messing with you while I am.*

I snapped my fingers. "Darn. And just when I thought we were becoming friends." My stomach grumbled. "So, what's a Red got to do to get some food around here."

"You may fix yourself a plate in the servants' kitchen down the hall on any day during most hours of the day. Now, I must relay this information to the Queen. Goodbye, Ivan."

I nodded. "Michael."

It took some wandering, but eventually I found the kitchen, and if this was for servants, I couldn't imagine what the kitchen for the royals looked like. Various types of cooked meats were lined up alongside fruits, vegetables, and starches, some of which I had never seen in person before. The aroma was wonderful and overwhelming at the same time.

My gaping awe must have been obvious, as one of the Green cooks came over and waved a hand in front of my face. "Earth to Red, Earth to Red."

I shook myself out of the daze. "Sorry. I, uh… I've just never seen this much food before."

He stood proudly. "Made fresh every day. The royal family wants to make sure we are well taken care of, and we," he gestured to a few other servants in the kitchen, "make sure the food is prepared and, if I say so myself, of the highest possible quality."

"Wow. Uh, thanks." I reached out my hand. "Ivan."

His eyes narrowed, ignoring my offer of a handshake. "Arthur, and don't thank me. This isn't supposed to be for the likes of you. Grab what you need and get out of here, Red." He pushed his way past me and over to the Blues and Greens at a nearby table.

I sighed as he walked away and dropped my arm. *Why would he be any different than the others?* I piled my plate probably a little too high with food. Technically, I was still a slave, but I was determined to eat like a king while I was there. I looked over at the other servants, who were attempting to ignore my presence, and shuffled back towards my room to eat. *One little event has changed so much, but some things never change.*

Sitting there, I felt lonely. My closest friends were miles away, struggling in the Enclave while I was eating in the palace. I was determined to make my time there worth it, though. Delivering that letter I hoped would bring me one step closer to the King and the important information that surrounded him.

Chapter 14

As the days went by in preparation for *The Cherry Orchard*, I grew more accustomed to the theater, the palace, and their inhabitants, even if they were not becoming more accustomed to me. Everywhere I went, eyes were averted, people whispered, and the occasional White spat at me. It had become almost a game to me, though, and I strengthened my resolve to show that they weren't getting to me. That face held on the outside, but it was wearing me down inside. Even if you've taken verbal abuse your whole life, an increased volume of blows will bend you; the key for me was not to break. I clenched my teeth and created a mental list of who had messed with me. They could spit at Ivan, but Coyote would bite back when the time was right.

Within the previous week I had also been given one more task by the Queen. It was rather simple but important: report on interactions and conversations of Duke Richard Bilgram, the head of one of the most powerful royal families, second only to the Hughes family, at the opening night party for *The Cherry Orchard*. Queen Vera had suspicions that the Duke was working with certain minor royal families to create a coalition to take the throne for himself, either by force or via the electors whenever King Timothy died. She wanted me to find out which families those were, so that the correct pressure could be applied to break that coalition.

To me, it all seemed petty. The throne was nothing but a title for the Whites to distractedly squabble over while the socialists held the real power. King Timothy III was no abolitionist, but he seemed more pragmatic than the alternatives. The Bilgram family had been the largest royal advocates for the initial creation of the Prism, and the Duke had a private army along with large funds from Red Tag slave trading dedicated to ensuring that the Prism Test never ended. If I wanted to make a difference while with the royals, the Hughes family needed to remain in power. Even after such little time with them, I had already learned that the royal game was hardly ever all or nothing. *Welcome to politics...*

As a crew member not part of the show's run-crew, I had been assigned as an usher for the show itself and as a general server during the after party, which would take place in the palace's ballroom. As per the tradition with royal events, all servants were to wear white masks, which not only concealed our faces but our tags as well. The Queen believed this positioning, combined with the mask's added bit of anonymity, would put me in a suitable position to keep tabs on the Duke without arousing suspicion. Apparently, she trusted me more than the average crew member: both because of my previous actions and because she knew that I understood betraying her family would lose me everything I'd gained and probably more. Our second meeting had been shorter than the first, but that point she had made clear.

Before the audience was to be allowed in, the house manager called us to the booth to give our final instructions. Due to my lower status I was to seat the people in the back-left corner, far from the Duke's seat near the front. I would have better luck overhearing his conversations at the after-party.

Following the briefing, I leaned against the railing on the balcony outside the booth, looking over the empty theater and its velvet ice-blue seats, soon to be filled with the richest and most powerful people in the country: royals, UPF elite Purples, and a few foreign ambassadors. If there had been more time to plan and I had not been given this task by the Queen, I could have gained something from my close proximity to the UPF high-ups, but that would have to wait for another time. I had my objective, and one objective was enough for the night. *One step at a time.*

The pre-show music began to play through the speakers, filling the vast, beautiful room. It was a moment of tranquility. I felt like I could fly up there and wished it could last even a few seconds longer, but I was ripped from that peaceful place by Archibald and yelled at to "get my ass downstairs."

I assumed my position in front of my section just as the doors opened and the guests entered. After examining many tickets, most of which were in fact not in my area, I was beginning to suspect that most of the guests were already drunk. A faint aroma of wine filled the air, and I couldn't help but smile behind my mask at the ridiculousness of it as they stumbled through the aisleways. These people had the honor of seeing one of the world's most famous shows performed by the country's best entertainers, and they probably wouldn't even remember it.

The guests in my section were mostly obese minor royalty and unimportant bureaucrats within the UPF's government. The former group was mostly asleep by the time the show started, while the latter sat as if they were at a military gathering.

As I scanned the crowd, I only caught a glimpse of the Duke out of the corner of my eye. He was tall and handsome, striding along with the beautiful Duchess Ilana by his side. They circled through the room like vultures as they interacted with the other guests, their gold and obsidian family rings glistening on their hands. Even from that short moment, it was obvious they wanted to make a scene.

The last of the guests settled in, and I stood alongside the edge of the chairs as a man walked across the stage and greeted the audience. A spotlight struck the main doors in the center aisle and they opened as the Hughes family was introduced by the man. The audience promptly stood and placed their hands over their hearts as the mellow Royal Anthem played slowly in the background. I followed suit, while scanning the members of the Hughes family as they made their entrance, a sea of blonde hair and ice-blue clothes. The King and Queen pridefully led the procession, followed by the two oldest daughters, Natasha and Alexandria, while Julia walked next to her youngest sister, Helena, in the back.

This was the first time I had seen Julia since the throne room, and my heart raced as a genuine smile crossed her face. She was enjoying the spotlight. Then I remembered that this was probably the closest I would ever get to her, and my heart sank at the thought.

I didn't know what to think about Julia. She was why I was where I was. Plus, she obviously cared enough to request that I be in her service, pushing back against her dad's interrogation, but what did that mean? Was it just repayment for saving her? Those were questions for later. Now, I had a job to do.

The music faded, and the audience applauded as the royal family took their seats. Shortly after, the spotlights returned to the main doors for the entrance of General Secretary Lawrence Bachton to the UPF's bold and brash National Anthem. The General Secretary was the head of the government and the most hated man among the Militia. It took every fiber of my being to not run across the theater in a foolish attack as I bit my cheek and clenched my fist in anger. *You can't kill the hydra by cutting off its head.*

The audience stood at attention and sang loudly, though the royals seemed less enthusiastic than the bureaucrats as he marched proudly down the aisle, the spotlight reflecting off his bald head and shiny purple tag. Lucky for me, again, the mask covered my face, so I could just stand and scowl at the man who represented everything I hated about the world. *Even here, I wait in the shadows.*

When the General Secretary was seated, I followed my fellow ushers to the lobby. The Blue and Green ushers gathered on the other side the lobby around a smuggled fifth of vodka, fitting of the theme, and occasionally shot glares at me. We would not be of use again until intermission, when our goal was to ensure the drunk guests knew where the bathroom was, where their seat was, or what their ticket even said.

Finally, intermission came, and we opened the doors and stood formally, waiting. I kept an eye out for the Duke, though he never emerged and was likely frolicking with other royals inside the theater. Part of me hoped that Julia would walk past on the off chance, but part of me wished she wouldn't. It was impossible to know if she would look for me or if she even knew I was working the show. *You have bigger concerns than her right now, Ivan...* She never emerged from the crowd, though the Queen did momentarily, her eyes meeting mine for just a second before moving on. Her stare sent enough of a message. My time was coming to execute the plan. When the show was over, the games would begin.

Chapter 15

As we relocated to the ballroom across the gardens, I tailed the Duke while he walked with Franklin McGill, a minor royal. I made a mental note and tried to listen in on the conversation while not following too closely. They were discussing a trade deal of some sort, with Bilgram offering Reds in exchange for supplies of the McGill family whiskey. The UPF have put a tight lid on alcohol sales, so the liquor smuggling business had become big. Enslavement of Reds, on the other hand, was perfectly legal. While this wasn't definitive proof of any conspiracy against the throne, the information could be used for blackmail, if necessary.

The Duke kept looking over his shoulder as we approached the ballroom, and I slowed down to avoid suspicion. Better to not risk getting caught so soon in the evening.

In the ballroom, I received a plate of hors d'oeuvres and began walking through the guests, offering one to each as I passed by them. It would be difficult to find the Duke again in the large ballroom with only the soft lighting from the chandeliers and the moonlight through the windows to illuminate the guests' faces. The room was massive, loud, and packed with similarly dressed royals and Purples speaking loudly about this bullshit or that bullshit while live classical music filled the gaps. *Where are you Bilgram?*

Everywhere I looked there were well-known faces: UPF military generals gathered in circles, Whites gossiping, and more. Among the crowd I noticed the infamous Baron Wilhelm Preus, the head of the third most powerful royal family. His sharp green eyes were focused on some conversation, and his white gold and green family ring was wrapped like a tiny snake around his finger. *Well, at least he isn't scheming with the Duke.*

Eventually, I spotted the Duke's signature goatee near one of the windows and began towards him just as the King clinked his glass for a toast. Even with the crowd quieting down as the King's deep and powerful voice filled the room, I needed to close the gap between Bilgram and me. "...yet another fantastic royal event..." I couldn't quite hear them yet and inched closer, almost losing my balance as a drunk uniformed Purple toppled into me and muttered some obscenities. "...appreciate each and every one of you..."

Finally, I was close enough to notice who he was talking with and overhear some of what they were saying. Tia Lin, a member of one of the few royal families not of European descent, was speaking, "... with the Chinese Mafia..." The audience laughed as the King made a joke. "...PL-47 model micro-camera..."

The King finished. "Cheers!"

The Duke looked at Lin, nodded, and they shook hands. *Not much, but it's something.* I offered the Duke an hors d'oeuvre as he turned his head towards me with a raised eyebrow.

He spoke with an almost German accent, "What is this?"

"I don't know, sir. I'm just a server, but I could ask the kitch..."

Suddenly, he grabbed my right ear and pulled my tag from underneath my mask, knocking me off balance and sending the hors d'oeuvre plate flying into some poor lady nearby. His face was red with rage. "What is this?"

I was too stunned to respond. He was not a tall man but, in the context, he was intimidating. *It's gone wrong...*

He stomped his foot, shouting. "What is this?!?" The room became silent. Bilgram ripped off my mask and threw it on the floor before turning to the crowd that had formed, gesturing outwardly. "They send a Red Tag to serve food to royals and the leaders of our government? Is that what the King thinks of us?"

This is bad. I held my hands up in surrender, trying to formulate a response but was paralyzed in fear. I could only look around in shock as every face in the room was turned on me. Out of the corner of my eye I saw Julia, and we made eye contact. She looked as helpless as I did, her narrow eyes filled with worry. She couldn't save me this time.

I finally managed to whimper. "I... I'm so sorry sir."

"Shut up, *boy.*" He hit me with a backhand, his family ring striking me in the temple and knocking me off my feet, though, the "boy" stung almost more than the slap.

Rage filled me as I smacked into the marble floor. *I could kill this bastard right now. Slave trading piece of shit.* I glared but didn't get the chance to seriously consider reacting as the King plowed into the circle that had formed around us, his large frame filling the space. "What is the meaning of this, Richard?"

The Duke tore his attention from me and fired it at the King instead, meeting his eyes of ice and a mental clash occurred ahead of the physical one. Approaching the King and pointing at his adversary's chest, the Duke continued yelling, "Did you invite us all here just to insult us by being served by *him*?" He pointed a finger at me at the end of the sentence. "What is this, a St. Paul diner? Could you not afford to hire any more actual servants while you wildly spend away the royal treasury?" There were murmurs in agreement from many in the crowd.

The King stepped towards Bilgram, his voice filling the whole ballroom. "That is enough! You are in my house and you are talking to your King!"

Bilgram hesitated, vocally overpowered by the King, before recovering his poise and holding his chin high and his arms out towards the crowd. "Timothy, you have a choice. Either he goes, or we go."

Crap. He doesn't have a choice. The King was caught off guard, and I could tell from the look on his face that he knew he was backed into a corner. I realized in that moment why the Queen was desperate for information. There were threats everywhere, and the Duke felt powerful enough to stand up to the King in his own home.

The King sighed and looked at Jonah, speaking reluctantly, "Please escort Ivan out." His cold eyes returned to the Duke and his voice recovered its sharpness. "We will discuss this later, *Richard*."

Jonah stepped forward and bowed. "Yes, your highness." He approached me and spoke in a hushed tone, "C'mon, Ivan, let's get you out of here."

I felt like I'd been brutally beaten. It was hard to move, hard to even think. I shakily reached down and grabbed my mask before following Jonah towards the hall. Along the way I was met with a mixture of pitied looks, mostly from the women, and glares, mostly from the men. The looks, the pain from the hit on my temple, and the overwhelming smell of alcohol was too much. In my life I had been stabbed, shot, and hit by a grenade, but that moment hurt the most. I was ashamed of myself for embarrassing the King, for failing the Queen, and for embarrassing Julia by my inherent connection to her. The most important people in the country had watched and even encouraged my defeat. *Some hero.*

Visibly shaking and barely able to hold my own weight, I stumbled into the hall with Jonah's help before sliding down the wall, my head in my hands. Jonah grabbed me. "Are you alright? That was pretty rough."

I hesitated for a second, breathing hard. "I... yeah, I'll be fine. Just... holy shit."

"I know. I've never seen anything like that. You have struck a nerve for some people, especially Duke Slave Trader."

"It seems I have."

"Well, looks like you're done waiting tables for the night. I'll make sure you get back to your room, okay?"

"Yeah... yeah, okay. Thank you, Jonah. I really appreciate this."

He shrugged. "No problem. Just doing my job."

We slowly and silently walked through the halls back towards the servants' chambers. When I returned to my room, I tore off my clothes, grabbed a towel, and headed for the showers, where I stood under the warm water, trying to process what just happened. I failed to watch the Duke the whole evening, to go unnoticed, and to even be a waiter. *Smooth.* Luckily, I did get some useful information. I hoped that could be my saving grace when I would be inevitably called before the royal family to be chastised for embarrassing them. *Damn it.*

I rested my head against the side of the shower and soaked in the feeling of the warm water rolling down my head and back. Blood trickled from my temple and dripped into the drain, but I didn't care enough to fix it. A tear rolled down my cheek. *Am I crying?* Everything was emotion in the moment, which was weird for me. I considered myself a rational guy, but the events of the past two weeks, culminating in that evening, had been a lot. For the first time in my life I really had something good to lose, and I had blown it. I'd gone from the savior of the princess to a disgrace in less than two weeks. *What goes up must come down.*

After an eternity, I shut off the water and looked at myself in the mirror. The red mark on my temple contrasted harshly with my pale forehead. *Great, just one more scar.* I slammed the outside of my fist against the wall next to the mirror, holding it there as I looked at myself one more time. I analyzed the scars across my chest and abdomen and tried to understand what they all saw in me: an undesirable, a freak. *Maybe I am.*

When I returned to my room, I quickly changed, turned off the light, and lied down facing the wall. After a few moments I sighed. "What am I doing here?"

A voice came from the doorway. "That is a fascinating question."

Chapter 16

*J*ulia. I didn't move. "You can't be here." *How did she get in here without me noticing?*

Her smooth voice cut through the darkness. "Says who?"

"Your dad, the King, who probably already hates my guts after tonight."

She laughed quietly and flicked on the light. "You have a lot to learn about my father, Ivan." She paused, and I heard her step closer, speaking tentatively, "How are you?"

I rolled over and swung my feet over the side of the bed. Looking at them, I responded, "To be honest, I'm not sure."

Her voice was calm and reassuring. "That's understandable."

I finally looked up at her, still in her regal ice-blue formal dress from the evening, a matching crystal necklace glistening on her chest. "Why are you here? The party can't be over yet; they'll know you're gone."

She smiled, the cute kind of smile with just the edge of the mouth when someone is holding in a laugh. "Is it that hard to believe I just came to see how you were doing?"

My mind was scrambled with the emotion of the evening, and I held my hands up near my head intently, trying to grasp the situation. "Yes. No. I don't know. You're a princess. This is all insane."

She giggled, her eyes entertained but her brows perplexed.

"What is?"

"Why am I here? Sure, I beat up a few goons who were attacking you. Great. Why am I here, right now, talking to a princess after creating drama between the two most powerful royal families. I'm just a Red. What the hell am I doing here?"

She gestured softly to the other end of the bed and responded in a soothing voice. "Can I sit?"

I nodded. What is going on?

She sat down gingerly on the edge of the bed and thought for a minute. She kept looking down as she spoke, less confident than I'd seen her before, though her voice flowed like a river. "I'm not sure what put you on that corner that night. If it was fate, luck, or just a coincidence; it doesn't matter to me. What matters is that instead of walking by like so many people would, you risked your life for a stranger." She met my eyes before I looked down at my feet sheepishly. "Ivan, you saved my life." She paused. "I don't know how to repay you for that."

"Well, you saved my life in return, so I guess we're even."

She scoffed. "You were stabbed fighting off those thugs because of me. Bringing you to the hospital afterwards doesn't count."

I huffed and threw my arms out. "So what?"

She laughed sharply, almost sounding offended. "So what? I don't care about a stupid embarrassing incident that wasn't your fault. That fool is a slave trader, and he believes that he belongs on the throne. All he would do is encourage the UPF to make more Red slaves for him." She huffed, frustrated. "I hate what he did to you, and I can't believe dad gave in to him. Someone needs to put the Duke in his place."

I smiled wryly. "I can probably help with that."

She sighed, and her voice became more questioning. "Does this have to do with my mom's 'secret' meetings with you?" She noticed my surprised look. "I may not be the Queen and may only be the third oldest daughter, but I have my connections."

Cunning, I'm impressed, but do I trust her? "Yes." Guess I do.

A light lit behind her eyes in curiosity, and she spoke intently, "Tell me more."

I scoffed. "And face the wrath of your mom?"

She responded softly, "Ivan, I'm on your side. I can keep a secret."

Do I have a choice? "Fine." I explained the tasks the Queen had given to me and the information I had discovered on the Duke that night.

She nodded occasionally throughout the story and then pursed her lips, pondering. Eventually a smile came over her face before she crossed her arms and looked at me, her eyes analytical. "Mother must see something in you. She has very few servants she trusts to run on her missions apart from dad's knowledge."

I shrugged dismissively. "Eh. She seems skeptical."

"She is that way with most people, and everyone is a little wary of the Red in the palace..." She rocked her head to the side, thinking. "My mom has to deal with all the official business and the interests of the royal family. Behind the scenes she is always scheming for whatever she thinks is best, which can be problematic."

I huffed. "Seems like a lot of drama."

She lowered her head, breaking the princess guise for a moment before recovering. "Too much sometimes. I do everything I can to break from my royal bubble and into the real world. It's difficult with everyone's judging eyes watching me."

"Sorry."

She shook her head. "For what?"

"I don't know, for having to deal with this crap."

Julia half-scoffed half-laughed and smiled, dropping her guard again and fidgeting with her family ring in her lap. She looked down hesitantly before returning her gaze to me. "You're a Red Tag and you're apologizing for what I have to deal with?"

I smiled before returning to a more serious tone, looking at my feet and then back at her. "One of the few lessons I've learned is that everyone has their struggles and comparing mine to theirs, or yours in this case, isn't productive."

She giggled. "I thought you were supposed to be some backwater rebel kid, not Aristotle." *Who?*

"It doesn't take a genius to take a step back and see the positives and negatives of every situation. Little girls dream every day of being in your shoes. That doesn't mean you haven't dreamt of a life outside of the spotlight." I reached my arm out at the last bit as if calling to the outside world.

She looked down and then back up at me, biting her lip and fiddling with her hands. I was surprised by the sudden surge of emotion through her face. "Thank you, Ivan. I appreciate that. I'm grateful for my position in life, but yes, sometimes it is awful to have my every move be watched." She breathed in and out heavily, trying to calm herself.

What am I supposed to do here? I reached out and touched her arm for support.

She looked up at me and our eyes met for a moment before she stood quickly and responded sharply, "I need to get back to the party before people start asking questions."

I stood, slowly and cautiously, before bowing. "Of course, m'lady."

She responded forcefully, "Stop. Just call me Julia."

I smiled. "Okay, Julia."

She turned and opened the door.

"And Julia." She looked over her shoulder. "Thank you for stopping by. I appreciate it."

She gave a slight smile, looked down hesitantly, and continued into the hallway.

I collapsed back into my bed in exhaustion. *What am I doing here?*

Chapter 17

I woke up like normal the next morning and began changing into work clothes. There was a knock at my door as I was finishing up. "Come in."

Michael appeared at the door, though he did not step into the room. He looked more agitated than normal by my presence, if that was possible. "Your presence is requested."

How is this guy so proper in the morning? "Should I change?"

He narrowed his eyes. "No. Come with me."

Crap. I knew what was coming, and it wouldn't be pretty. There was no way I could remain with the theater crew after last night. I had been a joke before. Now I would be a hindrance to the theater's success. The King would not be pleased with last night's disruption, and he was unaware of the information I was able to gather for the Queen.

Following Michael sheepishly through the halls, I wondered if this would be my last day in the palace. "What have you heard about last night?"

He continued ahead undeterred. "It is safe to assume, Ivan, that everyone has heard about what happened." *Great.*

We arrived at the small parlor, and Michael opened the door. "I will be waiting outside to escort you afterwards." *Another bad sign.*

I took a deep breath and entered the parlor, which felt small and suffocating compared to the hominess of my previous visit. The King was seated on one of the couches near the fireplace, his wife beside him. He did not look happy, or well rested, and his eyes sent a chill down my spine. "Sit."

I am so screwed. I took a seat in the chair he gestured to, trying to avoid shaking in the process. Last night I was rattled. This morning I was nervous, more nervous than perhaps any other time in my life.

The King sat, legs crossed, hands folded, his thumbs circling around each other in thought. The Queen seemed more relaxed, though that was relative compared to her normally stern demeanor. I was glad she was there, perhaps she could divert some of her husband's upcoming verbal attacks.

"You know why you are here," he began. I nodded. "The events of last evening were a complete and utter embarrassment to the royal family. You have been here but two weeks and already you have helped create controversy around my rule. I hope you understand how humiliating that was."

I nodded and responded shakily, "Yes, your highness."

He raised his voice, and I slumped back into my chair. "Did I ask you to speak?" I lowered my head. He coughed and continued. "There is no way for you to continue as a member of the theater team. Archibald did vouch for you, but he also admitted that your presence would be a distraction in the future." He sighed. "Honestly, I do not know what to do with you, Ivan."

I hung my head even lower. *He's going to send me back to the Enclave.*

"I'm not sure I have much of a choice but to expel you from our service." *It's over already?* My heart sunk, and I closed my eyes, trying to hold back any physical signs of emotion.

The Queen stepped in. "Wait a moment, Timothy. Don't you think you're being a bit harsh on the boy? The Duke was the one who made a scene."

The King looked aggravated and almost winced at the interjection, though he softened his voice for her. "Yes, and he will be dealt with in the proper time, but Ivan is my servant, and I must handle him."

"What if I told you that at my request he was gathering crucial information that could help us bring down Richard, and that is why he was in such close proximity to the Duke?" *Thank you.*

The King looked even more annoyed and took a deep breath, the softness towards her was gone. "Why do you do these things without my knowledge? What are you trying to accomplish?"

She looked at me, ignoring his questions. "Tell us, Ivan, what did you learn?"

I did not appreciate the anger of the King being deflected back upon me, but I complied and described the conversations I heard that implicated Richard as well as the McGill and Ling families, albeit with some limited content on the latter. "… and I likely would have learned more if he had not discovered my tag."

The King sat back, pondering and running his hand through his bright hair. Eventually he leaned forward. "Well then. At least we have identified two of Bilgram's allies and probably have enough to blackmail them out of their agreements, but there must be far more. He is too smart to interact with his strongest allies at a public gathering." He sighed, frustrated. "Very well. Ivan, despite the embarrassment, you did decently well retrieving this information, even if my wife failed to inform me of her scheme," he growled. "The question still remains, though, what I should do with you." He fidgeted, seeming uncomfortable.

The Queen spoke charismatically, "We have discussed this, Timothy."

He sighed and thought for a moment before he spoke, gesturing with his hands, soft but firm, "Alexandria told me how you helped her get her friend released, saving our family from another embarrassment. It seems that my wife and two of my daughters have decided you are worthy of their trust. I am still skeptical of your past, but you have proven yourself to be of use. I do not like it, but I will grant my wife's request." He paused, as if considering whether he would regret his next statement. *Man, he looks like someone stabbed him in the gut.*

He sighed and continued slowly, obviously not ecstatic. "You are to be a bodyguard for Julia. Additionally, you will execute any requests she has of you to advance the interests of our family. As you're aware, there are many threats to us, so we need trustable people in key positions. We will allow you to carry limited weaponry, as well. Despite my discomfort with that, my wife feels it is needed for you to execute your assigned duties. Do you understand?"

Wait what? I sat there with my jaw dropped, probably looking like an idiot, too stunned to respond. In a quick exchange I went from fired to becoming Julia's bodyguard because of the Queen.

He grimaced and continued. "This is probably a lot to take in, but it has become... apparent... to me that you have the trust of

86

much of my family and that you can be of use away from providing service for guests."

I shook my head in shock. "I... I... Thank you, your highness. I don't know what to say."

He groaned, almost sounding like he was already regretting the decision. "Tell me that you will protect my daughter with your life and won't make me regret this."

I dropped from the chair to a knee and bowed my head. "I will serve with everything I have your highness. I am honored by your mercy for my mistake."

He nodded. "Now go. Act on those words before I think twice about this. Michael will direct you from here."

I stood and bowed. "Your highnesses."

Michael was waiting for me in the hall. I looked at him. "Did you know?"

He kept a straight face. "There is a reason the Queen trusts me, Ivan. But, no, I did not know what the King would decide. I only knew what the Queen would make him do in the long run."

I nodded, acknowledging his statement and laughing a little.

He looked around to make sure no one was in ear shot before whispering, "For the record, I wish you had punched Duke Bilgram in the face, but you didn't hear that from me."

I smiled. "Me too, though I would probably have been hung if I did."

His eyes narrowed. "Indeed. Follow me, I will give you a brief introduction to your duties." He showed me the halls around the royal family's rooms in the restricted upstairs portion of the palace, pointing out where the guards and personal bodyguards were to be posted. "Your position is unique, as you will be the only official bodyguard assigned to Princess Julia. Though she will often be around other royal guardsmen, you are the one who will be travelling with her to ensure her safety. It may be difficult for you, as I'm sure you are aware that people won't appreciate being told what to do by a Red. Just... do not agitate the other guardsmen. You have a way of being too casual, and they are not happy that she was away from them and almost killed. They take the job seriously, which is good, but that means they may see you as a threat. Just a warning for you."

"Thank you, Michael. This all helps a lot."

"One last piece of advice. Don't let people know how close you've become with some in the family. For their sake and yours, that kind of publicity is dangerous with rival families and the UPF looming."

"Noted. You sure you don't want the job? You seem like an expert more than just a butler."

He clicked his tongue condescendingly. "Like yourself, appearances can be deceiving. I may have been wrong about you, but time will tell. Now, I must return to my duties. Good luck with your new position, Ivan. You should see Princess Julia along the lake front for instructions from here."

"See you later, sir."

He smiled slightly, the first time I'd seen him do so. "Glad to see you remembered some formalities." He left, walking with a purpose down the stone hallway back towards the Great Hall.

Chapter 18

I found Julia sitting on the edge of the pier, her feet in the crisp cool water, gazing across the lake. Her bright blond hair shone in the sunlight against the water. This was the most casual I had seen her, wearing rolled up jeans and an ice-blue knit sweater. For just a moment, she looked like a regular girl before I remembered she was a princess. Her two Blue handmaidens stood at the start of the dock. They looked surprised to see me when I walked past but did not interject.

The boards creaked under my feet as I approached. She heard but didn't look up. "Dad got rid of him, didn't he?"

She thinks I'm Michael. I imitated his snobby voice. "Indeed, m'dam. They threw him into the dungeon to rot."

She turned around quickly, obviously shocked to hear my voice instead of the butler's. A big smile came over her face, and she ran towards me, giving me a hug. I stood there, stunned, for a second before returning it. It isn't often you get a hug from an attractive princess. After a moment she let go and stepped back quickly, self-consciously scanning the shoreline to see if anyone was near.

She nervously brushed her hands against her pants, her face a mix of relief and surprise. "After our family meeting last night, dad didn't seem very keen on keeping you, even though Alex, mom, and I tried to convince him."

"Well, you're not going to get rid of me that easily."

Her face kept flipping between analysis and shock, her eyebrows struggling to keep up with her mental confusion. "What? How? Tell me everything."

"The combination of the support from you three plus my information on the Duke convinced your dad that I was 'useful.'" I made air quotes around the last word. "He agreed with the Queen's request."

Now her eyebrows were just scrunched in confusion. "What request?"

I cocked my head to the side. "You didn't know?"

She was suspicious. "Know what?"

Wow, I'm actually in-the-know for once. "She wants me to serve as your bodyguard."

Her reaction was a mix of rage and surprise, and I could see the gears turning rapidly in her head as she paced around the dock trying to calm herself down. The river of her voice turned into a broken dam. *If she didn't know...* "Why wouldn't she tell me this? She thinks I need a bodyguard? What are people going to think? Ugh! Why does she hide things from me?"

I rubbed the back of my neck. "Oh. Uh, sorry to disappoint."

Stressed, she ran her hands through her hair. "No. I'm not mad at you. Just, my mom is trying to keep an eye on me and I wasn't prepared for this." *A princess losing her cool is surprisingly adorable.*

I shrugged. "You did just get attacked."

"Yes, but... I'm sorry. I'm actually happy about this, but I just wish I knew ahead of time. Now it just looks like a scheme from my mom to get information about me."

"Well, I won't tell her."

She lowered her head and then looked at me, inquisitive. "I may be a princess, Ivan, but my mom has way more influence than me. It will be hard for me to protect you, if you don't go with her unspoken plans. Not to mention the other royals."

"My job is to protect you, now. Let me worry about my own safety. I've been doing it for the last twenty-one years. Besides, I think you have more influence than you know."

She was caught off guard and crossed her arms. "How so?" "You may not hear what the average people say, but I do. We've heard your quiet calls for reforms."

She quieted her voice, as if someone could hear her. "I try not to be too loud about politics."

"I know, and that's smart. But heard what you have said, and that has earned you a lot of respect among the Yellows, Oranges, and Reds."

She looked along the shoreline again and bit her cheek nervily. "I... I'm honored to be respected but influence among the royals is a whole different thing."

"Is it?"

She shook her head sharply. "What?"

"Is it? The monarchy has been extremely isolated since the civil war, but that doesn't mean you have to be. You were breaking through the divide between the royals and everyone else by being out there the night you were attacked. Now, just do it in the light more often. The media, state-run and underground, would fight for an interview with you. You're a princess, you can make your own influence."

She looked confused but also somewhat impressed. Shaking her head dismissively, she lowered her arm sharply. "That's a conversation for later..." She looked around, checking that the handmaidens were out of earshot and whispered, "...and in private." She took a deep breath, calming down, but her eyes flickered back and forth as she pursed her lips and tried to think things through. "For now, just be aware of the caveats that come with anything that has to do with my mom. My dad may be the King, but she is a puppet master behind the scenes. I love her, but I pick my inner circle carefully to prevent control by her or anyone else."

I nodded. "Makes sense. If you'd like..."

"No, Ivan. I already said, I'm happy about this, but you... we... need to be careful. Come. I assume Michael showed you around upstairs. I'll show you the daily parts of my routine, so you can have an idea of where you'll be." She put on her shoes and socks before leading me back down the pier. "Have you been formally introduced to my handmaidens? No? Okay. Rachel, Anne, meet Ivan."

I shook both of their hands, bowing ever so slightly while doing so to signal that I still knew my place. "Nice to meet you both, officially."

Julia's proper princess demeanor returned. "You two can go to lunch. I will be running Ivan through his responsibilities." They both bowed and headed off towards the servants' wing.

We walked back towards the palace, heading through the garden. Julia seemed to be pondering something, and she gently fiddled with her family ring as she held her hands in front of herself. Her brows were furrowed in analysis of some kind. Eventually, she stopped to look at some of the flowers along the way and cupped a purple one in her hand. Her expression softened. "The first snow will be here soon. It always amazes me how the beautiful colors of this garden are replaced by a blanket of white, yet it manages to be just as stunning."

I nodded. *What do I know about flowers? Nothing...* She was right about the temperature, though. It was a cool day, and I rubbed my still bandaged left forearm. I had been replacing the gauze every few days, but it was becoming apparent that an ugly scar would remain.

She looked at me inquisitively while still crouched. "I had meant to ask, what did you do to your arm?"

I looked away, uncomfortable. *When do I tell her? Can I tell her?* I deflected jokingly, mimicking her tone from earlier. "That's a conversation for later, and when we are alone."

She giggled and smiled for a moment before becoming more serious. "I figure there's a lot you haven't told anyone."

I crossed my arms defensively. "We all have our secrets." *Some more than others.*

Julia was silent for a bit, examining a few other flowers and considering that statement. Then, she stood and sighed before giggling softly. "So many guys are going to be mad that you're my bodyguard."

I raised an eyebrow. "Why?"

She began walking up towards the palace and I followed.

"Royal girls, especially us as princesses, get constant suitors. You don't think they're going to be angry when they see a Red Tag guarding a girl they're chasing after?"

I laughed. "I didn't think about that. They must have a pretty low self-esteem to be jealous of a Red."

Her cheeks became a little red, and she looked away. "Or to walk up to the palace with flowers expecting us to fall for them."

I chuckled. "That's a thing?"

She shook her head dismissively. "Yes, especially with some of the minor royals, Blues, and well-off Greens. It's so hard to know who actually cares about me as a person instead of as a princess." She pushed forward as passion filled her voice. "Everyone is so *fake*. I hate it. The world seems to care more about status than who we are. So many people don't seem to get that we're not all that different, you know? White, Purple, Red, whatever. We're not that different."

She is way too down to earth to be in the royal family.

Chapter 19

When we reached the palace, Julia pointed out parts of her routine and explained where I should be for certain meetings. "I also want to give you some level of freedom, Ivan. If you need to go into the city, just let me know. I'm sure you have some people you'd like to see outside of the royal territory. You're not a prisoner, even if that seems hard to believe after the last few weeks."

We moved upstairs and towards her room. She opened the door and gestured for me to enter. "Take a seat. We have a lot to talk about still."

Her room was massive, with a small sitting area, and expensive furniture only a royal could afford. Ice-blue decorations and carpets covered the stone floor and bed, and for the first time I felt like I was in someone's home. A soft Fall scent that I couldn't recognize wafted through the air.

 She hesitated for a moment before sitting on one of the couches. After waiting for her, I sat on the one across from her. "I'm surprised you're willing to trust me with all of this."

She looked down, rubbing one thumb along her ring in her lap. She responded cautiously, "If I didn't trust you, Ivan, you wouldn't be sitting where you're sitting. I may be more trusting than some in my family, but, like I said, I pick my inner circle carefully. It is like a team of sorts, which you need to survive around here: in both reputation and actuality. So, on my 'team' you work for my interests, but it is not a one-way street. If there is anything I can do to help you, you can ask."

I nodded. "Understood."

Julia ticked her tongue, analyzing something. "Like I said on the pier, I believe my mom sent you to keep an eye on me for some reason. I'm sure she claimed it was for my protection, but there is always an ulterior motive with her." She paused, carefully planning what to say next. "I need you to return to her. Tell her that I am skeptical if I can completely trust you, despite you saving me, and that you need an idea to convince me to go along with having you as my bodyguard."

Confused, I shook my head. "What does that accomplish?"

She gave me a look that told me to be patient. "I am not all that interested in what she says to do to help me, though I am a little curious. What matters is that she will request that you do something for her in return for this information, likely something pertaining to me. It might be a small piece in the puzzle to figuring out her schemes involving me."

"And you want me to bring this to you, so you can decide what we should do in response, right?" *Why do I feel like she's not telling me something?*

She straightened her posture and nodded her head. "Precisely. I'll be here when you're finished."

I lightly hit my hands on the top of my knees and stood. "Your wish is my command."

She crossed her legs, maintaining her royal poise. "And, Ivan. Try to take a non-direct route back here to avoid any suspicion."

I bowed. "Of course, m'lady." *What's the real reason for this?*

After some searching, I found the Queen conversing with some minor royals just beyond the gardens. I caught her attention and casually leaned against a tree nearby until she had a chance to break away. *Don't want to look too eager.*

Eventually, she wandered over, and her smooth Russian accent cut through the air. "Let's take a walk, Ivan." We turned down the path back towards the palace. "How is Julia handling your placement?"

Placement. She thinks I'm her agent. Ha. I spoke as formally as I could. "It is going well, though she is having some doubts whether I can be completely trusted. She said she is very careful with whom she lets into her circle."

She looked towards the lake to our right. "I had feared that she may have doubts, especially considering I initiated your appointment as her bodyguard. Did she mention anything about that?"

I shook my head calmly. "Not at all, your highness."

She thought for a moment. "She is paranoid that I have some type of grand plan for her life." She chuckled. "Here. You can tell her that you discovered this when looking for me in the small parlor." She pulled out an unsealed letter from her jacket pocket and held it out for me. "Burn part of it so it looks like I failed in an attempt to discard it. That should convince her that you are on her side."

I took the letter and wondered whether I should read it.

She read my mind. "It is nothing special, just a correspondence from a friend regarding yesterday's party. You will not be surprised by the content."

"Understood. Thank you, your highness."

"One more thing, Ivan." She stopped and examined the statue of her husband riding a horse in the garden. *Here we go.* "I would *appreciate* if you could keep me informed if she tells you about her plans regarding the throne, Natasha, or any other political matters. If any of my younger daughters have the ambition to challenge my eldest, it would be her. I want to know if she is getting any ideas."

"Of course, your highness. I appreciate the help and will see what I can do."

She looked up at the statue and her eyes narrowed. "They got the nose all wrong."

I took the letter and returned to Julia's room, stopping in the small parlor first to fake burn the letter in case anyone was watching me. I made sure to read the letter along the way as I wanted to ensure that the Queen wasn't lying about there not being any crucial information. She wasn't.

Julia scanned the letter quickly before setting it on the coffee table following my explanation. "She was right that this would have helped convince me to trust you, even if there isn't much to it. Now, what of her plan?" Her icy-blue eyes were swimming with anticipation.

I sat on the couch across from her. "The Queen has requested that I report on any political ambitions that you express, specifically related to Princess Natasha and the throne."

She pondered for a second and pursed her narrow lips, her eyes focused on nothing as the cogs turned in her head. "Interesting." She turned to me and smiled. "Well, thank you, Ivan. And congratulations, you passed."

Are you joking me? I lost my cool and stood quickly. "That was a test?"

She responded diplomatically, her eyes putting me back in my place. "Yes. I needed to be sure that I could trust you to be honest with me instead of doing just what my mother said, even though she suspected that I was onto her."

I slumped back into the couch and crossed my arms. "You said you trusted me. After saving your life you needed this silly test?"

She responded cautiously. "I did, and now I can be sure that I can trust you with my secrets without you spilling them to my mother. I'm sorry, Ivan, but you are new here still. Planting an agent in someone's inner circle is what my mom does."

I narrowed my eyes. "Fine. Hopefully I can trust you to be honest as well."

"No more tests, Ivan." She paused before continuing. "Now, for you to be my bodyguard, you need to know some of the details regarding my family, though I'm sure you've already figured out some yourself."

I sat forward again. "Only a bit."

"We have already talked about my mom. She is manipulative. Her charisma masks that, but we are on good terms as long as I don't mess with her grand plans."

"And what are those, besides the obvious plans to prevent the threats to your family's hold on the throne and to watch your political ambitions?"

She sighed. "Most of her schemes involve the throne, which can be productive but also cruel at times. She also has smaller plans surrounding my sisters and me, most of which we don't even know. The rest tend to involve information gathering through her various pawns throughout the palace and beyond. Be careful what you tell them, or anyone in the palace. Some, like Michael, are great people, but they ultimately report back to her. Other people you need to be aware of within her sphere of influence are many of the guardsmen, Chief Chef Oliver, a few members of the local police precinct, including Officer McBart, as well as minor royals such as Alexander Hamilton V…"

"Wait, the descendant of the second King of America?"

"Yes. Some of the Hamilton fled to Minnesota before the war to avoid the socialist uprisings in New York. They're not as powerful here as they are out east, but they are still key players."
"Holy shit… I mean, excuse me m'lady."

Julia laughed, surprisingly breaking her regal demeanor for a moment before biting her cheek and collecting herself carefully. *There's a different girl behind her princess front that she is trying to hide.*

She gave a slight one-sided smile and spoke softly. "Call me m'lady in private one more time, and you're fired."

I smiled. "Of course, Julia. I'm just creating a mental target list."

She gave me a wary look before continuing. "My dad's circle is more obvious: all of his council members, most people with official positions, some of the butlers and people like Phillip, and also the Preus family. Dad is intimidating but not cunning, so don't worry about him scheming much, though he may be looking for opportunities to get rid of you if you mess up."

I rolled my eyes. "Of course he is."

She was quick and direct. "A lot of people are. You're a Red and many people around here will not hesitate to take you out if you're not careful." She hesitated to collect her thoughts. "Now, Natasha, my oldest sister, is mainly under my dad's wing as his desired heir. He is using his influence to ensure that the royal electors pick her whenever he dies. Because of that, she lacks a unique circle on her own besides her husband, Benjamin, and his minor royal family, the von Heusbarns. You really don't need to worry about her unless you decide you want 'her' throne, as she is more focused on being proper than political drama."

"You don't want the throne?"

She laughed. "Hell no." Her eyes widened with a bit of surprise. She bit her cheek and looked at her hands again. *Wow, didn't know princesses could swear.* She took a breath and regained composure. "You can tell my mother that, honestly. I have no desire to take the throne. I want to help change things, but I don't think controlling squabbling royals is the way to do that. She can have it."

I nodded. *Glad to hear it.*

A slight smile crept over her face, and she looked off to her right. "Alex is the rebel child of the family and I love her. She has had and will have more boyfriends than you can keep track of, not that she sleeps around. Mom struggles to keep her reined in. Parties and drinking are her scene." She looked at me. "You wouldn't notice it from how she holds herself, but she is also a huge metal fan, so if you want to get on her good side, mention some music. She couldn't care less about 'influence.' She just wants to have fun and cause problems."

I laughed. "I got a bit of that vibe from her."

She bit her lip. "Don't get me wrong. If I ever want to have some fun, she is the first person with whom I go. In fact, she was at that same party the night I was attacked, though she stayed later. She could learn the art of diplomacy and poise, but we need her to break the mold occasionally. Her only people in the palace are a guard who helps her sneak around and one of the chefs who sneaks in her booze. Neither of them are of any concern. If anything, she and I are on the same team."

"Understood."

"The last is Helena." She smiled cheekily with a little pride. "She's only fifteen but she is becoming a bit of a political animal. Things are hard for her right now, as she can't help but think what would happen if she had to pass through the Prism like some of her friends. Despite our closeness, though, mother has a lot of sway over Helena and will use her in her political games. Helena's little inner circle includes one of the gardeners and Arthur, who I'm sure you've met in the servants' kitchen.

I rolled my eyes. "Oh, I've met him."

She giggled. "I figured. He can be brash."

I sat back again, taking it all in. "I didn't realize all the interconnecting loyalties. From the outside we never see all of this." All my life I had imagined the royalty as a united block. The last few weeks had exposed how much I was wrong about.

She crossed her legs. "That's because most people are quiet about it, but those circles spread. Pretty much everyone in royalty is either a major player or part of someone else's sphere of influence, if not in their inner circle. Now you understand why I feel caged in this place. Everything is part of the game." Her face became weary. It was obvious that royal life took an emotional toll on her, but it felt nice that she was comfortable opening up to me.

"So, besides me, who else is part of your 'team.'"

With some effort, she regained her focus. "Yes, you, my hand-maidens, also Jonah, one of the guards I'm sure you've met..."

"That explains why he was helping me so much."

She smiled and blushed a little, another real moment. *Was she spying on me?* She bit her lip. "I needed someone who could be near you, and Jonah is the nicest guard you'll find. He genuinely wanted to help."

I smiled. "Glad to know there are some good people around here. I owe him one."

"I try to ensure my inner circle is filled only with those types of people." She thought for a second. "Let's see, also Maria, who is a maid, the families of my friends within royalty, and a few people around the city in the UPF's bureaucracy and police."

I was surprised. "I thought you didn't like the socialists."

She clicked her tongue and was quick. "I don't. Not everyone involved in the UPF believes the ideology. They keep me informed on what's going on throughout the city. As we both know, the real power is not here, despite what so many of the royals believe in this bubble. I haven't reached for any power myself, but I still want to know what is happening."

I nodded. "It definitely is a bubble. Between all the money they receive from taxes, the few private companies left, and the black market, I imagine it is hard for the Whites to see that there is a starving country out there."

"Exactly." She sighed. "I've seen more than most, but there's still so much I've been sheltered from... so much I don't know." She stood and walked over to a pitcher of water on a nearby table and poured herself a glass. "Would you like some?"

"Yes, thank you. Though shouldn't I be doing that?"

She responded, slightly offended, "Unlike many in this family, I'm happy to do some things for myself. Here." She handed a water to me and then placed her glass on the table before sitting back down. "Do you have any questions about who works with who?"

"It is a lot to take in, but for now I think I'm keeping up."

"Good." She took a sip of water and then shifted uncomfortably, fidgeting with her ring. "There is one more sensitive thing that you need to know in order to fulfill your duties."

I nodded, trying to look understanding.

Her brow furrowed. "Nothing I have said can leave this room but everything from now on is top secret."

"You have my word."

"Okay." She stood and then hesitantly sat on the couch next to me instead. She pursed her lips and took a deep breath. "Well, a few days ago, my parents told me they are planning an arranged marriage for me with the Preus' oldest son, Isaac, in order to ensure an alliance between our families and put old feuds behind us. Isaac is a renowned socialist and has been placed among the elites in the UPF's air force production division, so he is a big deal to them. He is also creepy, and I don't want to marry him. My parents see it as an opportunity to consolidate power, but I can't do it.”

I shook my head sharply. “An arranged marriage. What is this, medieval Europe?”

Her ice-blue eyes began to fill with tears and she fought to retain her poise. “It feels like it sometimes.” *What do I do, what do I do, what do I do?*

“I… I’m so sorry, Julia. Is there anything we can do to stop it?” I noticed a tissue box on the table and grabbed it for her.

She sniffled and grabbed a tissue. “No. I’ve already fought with my parents over it. When they want something like this, they get it.”

I just sat, looking at her sadly. We both said nothing for a few moments, she sobbed, justifiably. *Life is unfair for everyone it seems.* Eventually I spoke with a bit of anger. “Each of us has our struggles. My chains are wrapped around my ear, yours around your finger.” I gestured to my tag and then to her ring. “We are not free without choice, and your parents have taken one of the most important choices away from you.”

She nodded and put her head in her hands, sobbing.

“I… I can go if you’d like to be alone.”

She took her head from her hands and grabbed one of mine before quickly recoiling and letting go. After a moment, she leaned forward, thinking hard. “Please stay. This might sound stupid, but you’re one of the only people I can talk about this with.”

“Why? I mean, why me?”

She sighed, still not looking at me. “My friends would love to be in this situation, getting betrothed to a successful man from an influential family. It's the mentality of this place. You're one of the only people I trust that still has a foot in the real world."

I nodded. "Okay, then. I'm here for whatever you need."

She sniffled and took another tissue. "Thank you, Ivan."

In that moment she was a girl, not a princess. I was starting to understand the split in her life, not all that different than mine. She seemed willing to trust me with both sides of her. That meant a lot, but it also meant I had to decide if I could trust her with all of me.

In an effort to lighten the mood, I stood up and got her more water, joking softly, "See, I can do my job. Learning already." *The least I can do is make her laugh.*

She giggled through the tears, her emotion opening up her cute authentic side. "Thank you. What are the odds the random Red boy that saved me would also know how to listen?"

I handed her the glass and sat back down, trying not to blush. "I don't really know how to take a compliment like that."

She laughed a bit and retook my hand tentatively for support. "I bet not, especially with the elitists around here. I've seen how they treat you, Ivan. I'm sorry."

I squeezed her hand for reassurance. "Don't worry, I'm used to it, and hey, now I have some palace friends, like you."

She smiled softly and cleared some of the final tears from her face. As she shifted back across the couch, she put her hair into a ponytail. An idea must have popped into her mind, because her eyes lit up with a bit of excitement. "Phew. Okay, I gave up one of my secrets, your turn."

I shook my head sharply, surprised. "Wait, what?"

"We're a team now, Ivan. I need to know if there's anything that could impact how you do things here." She thought for a moment and looked at me with a smirk. "Besides, I need a distraction."

I slouched back in the couch uncomfortably. *I don't like where this is going.*

She flicked a hair from her face. "Tell me something about you. You haven't told me much about your past besides where you worked and kind of where you lived." *Like being a lieutenant in the Militia?*

"And nothing leaves this room?"

"Promise."

"And you promise to let me explain?"

She cocked her head to the side. "Should I be worried?"

"Is that a yes?"

She shook her head. "Fine."

Don't you do it. Don't you... "I am a member of the Militia."

She tensed up and remained deathly still for a moment, processing it. When she spoke, her voice was inquisitive and careful. "I had always suspected it with the knives, the radio, the red tag, the sneaking around at night..."

"And you don't want to kill me?"

She met my gaze, her narrow eyes studying me carefully. "I mean. Do you actually do the things that the UPF claims?"

"No, we don't kill innocent people. Most of our missions are done with no casualties, and always done to avoid civilian casualties. We aren't terrorists. We just want freedom from the Prism."

She considered that for a second, looking at her hands nervously. "And can I trust you to be honest even now?"

"Have I given you a reason not to be?"

She stood quickly and paced around the room. I could almost see the gears working in her head. When she spoke, her voice was stern, "No you haven't, but you do realize how serious this is, right? You just told me you're part of a violent rebel group, Ivan! I've talked about reforms, but a terrorist group trying to destroy the Prism?"

I looked down and then back at her. "Ask me anything. If I lie you can throw me into the Mississippi."

She crossed her arms and bit her cheek, thinking. "What's your codename?"

I smiled with just the right side of my mouth. "How did you know..."

She rolled her eyes. "Oh, come on. Everyone knows you have codenames."

"Fair enough. Coyote."

She scoffed, and sarcasm flooded into her voice. "Oh, so you're not just a member of a rebel group, you're a leader."

I shrugged. "Kind of."

She groaned and paced a bit more before looking back towards me with her arms crossed. "What does it mean? Why 'Coyote'?"

I smiled and looked at my feet. "When you're recruited into the Militia, your officer gives you a codename that they think fits you in some way. It replaces any real name you have when it comes to Militia operations. Poseidon was my officer because he pulled me out of a tough spot when I was little and brought me in. He named me 'Coyote' because apparently it is a spirit animal for those that can see humor in the worst times, are tricksters, and are also teachers."

"Huh. That is deeper than I expected. It suits you." A small smile broke through her seriousness, though it faded as she thought for a second and cocked her head. "Aren't you on the most wanted list?"

"Yes, I believe I was moved up to number six on the rankings."

She scoffed again, her brow furrowed. "You keep track?"

"Yeah, it's kind of like a leaderboard." I noticed her concerned look. "You see, if someone in the Militia kills a civilian or commits some nasty crime, we kick them out, and they're caught quickly without our protection. Those of us that are high on the rankings have pissed off the UPF, but we haven't done anything really bad."

She shook her head. "So, you're a bunch of guys comparing your missions via the most wanted list? That's ridiculous. Don't you want to live?"

"Most of us don't have much to live for." *That hurt to admit.*

That hit her, and she waited before taking a seat at the other end of the couch, pulling her legs in close and holding onto them defensively. She looked down before making eye contact, her eyes sharp. "So, everything you've been doing here, it's not some type of mission, right? You weren't following me that night?"

I raised my hands in defense and responded emphatically. "No! Not at all. I... dang that was a long night. I was coming back from visiting my friend who runs the St. Paul Free Press, after running a mission. I had no idea who you were until they told me in the hospital the next day. I swear."

She looked relieved. Then, a slight smile crept across her face and she looked around, like for some reason this was the first time she was worried someone was listening. "You know the guy who runs the Free Press? I love it. I always have it smuggled in. It's the only real glimpse I get into the real world now that I'm out of college." *Aw. Cute. She thinks she is rebellious.* She thought for a second. "Coyote, so you're the one who wrote the op-eds about how reforms can be done peacefully still."

I smiled softly. "Yes."

She cocked her head to the side. "Do you believe that?"

"With the monarchy's help I do."

Her eyes narrowed skeptically. "So, what you said on the pier..."

"I meant what I said. You have a lot of influence."

Julia considered everything for a bit longer, her eyebrows furrowed in concentration. "How many people have you killed besides the one that night?"

I sighed and looked at my feet, thinking for a moment. "More than I'm proud of. Unlike some, I don't take pride in killing someone's dad, husband, or brother. I picture their faces sometimes..." I trailed off for a second. I'd never told anyone how it felt to have killed before, and I didn't know how to finish, so I deflected. "Like I said, I want a peaceful solution, and a lot of my strategies have been working for that."

She pondered that. Obviously, she knew I had killed people since she had seen one of them but having me admit that it was more often seemed to take a hit. Shifting uncomfortably, she avoided eye contact. "How does it feel?"

"What?"

She hesitated. "Killing someone... how does it feel?"

I sighed. "I try to avoid killing unless necessary, so it is normally in defense, which means I'm relieved to be alive myself at first, but later... it's awful. Like I said, they're all someone's dad, husband, or son. You don't just kill a person, you kill that part of everyone they're connected to, and that... that is the worst feeling in the world. I pray you never feel it."

She looked at me with pity before looking at her legs. I could tell that she was reflecting on everything as she fidgeted with her ring before changing topics. "You said you had peaceful strategies. Like what?"

"Confidential."

She seemed annoyed. "Oh, come on, *Coyote*. If I was going to turn you in, then I already have enough information to do it."

I thought back to the few conversations that I'd had with Delaware via radio since our last meetup. Things were coming along well, and if I could trust Julia with me being Coyote, I could probably trust her with this. "Fine, but don't mock my codename." She rolled her eyes. "We've been working for the past year on this. It's called Operation Blackout."

"Do you name all of your missions after some spy movie?"

"No, just this one, because it's important. Can I continue?"

She rolled her eyed again. "Go ahead, spy boy."

"On the night that we met, I was running the last setup mission that we needed before the big one. We had to get the locations for the UPF's security cameras in the cities and the coding information for their systems used to spy on people's computers and phones. Someone must have tipped off the police about the transfer we had arranged. We escaped, but somehow they found us at our safehouse." I hesitated. *Damn it.* I took a deep breath and continued, "Southpaw and Bobcat were downstairs when they came through the front door. They never had a chance..." Tears filled my eyes a bit. *Why now?* "Three of us barely survived hiding upstairs before they torched the place. Delaware was helping Razor up the stairs and needed help, but when I forced them out onto the roof, I fell back down into the flames. That's how I did this to my arm."

She looked at me with concern and hesitated. "That's awful, Ivan." After a moment, she looked at my arm. "Can... can I see it?"

"If you want. It isn't pretty."

She let her legs back down before cautiously and slowly beginning to unwrap the gauze from my arm. Her face was a mix of curiosity and caution. As I watched her expose the burn, she became more worried and hesitated. *Is she actually worried about me?* "Does it hurt?"

"Not anymore really. I doubt it'll heal much more than that. I'm lucky it was just that forearm."

She held my wrist with one hand and reached out to tenderly touch the burn marks with the other. Her hand shook. It felt weird to have her doing it, but it also felt good being open with her. "So, you helped save three people in one night."

I looked away from her, my eyes tearing up again. "I'm glad I was able to save you, but they were my team. It was my job to keep them alive. Two out of four is not a success in my book."

She tenderly held my arm for reassurance. "There was no way

for you to know they were coming, was there?”

“No, but…”

She cut me off. “You can’t blame yourself then.”

I just looked at my feet.

Her eyes studied my face. “Is it really that bad where living your life in fear of death is worth the risk?”

I bit my lip to prevent any more emotion from showing. “It’s awful. People die every day without enough food, medicine, or clean water. If you’re going to die anyway, might as well die fighting for something, right?”

Her voice was shaky, and she looked away before returning her eyes to mine. “So, the articles, the rumors, it’s all true?”

I replied, deathly serious, “All of it.”

That hit her, and she broke our eye contact. We sat there in silence for at least a minute as she tried to process things, obviously uncomfortable with all the information being thrown at her. Eventually, she looked at my arm again, analyzing it before changing topics. “I think I need to get you a new jacket, and some better clothes, if you’re going to be around me all the time.”

I hesitated. “You don’t have to…”

She cut me off sharply. “Ivan, perception is important, and how you look is a reflection on me.” Her stern look was replaced by a smile and a softer tone. “Besides, it’s my turn to help you, and this I have experience with.”

I bit my cheek and looked at her, giving in reluctantly. “Fine.”

A small smile of victory crept over her face. “Good.” She thought for a second before returning to the topic of Coyote. “You said the mission that night was for this big plan. What did the camera information get you?"

I sighed and looked back at her holding my arm and looking at me with care. "That information allows us work our virus into their system, eliminating their cameras. We will insert the virus during Operation Blackout, which is a series of targeted strikes against their four operation centers: Minneapolis, St. Paul, Milwaukee, and Des Moines. If we can take them down, then they are blind to our movements throughout the whole country. Plus, they can't use the surveillance to spy on people for the Prism. We will have destroyed their strongest weapon against the people and weakened their legitimacy."

"But can't they just turn the cameras back on and reactivate the systems?"

"No, the virus will overheat any cameras, new or old, on the system. They would have to rebuild the entire program and reinstall thousands of cameras, which they won't do easily with us stopping them at every turn."

"That is fascinating, but how does that bring a peaceful resolution to the situation?"

I smiled. "That's where you step in..."

Chapter 20

"You want me to do what?" Julia was on her feet and pacing around the room.

"It'll work." I stood.

She looked at me sharply, sending a shiver down my spine. "You think that somehow I can convince my dad to force the UPF into ending the Prism and reforming the government just because they lost their ability to spy on people?"

I hope. "Yes."

She ran her hands through her hair, letting her ponytail down in frustration. "What have I gotten myself into? You're asking me to risk everything to help you further fracture the Prism. This is insane!"

"I won't force you to do anything, Julia, but with you and your father's popularity, the mere potential of using your army will be enough when we take out their cameras. Together, we can actually change things." I stepped closer to her to try to calm her down. "And like I said, this plan is long term. This isn't something you need to do tomorrow."

She was hesitant and crossed her arms defensively. "You said I wasn't part of some mission."

"You're not. I just thought this was a way to advance your family's interests and our interests. It is separate from Operation Blackout, which we will be doing either way."

She sighed, letting down her guard slightly. "Fine, I will consider it, especially if everything you've said about the conditions out there are true, and you think I can actually make a difference. My dad will be a whole different problem, though. He is very passive in these types of political matters."

"I'm aware, but the goal is for him to see the personal advantages he will gain. His passiveness is actually an advantage here, because any alternative king would be solidly against us."

She nodded and checked her phone. "Shoot, I have to get to a lunch downtown." She stood. "Come along, *bodyguard.* We will have to discuss this whole Militia thing later. Understand?" *Of course she's still uncomfortable.*

I nodded, "Understood," and grabbed my gauze on the way out, starting to rewrap my arm. I wasn't ready to show that scar to anyone else quite yet.

When we reached the garage, Julia looked at the cars quickly. "Which one should we take?"

"You're asking the poor kid that's only driven old public-built beaters which car we should take?" I hesitated. "Fine, that one." I pointed to the Italian car in the corner.

"No, you do not get to drive the Lamborghini on your first day." *Worth a shot.* She grabbed a set of keys from the wall and pointed to the dark blue sedan just in front of us. "You do know how to drive, right?"

My mind went back to the Militia's beaters and I wondered if they actually fell under the same category of driving as these supercars. "Yes, I do."

"Great. Don't kill me or crash the nice car, and you pass." She tossed me the keys. I opened her door and shut it behind her before getting in the driver seat.

The inside was a space ship, not a car. There were more settings and dials than I knew could exist and it smelled like leather mixed with expensive, if expensive could itself be a scent. I hit the garage door opener and started it up. *At least I know what those two things do.* The sound of an obvious V6 below the hood roared to life, and I smiled a little too much. Julia just shook her head as we pulled out into the world.

Chapter 21

My first bodyguard mission consisted of standing in the corner of The Capital Grille, a fancy restaurant downtown. My job was to constantly scan the room for potential threats, of which there were none. The biggest problem was actually getting into the place, as the manager insisted it was for Yellows and above only. Julia eventually persuaded him with a generous bribe, but I felt bad being a burden on her. *I'm supposed to be helping...*

Honestly, with Julia's casual attire I doubted that many people would recognize her without her usual regal attire. She was eating with two friends, a Blue and a Yellow, that she had met while studying the sciences at the University of Minnesota. Apparently, she had wanted a degree and decided that science was one of the few areas that wouldn't involve extensive propaganda from the People's Front. *Smart and attractive... Stop it...*

This gave me time to think, something I had been lacking recently. In a whirlwind I went from almost fired to Julia's bodyguard and apparently one of her best friends that she can open up to. It all felt so alien to me, but it also felt like the easiest thing I'd done in my life. If I wanted, I could have forgotten about my old life and Coyote, but I was determined to use this new, comfortable position to help the cause. I just hoped that I wouldn't have to choose between my two loyalties.

Standing back, I was giving the girls their space. Based on the occasional look that came in my direction, though, I was the subject of some type of conversation. I didn't know if that was a good or a bad thing. Delaware had been the only girl I was close to, so I wasn't exactly acquainted with their social habits.

I looked out the window just in time to see a Yellow with a camera getting out of a car, his eyes fixed on Julia. *Well, it's show time.* I jogged out the front door onto the busy downtown sidewalk and stepped in front of him as he prepared to take the pictures.

Taking off his sunglasses and pushing at me, he still tried to get a picture around me. "Get the hell out of here, Red."

I stood my ground. "The princess is trying to enjoy her lunch, so I recommend violating somebody else's privacy."

He kept moving the camera around to get a pic, and I matched him each time. "Who do you think you are?"

"I'm her bodyguard, so scram."

A smirk came over his face. "Since when they getting Reds to guard royals?"

I grabbed his arm forcefully. "That's a nice camera you got there. It'd be a shame if someone broke it."

He was taken aback and shook his arm free. "Fine. But just know you're going to end up in the papers instead of her soon." He walked back to his car, snapping a poorly angled pic of the girls on his way.

Onlookers hesitated in confusion as I called after him, "Maybe if your papers bothered to cover the government's corruption you wouldn't need to report on what the princess is having for lunch."

He just shook his head and I waited until he drove away before heading inside, ignoring the looks from the crowd on the sidewalk. I looked around the restaurant full of Blues and Greens one last time as they finished up. It was quite amazing that the socialists had managed to replace the corrupt monarchy of the past with a system that had an even more rigid social structure, the exact opposite of what they claimed they wanted. If people weren't starving it would have been funny.

When the girls were ready to leave I met Julia at the table and we walked out towards the car. She looked around inquisitively. "Thanks for handling that paparazzi. On casual Saturdays with friends like this I'd rather not have a ton of pictures taken, considering my lack of make-up and everything."

"Understandable, though, I think it comes off as more authentic to people to see a princess dressing like the average person."

She laughed. "Did you just turn a compliment into calling me average?"

I chuckled. "Don't underestimate my ability to be awkward."

She smiled and shook her head. "It's fine. Now, let's head back to the palace. I need to get ready for a gathering with some of the foreign diplomats."

I let her into the car and then jumped into the driver's seat. "How often do you have events like this?"

She looked out the passenger side window as I pulled into the street. "Someone from the family is attending an event at least once a day normally, not necessarily all in royal territory or even in Northern Mississippi, since dad has a lot of trips out of the country. I have maybe two to four formal events a week and normally a few more informal ones. It's part of the life. Problem is, the conversation is dull and the gossip is merely drama. We should have more events with real people." She smiled and hesitated. "For example, talking with you today has been refreshingly *real*. Everyone always has certain expectations for me to meet. It's tough, trying to please everyone. Thank you, again, for listening."

"Well, it is my job to talk to you. Plus, the alternative is talking with the cranky mechanic, so you surpass the expectations."

She smiled and laughed. "Well I'm glad to be above a cranky mechanic."

I laughed. "Don't flatter yourself. It's a close race."

"Ouch."

Chapter 22

We pulled through the gates, and I let her out at the front. She smiled softly at me as a butler opened her door, "Wait for me outside my room."

"Will do."

I ran into Jonah on the way from the garage. He was grinning. "Heard you're Princess Julia's new bodyguard. Congratulations, my friend."

"Thanks, I'm still kind of shocked by it all."

"I bet, but it is great to have you as a fellow guard now! Also, Julia told me about the weird fighting style you used to take out those thugs. Teach me sometime?"

I was caught off guard by that. I'd never really thought of my fighting "style." "Sure, and you can teach me how to fight the right way instead of how I taught myself to."

He smiled. "Sounds like a deal."

He started to continue his route before I grabbed his arm. "Also, Jonah, I wanted to thank you for last night. I'm not sure how I would have made it out of there without your help."

He gave a slight smile. "No worries. It's my job. Now that we are both connected to the princess, I'm sure there'll be a time in which I will owe you back. You feeling okay today? No fights with Dukes?"

I laughed. "No, just with paparazzies!"

"Ah, yes. Ivan, the hero we need but don't deserve, fighting the crime of photography. Well, I have to continue on my patrol, but it was nice running into you. We will have to talk about that training later."

"Will do. See you around Jonah."

Julia was right – Jonah was truly a kind and helpful guy. I just hoped I wouldn't make a fool of myself training with him.

The rest of the guardsmen must have heard about my new job too since I was met with sneers and sarcastic comments as I walked through the Great Hall and upstairs towards the family's rooms. I waited outside her door for a while. Eventually, one of the handmaidens, Rachel, came out. "Apparently Isaac will be attending the party tonight."

"Dang. Is she okay?" *Can I kick his ass?*

"As you'd expect. I need you to run and let the King and Queen know that she is running late due to… I don't know, come up with an excuse."

"I can tell them her dress was misplaced or something?"

Her eyes lit up. "That'll work. I think they're in their room. Thank you, Ivan. Besides, you owe us for having to deal with that blood you got on her jacket."

I laughed. "No worries."

"Also, since the event is more formal, Julia had a suit sent to your room for you. Pack a bag too. You all are staying at the hotel overnight."

"Oh okay, thanks." *How did she get a suit ready for me so fast?*

I headed down the hall and made the few turns to get to the King and Queen's room. The Blue guardsmen outside did not seem excited to see me. "What do you want?"

"Uh, I have a message from Princess Julia for the King and Queen, sir."

He huffed. "It can wait."

"Can I leave the message with you?"

"No."

I got impatient. "How long will they be?"

"However long I want to make you wait."

I crossed my arms. "So, I could just go in."

"No, you..." The King exited as he was speaking, "Your highness."

The King nodded to the guardsmen and then looked at me, confused. "Ivan, what are you doing here?"

"Your highness, Princess Julia wanted me to inform you that she will be a bit late. Her dress was apparently misplaced, and it took a while to find it."

The King considered that for a second before examining my clothing. "Huh. Fine, and I hope you will be wearing something more appropriate for this evening. That jacket is atrocious."

"I believe the princess sent a suit for me, your highness."

"Then go on. I can wait for my daughter, but I will not wait for you."

"Yes, your highness." I bowed and walked quickly back to my room, where I found a white blazer and navy slacks along with an ice-blue button down shirt laid nicely across the bed. On top of it was a platinum pin with an ice-blue lion to symbolize I was one of the royal family's personal servants. Slid under my bed was a box full of more imported clothes, ranging in styles and way more expensive than I could have ever afforded. My old clothes were nowhere to be seen. *How did she set this up so quickly? My size too. Weird.*

I dressed as fast as I could. These were the nicest clothes I'd ever worn. Sure, the uniform from the night before had been significantly better than my normal clothing, but it definitely was not well-fitted. This outfit, though, was some serious designer quality stuff, from out of the country obviously. Nothing made in Northern Mississippi was ever that nice.

Throwing some of the spare clothes and the few toiletries I had into my bag, I set off, stopping by the bathroom quickly to make sure my hair didn't look like crap. I looked like a whole different person: put together. It felt unnatural and good at the same time. As I finished, I touched my tag. *No clothes can change that.*

After winding through the halls and up the stairs back to Julia's room, I knocked at her door. Rachel popped her head out. "Almost ready." She looked me up and down, "You clean up nice, Red Tag," and slid back into the room. That was the first time I had heard "Red Tag" in an endearing way.

I stood formally, hands behind my back, outside the door. A few guardsmen passed by and looked surprised to see me looking decent but didn't say anything. *That's a first.*

Eventually, Rachel opened the door for me. Inside, Julia was wearing a light blue strapless dress that matched her eyes... and my shirt. *That's not a coincidence.* She looked like she had pulled herself together emotionally, and Anne was finishing her hair up in a braid that wrapped around her head. She looked beautiful. *No, stop. That isn't a possibility, especially now.*

When Anne finished, Julia turned and saw me, looking proud of herself. "So that's what you look like with two sleeves."

I laughed. "How did you have all those clothes ready so fast?"

"You'd be surprised what I can do with a cell phone and a few hours."

"Apparently, though I do want my old clothes back." She just rolled her eyes. "Also, it looks like your handmaidens did a good job finding that misplaced dress."

"What? Oh, I see." She blushed shyly before regaining her poise. "Thanks for covering for me."

I bowed. "My pleasure. Ready, m'lady?"

She smiled softly. "Yes. Let's go before my dad kills me for making him late for his chat with the Chinese Premier." *Because that's how I expected tonight to be going when I woke up this morning.*

We met the rest of the family and their respective bodyguards in the Great Hall, in addition to Natasha's husband, Benjamin von Heusbarn. We were spread between four cars. I sat next to the chauffer in the front of one, with Julia and Helena in the back.

The event was to be hosted by the General Secretary himself at one of the fanciest hotels in Northern Mississippi, though it was a bit of a drive up to St. Cloud. Yesterday had been mostly Whites and UPF elites, but tonight many foreign heads of states would be there as well for a bit of diplomacy.

During the hour or so drive I noticed the worry creeping across Julia's face. *This must be her first time seeing Isaac since she was told of the arrangement.* I pondered what could possibly fix the situation but was coming up empty. *This sucks.*

126

The convoy pulled into the hotel, and the bodyguards opened the doors for the family. I opened the door for Julia and Helena, who did not have a bodyguard of her own yet. Alexandria looked annoyed as she ignored the assistance of her own guard. I chuckled to myself. *Poor guy. She probably ditches him constantly.*

I whispered to Julia as she exited the car, "You doing okay? Give me a signal or something if you need me to pull you out of anything."

She took a deep breath and looked at me sharply. "I'll be fine." I had a weird feeling that tonight wouldn't be.

The hotel itself was fit for royalty, with gold plated everything and marble covered everything. *Excessive plated excessive.* Massive arches welcomed us at the entrance and things only got fancier inside. *Hey, they need to be impressive to host the "Great Leader," right?*

The ballroom was an obvious attempt to put the royals to shame. A giant red carpet flew through the center of the room as three diamond chandeliers hung from the ceiling. Marble columns accented in gold lined the walls. A square foot of the place was worth more than my life. *Not that my life is worth much to these people.*

Live classical music met us as we entered, and a de facto line formed to greet the King and Queen. Each of the dignitaries wore a pin for their respective countries: the General Secretary of the Soviet Union, the Premier of China, the Prime Minister of India, the General Secretary of California, the Prime Minister of New Lombardy, the Prime Minister of France, and the President of Brazil, among others. They all led countries within the socialist

Fifth International or were friendly to its intentions. With the tense state of world affairs following the British and Scandinavian plays in Denmark and the Netherlands, the Fifth International needed to prepare a response. The party provided suitable cover for the socialist leaders to meet without a publicized formal conference. *The most powerful leaders in the world all together in one room to discuss how to further destroy it, great.*

Standing at attention in the corner of the room, I watched while Julia followed behind her parents, greeting the dignitaries impressively in each of their languages. She didn't see her political potential yet, but I was becoming ever more convinced that she could be the answer to so many problems if she could just reach out and take the opportunities in front of her. She had the charisma, poise, diplomacy, determination, and, well, the looks. The only problem holding her back was her desire to be loved by everyone, which is impossible in politics. As much as she could impress here, though, she lived in the shadow of her parents and older sister. She was a princess, not a head of state or a future one.

It was ironic that Julia was in Natasha's shadow, as Natasha did little to impress. She played everything by the book. It was one thing to want to be loved by everyone, but Natasha's goal was to not be hated by anyone. She never strayed from her passive and usually non-controversial father. It was a safe way to become queen, but apathy is a poor trait for a ruler.

Time passed as the guests became drunker and drunker, filling the air with senseless noise, the smell of fruity liquors, and heavy cigar smoke. Julia meandered through the crowd, sipping on her one cocktail while others drunk themselves into oblivion. *Smart.*

Meanwhile, heads of state whispered in corners, looking over their shoulders to ensure no one was listening. I was so close to the heart of political power, yet I felt like little more than a fly on the wall.

Purples and foreign politicians shot me looks as they passed by, surprised to see a Red Tag at such an event. It was starting to give me a bit of pride to stick out like that, a stain on their perfect evening, reminding them of what's out in the rest of the country. I was determined not to draw too much attention to myself. I did not want a repeat of last night.

Eventually the King directed Julia to follow him. *Here we go.* I slid behind them along the wall, staying close enough to step in if something went awry. They reached a tall, muscular royal, slightly older than me. The King did a quick, formal greeting before leaving them together. He kissed her hand gently, his wide green eyes looking up at her like a snake underneath his sleek black hair. *Isaac. Bastard.*

While Isaac pressed forward in conversation, Julia was obviously uncomfortable, fiddling with her own ring and looking around anxiously. Though she was trying to hide the discomfort, it wasn't working. She drank the rest of her cocktail quickly and made eye contact with me, her eyes wide. *I'll take that as a signal.* I slid through the smoky crowd and up to them, speaking as formally as I could, "Could you use another drink, m'lady?"

She nodded properly. "I would appreciate that." She looked towards Isaac and struggled to smile. "Isaac, this is my bodyguard, Ivan."

Isaac didn't seem at all interested in me. I reached out my hand and grinned cockily, using my numbers as a tool to make him a little uncomfortable. "Ivan 181375. Pleasure to meet you." Judging by his reaction, I could tell he was the arrogant first born who always thought too highly of himself. His fake smile and excessive usage of some type of expensive tropical cologne meant he liked attention, just not from me.

He looked at my hand, peaked at Julia, who was analyzing me skeptically, looked at me again, and uncomfortably shook. His voice was cold and raspy. "Isaac Preus."

I pointed my finger obnoxiously as I faked a thought. "Aha, Preus! Your great-grandfather was the last governor of Minnesota before the war, wasn't he?"

He gave me a look that asked why I was talking to him and sighed, reluctant. "Yes, he was."

Tapping my finger against my lips, thinking, I pushed with more fake curiosity. *Sometimes a little useless knowledge can be helpful. Good thing Poseidon taught me to read.* "I can never remember, did Minnesota have elections for governor or appointments from the king back then?"

Realization crept over Julia's face as she finally understood my plan, and she cut in. "I'll let you two talk for a bit. I can grab the drink myself." She gave me a thankful look and glided off. *This is going to be way too much fun.*

Isaac looked longingly after her before turning to me, a vein on his temple twitching. "He was appointed. Now if you'd excuse me..."

Where do you think you're going? "Huh, I always thought Minnesota had elections. I guess that's what you get when you didn't go to school!" I laughed, he didn't.

He quickly took a drink of what looked like whiskey and bit his cheek, looking around the room, desperate to get away.

"Surprising that your family doesn't have a larger role to play with the power you all had before the war. I mean, before I was brought into the princess's service I'd only heard a bit about your father."

His eyes narrowed as he aggressively downed the rest of his drink, the vein twitching with agitation. "Who the hell do you think you are?" *Your worst nightmare.*

I responded sarcastically, "Oh. Sore spot?"

His fist clenched, and he bit his cheek as he hissed, "My family deserved better, and we are going to get it. You wouldn't understand, *Red.*" *What does that mean?*

I cracked my knuckles. "I was surprised to hear that you were at an event for international politicians, *White.*"

He scoffed. "I build war planes. It is very important for me to connect with international buyers."

"Ah, gotcha, and princesses, apparently." He glared at me but did not respond. "I'm sure it's hard to compete with your prices since you use such… *cheap*… labor."

"I'm not sure what you…"

I rattled my tag obnoxiously and raised an eyebrow.

He rolled his eyes. "The Red Tags provide a fine service for the collective and are compensated for their work." *Fine service. What a joke.*

"So, how do you feel about Princess Julia?"

"I beg your pardon?" *There goes the vein again.*

"How do you feel about her?"

He coughed and narrowed his eyes suspiciously before clearing his throat and tightening his tie. "She's an attractive, young princess with a powerful family. What's not to like, besides her talkative bodyguard?"

"Oh, I see." *Fight me.*

Julia returned as Isaac appeared ready to assault me, but my job was done. *He got the message, and she got away for a bit.* While she was gone, she definitely had more than one drink, as the slight hint of fruity alcohol hung around her. She smiled at us. "Glad to see you two are getting on well."

Isaac just flicked his eyes between her and me as the vein looked ready to burst.

I exuberantly clapped my hands together. "Well then, I should head back to my post. It was nice meeting you Isaac." I reached out for a handshake, which he did not accept. I left it there for a few moments. "Hope selling planes to dangerous dictators, I mean other countries, goes well." *Bastard.* I turned to Julia and bowed. "M'lady."

Julia coughed, trying not to laugh and quickly regaining her poise. She sent a warning shot as I passed by, telling me to behave. *No.* Hopefully I could relieve some of the pressure. If he hated me, maybe that would give him a reason to stay away. *Shackles are off.*

I purposely bumped into one of the Purple UPF higher-ups on the way back, saying sorry very deliberately, so that he saw I was a Red. *I am the life of the party. So much for being low key.*

Eventually, the speeches started, and people gathered tightly around the various standing tables as the crowd quieted down. Julia used this as a good time to glide back to her family. I was proud of her for toughing through that without stabbing the guy. I really wanted to, and I actually had a knife hidden up my right sleeve. Bodyguards didn't get searched.

While General Secretary Bachton took the stage and began ranting about the unshackling of the proletariat or something, I slid over to the bar and signaled the Green bartender. "Hey, I was just talking to Isaac Preus, and he wanted me to let you know that he wants five bottles of your most expensive champagne sent to his room tonight. Something about a massive fighter plane deal."

The bartender looked at me skeptically before noticing the Hughes family pin. "Oh, well, okay then. We will have those sent up for him soon. Did he just want it put on his room tab?"

"Yes, of course. Thank you."

"No problem." *I'm an asshole.*

Eventually, the speeches finished, and guests began stumbling to their rooms. I moved towards Julia from my position, but Isaac beat me to her. He shot me a glare as I approached before returning his attention to her, wobbling on his feet. "May I have the honor of taking you back to my room this evening, my betrothed?" He reached for her hand.

Rage surged inside of me, and panic filled Julia's eyes. She stepped back, out of reach. "I think it would be best if we slept in our own rooms, Isaac."

Isaac stepped towards her, drunkenly grabbing her arm. *Oh no you don't.* I flew forward swiftly and ripped his arm away from her before he could speak again. "I believe the princess made herself clear."

As he stumbled backwards, I put myself between him and Julia. A mix of realization and anger crossed his face as he pointed at me. "You're going to regret this, Red." His expression softened, and he looked past me to Julia. "I'll stop by your room later, my princess." With a frustrated huff, he shuffled towards the doors.

I made sure he was gone before turning around. "You alright?"

Julia took a deep breath. "Yes. Thank you for intervening, though. I don't know what he would have done."

I smiled softly and shrugged. "No problem. Though, he did say he would be stopping by your room."

Julia hesitated, and worry crept onto her face. "He did, and we're on the same floor I think. What am I going to do?"

I pondered for a second. "Don't worry. I'll stand watch outside your door to make sure he doesn't do anything."

She pursed her lips in thought. "You are willing to stand outside the door all night?"

I shrugged. "It's my job, and if it makes you feel better, then it's worth it."

She smiled. She was slightly tipsy, and her guard was down more than normal. "Thank you, Ivan. I really appreciate it." She sighed. "Maybe I could actually get some sleep, then."

"I also have a surprise that I think you'll enjoy."

Her eyes narrowed skeptically. "What is it?"

"You'll see soon."

She groaned. "Ivan!" I just shrugged. "Promise me you'll avoid making a scene in the future, *please.*"

I laughed. "Fine. I promise."

She shook her head sarcastically before meeting my eyes. "Walk me up?"

I bowed. "It would be my honor, m'lady."

She rolled her eyes, and we walked towards the elevators.

Chapter 23

We arrived just as the chaos struck. Isaac was raging at a poor hotel staffer outside of his room, "I did not order five bottles of $5,000 champagne! How hard is that to understand?" *Hell yes.*

The worker sheepishly raised up his arms in defense and stuttered, "There's no return policy, sir. These were ordered for your room."

Julia's room was at the other end of the hall, so I slid over, smiling at Isaac and blocking him from her. She held back a smile as she realized that this was my surprise.

Isaac was on fire, and I loved every second of it. The forehead vein was this snake's rattle. "You, bodyguard, tell them to take this back."

I looked at the Yellow Tag hotel staffer and then at him, shrugging. "I think he was pretty clear. How much have you had that you don't remember ordering it? I was there!"

He slammed his knuckles into the wall in anger. "No, I didn't. Ah! Fine. It's just $25,000 anyway." *Okay. Rich bastard.* He looked at Julia, his green eyes a mix of rage and panic as he took a deep breath. "I'm sorry, my betrothed. I'm not an alcoholic, I swear."

Julia didn't respond, and I blocked Isaac as she glided by. He pushed against me for a moment before giving up and slumping back into his room. *Hopefully that's all the energy he has for the night.*

I escorted Julia to her room and unlocked it for her before taking my post outside. She smiled rebelliously before going in. "That was amazing, Ivan, but *never* do anything like that again."

I nodded and smirked. "Yes, m'lady. Have a goodnight."

She rolled her eyes and entered the room. "Goodnight, Ivan. Thank you again for offering to stand guard."

The next six hours were awful as I stood outside the room, bored out of my mind. It was me, the weird smell from the carpet, and the drum that was my heartbeat, which seemed deafening in the silent hall. The only other sounds I heard were the occasional whirring of the elevator shaft and the constant, ever so slight, buzz of electricity from the lights in the hall. I was left to think about everything that had happened, but Julia's arranged marriage was stuck in my mind. It didn't matter whether I had feelings for her or not. I was not going to let her be forced into marrying Isaac.

As I hoped, Isaac never came. He had probably passed out from the alcohol, whether he drank any of the champagne or not. Still, standing guard was worth it, just in case.

Eventually, the world woke up, and people started moving out of their rooms. Julia appeared at the door, wearing similar clothes to the casual ones she had on earlier yesterday. She rubbed her eyes. "Hey, Ivan. Any trouble last night?"

"Surprisingly, no. Seems like the alcohol got to his head."

She yawned. "I'm glad. Sorry you had to stay up all night, though."

I smiled reassuringly. "Don't worry about it. Though, I could use a shower to wake myself up."

She smiled softly. "I will have them bring your bag up. You can shower here. Isaac is still around, so I would prefer you stay close."

I cocked my head to the side. "Are you sure that's okay?"

She responded sternly, "I'm a princess, and I say it's okay."

Once my bag arrived, I showered and changed into my spare clothes. As I threw by bag on the couch in the suite and started packing up, Julia walked out of the bedroom and sighed. "You would think a hotel this expensive could get a princess a decent hairdryer."

I laughed and looked back at her. "Oh, how the monarchy has fallen."

She giggled. "Almost done?"

"Yup. Thanks for letting me use your shower."

She sat down next to my bag on the couch. "Of course." She hesitated, and her eyes searched for words. "Why did you try so hard to ensure Isaac stayed away from me last night?"

I considered the question for a second before deflecting. "It's my job to protect you, Julia." She looked at me disapprovingly. "And... I know how much this matters to you."

She sat, looking at her hands and thinking. "Ivan, what am I going to do?"

I moved my bag and sat down next to her, sighing. "I don't know. It pains me to say it."

She looked at me before standing, her hands fidgeting with her ring nervously as she paced around the room. Last night had been rough for her, and her eyes were irritated from crying, a sea of blue clashing with streaks of red. She spoke intently, "You came up with everything to stop it last night. You have nothing now?"

I looked down before returning my eyes to hers, defeated. "Making him hate me with stupid questions and sending a prank to his room is one thing. Convincing your parents is a whole different story. I'm sorry Julia."

She sniffled, and tears streamed down her cheeks as she held her hands tight to her chest, shaking. "I barely slept. I was just thinking about Isaac and our betrothal the whole time."

I sighed, stood slowly, and hugged her. "To be honest, so was I."

She kept her hands at her chest but placed her chin on my shoulder, her tears smacking into my jacket as she spoke hesitantly, "Pretty dedicated to your job."

"Yup."

She took a long breath, looked up at me in realization, and quickly backed away as she paced over to the window. "I'm so screwed."

I was determined. "We'll figure something out."

She dropped her hands in anguish, taking her ring off and examining it in the morning sunlight before placing it back on her finger. "Will we?"

"He could always fall out a window."

She was sharp, her eyes like daggers. "No, Ivan."

"Fall down the stairs and hit his head?"

"Ivan, I said stop. It's not funny," she snapped.

I bowed. "As you wish, *m'lady*." She gave a judging look and shook her head. *Not in the mood for jokes.*

Chapter 24

*D*ing, we stepped off the elevator to see most of the family in the lobby, ready to go. Only Alexandria and Helena were later than us. I could feel Julia's blood pressure rise as the Queen approached and started asking questions. "Did you have a good time last night?"

Her icy glare clashed with her mother's intensity. "It was *fine*, mom. Isaac tried to force me to his room. Luckily, Ivan was there to stop him."

The Queen looked stunned. "Hun..."

Julia stormed off. "I'll be in the car."

The King stepped in front of her, their eyes meeting. *Ice vs Ice.* "Do not talk to your mother like that."

Julia took a deep breath and came face to face with her mother, gesturing towards her coldly. "It was awful having to talk with him and all the socialist tyrants, pretending that I was happy to see them. I hated being grabbed at by my drunk arranged fiancé in front of a room of people, mom." She turned her head towards her father, her eyes narrow. "There. Happy?" *Ice cold.*

With that she did a quick about-face and stormed off with me in tow. I was sure to not make eye contact with either of her parents, though I could still see the shocked look on their faces.

I opened the back door of the car for her, and she looked

around for a second. "Can you wait outside, Ivan. I need a moment." *Understandable.*

"Of course. And if Helena comes?"

She was quick. "The sooner that happens, the sooner we can go home."

Nodding, I stepped back and let her have her privacy behind the tinted windows while I stood at attention with my hands behind my back outside the car. It would have been a beautiful morning under different circumstances, with the birds singing and gliding through the trees in the hotel courtyard.

Eventually the rest of the family emerged. Alexandria stumbled to her car, hungover, or still drunk... or maybe a bit of both. Her bodyguard was just trying to keep her upright.

The Queen approached and tried to peek in the window, her brow furrowed. Her voice was impatient, lacking understanding. "Do you think she will be alright?"

I kept looking straight forward, past her, and put as much formal bluntness in my voice as I could. "I believe the princess clearly expressed her thoughts on the matter."

She scoffed. "You may be her bodyguard now, but you're still just a pawn in a game far larger than you can see. Did you even try to do as I asked?"

I mimicked a royal accent, still facing forward. "You must not play chess often. A well-placed pawn can win the game or become a much more powerful piece." I turned towards her. "Anyway, if you just asked her, she would have told you the truth about the throne. She does not want it."

She bit her cheek before gesturing sharply to me with an open hand. "What do you think you gain in alienating me in favor of her? I put you here. Remember that. Do you think that stopping her marriage to Isaac would mean it would be possible for you?"

I just stared forward, past her. *Does she actually think I'm interested? Am I?*

"Oh. I see, or is it that you believe you're just doing your job and trying to protect her? Maybe it's a bit of both." She was trying to read my reactions, her eyes scanning my face. *What is it telling her?* "You have no idea how much danger you'll be putting her in if this marriage doesn't go through. You know bits and pieces of a grander picture, Ivan, that's it. Don't let this sudden loyalty to her blind you. She's *my* daughter, I love her, and I want the best for her. Don't overstep your role."

I looked at her blankly. "We should get going, your highness."

She made a ticking noise with her tongue. "Think about everything carefully, Ivan. I would hate for you to get hurt." *Was that a threat?*

Helena walked over, ending the confrontation. I opened the door for her before climbing in the passenger seat next to the chauffeur. I looked at Julia in the review mirror, her eyes shut and her head resting against the window. *I'm so sorry.*

Chapter 25

Over the next few weeks, I became more acquainted with my new position and stopped the occasional paparazzi, random suitor, or fangirl. Though, Julia was often accepting of any girls that looked up to her and wanted a picture, especially younger kids; she always smiled the most with them, and that made me happy. The most amazing thing is that she tried to ignore the color of the child's family's tag, no matter what. Reds rarely got near her due to area restrictions, but watching her attempt to bridge that divide brought a tear to my eye. If they were going to look up to anyone in the messed-up country that we lived, I was glad it was her. It was hard to think of something more adorable than a little girl dreaming about being a princess and actually getting to meet one, especially when she was a little future Red who was constantly told by everyone else that she didn't matter. *What kind of role model am I? I'm sure some future Red boys dream about fighting in the Militia with people like me. Is that a good thing?*

Isaac was now visiting the Royal Household every other day, sometimes for dinner with the royal family and other times for time alone with Julia. She hated it. It was becoming increasingly evident that we could do little to change her parents' minds, even after Julia used the champagne and Isaac's drunkenness as justification for her concerns. We would have to get creative.

Stopping Isaac, though, would have to wait a bit longer, as Delaware and I had been coordinating an operation to expose the UPF's invasions of privacy: recording people's phone calls, tracking their activity on computers, and monitoring their movements on the streets and within their homes.

One of our connections in the technical division of the UPF had confirmed that the Secretary of Intelligence, a Purple named Vince Heller, kept a hand-written journal of sorts in a safe in his home. It apparently held his observations, thoughts, and plans for the department. The plan was to scan the journal and publish it in its entirety. We would then print thousands of copies and spread them throughout the city. Excerpts of the important parts would also be published in the St. Paul Free Press. It was an ambitious undertaking, but one that could undermine the UPF's entire political base and make even some Greens and richer Yellows turn their heads.

Sitting in Julia's room, I was giving her a rundown of the plan so that she would know where I would be. She paced uncomfortably, still not acclimated to my missions. "Won't Secretary Heller have some type of security? Even at his home?"

"Yes. And that's why it will only be Delaware and me going. It needs to be as covert as possible."

"You've talked about her quite a bit since you've told me about Coyote. Who is she to you?" *Why do you ask?*

I crossed my legs, relaxing. "She is the closest thing I had to a best friend back in the Enclave. She is like my little sister. I recruited her into the Militia and have done everything I can to keep her alive since. She is overseeing my team while I'm here."

She pondered for a second, scanning the room for the next sentence. "Huh. How many girls are in the Militia? Based off your silly leaderboard it seems like most of you are guys."

"Most of us are, but we have a lot of girls spread throughout, even a couple lieutenants, and you don't know about them because most of them prefer to remain a secret. With Coyote, I chose a more public route."

"How many lieutenants are there?"

"Five in the Twin Cities, Five throughout the rest of the country."

She crossed her arms. "Huh, Mr. Big Shot then."

I scoffed, though I was glad she was slowly becoming more comfortable with Militia discussions. "It's not about being in charge. I want to be where I can have the biggest impact possible." I sighed and stood. "I need to head out to the Enclave. Is it okay if I take the older sedan?"

She hesitated. "Yes. Just don't actually use it to cause trouble."

"Trouble is my middle name. Wait, never mind, the UPF didn't give me a middle name..."

She rolled her eyes and shifted uncomfortably. "Is Coyote going to kill anyone tonight?"

"Ideally, no. Is Isaac coming tonight?"

She sighed and crossed her arms, noticing my deflection but ignoring it. "Unfortunately."

I smirked. "Well, then maybe one." Her glare in response sent an icy shiver down my spine.

I had taken a few independent trips into the city, but this was my first time returning to the Enclave since I had left Delaware in charge of my team. I wanted to visit more often, but I also didn't want to look suspicious with the UPF having eyes everywhere. Parking the car a few blocks from the bridge, I walked over it and stopped in the middle. *I've missed this view.* The sun was setting over the river and the array of colors across the water was a beautiful sight. I hoped to show it to Julia someday soon.

Delaware was meeting me at our headquarters, and I wanted to check in with El Capitan while I was there. First, though, I went over to my old house and switched into my black Coyote jacket before grabbing a few spare knives, my bandana, and my nine-millimeter pistol from out of the crevice in the corner of the room, though I hoped I didn't have to use it. Guns were noisy and messy. I preferred the silent route and, even better, the non-lethal one.

I looked into the broken glass mirror above the dresser. The mark on my temple was healing slowly. It acted as just another indicator of what I'd been through in my life. It felt freeing to be back as Coyote again, away from the eyes of the world. *Is Coyote me, or just Ivan's escape? Will Julia make me give him up?*

When I reached HQ, Razor was pacing outside the door, deep in thought.

I flashed a smile. "Hey! How's it going?"

He kicked the dirt, sending a haze across my legs. "Something is going on, and Delaware won't tell me anything. I'm guessing that's why you're back."

I sighed. "Yeah. Delaware got some intel and needs me for a mission. We need to keep it quiet for now, but you'll know when it's done."

He lowered his head and crossed his arms. "So, you don't trust me?"

I laughed. "It's not that. After what happened with the flash drive mission, El Capitan is keeping a tight lid on mission info. It's nothing personal, Razor."

He fiddled with his black tag, thinking. "I guess that makes sense. Anyway, it's good to see you back, Coyote. Delaware has missed you, we all have." He smiled.

I gave him a hug. "Missed you guys too. I've gotta go, but I'm glad I ran into you Razor. I'll see you around."

Razor nodded as I headed into HQ. He was too young to understand the need for the secrecy of information. We still had no idea who had leaked the information about the flash drive transfer and couldn't risk more agents getting killed.

As I turned to head down the stairs, I ran into Zeus, and his smoker voice provided a rough greeting. "So, the Coyote lives. Hopefully you haven't gone soft on us living with the princesses."

"We will see tonight." I hesitated before being more solemn. "Any news on Southpaw and Bobcat?"

He scowled. "No. We have given up looking."

Shit. I closed my eyes tightly before looking back at him. "I am so sorry. They deserved better, Zeus. It's on me."

He scratched his beard sharply and changed topics. "Hmm. The captain is waiting for you downstairs with Delaware. Welcome back, Coyote." *I don't blame him for being upset.*

"Glad to be back, even if it's just for a bit."

I walked down the stairs to the command center. Delaware and El Capitan were bent over the map, analyzing something.

"Glad to see this place hasn't fallen apart without me."

Delaware looked up and smiled before sprinting over and hugging me. "Welcome back!"

"Good to be back. I missed you Del." I walked over and gave El Capitan a hug for good measure. "Please tell me Delaware hasn't gotten my team into too much trouble."

He laughed. "Actually, she has done well. She was the one that led the effort to get the intel for tonight, as you well know."

"What can I say? I taught her everything she knows."

She piped in, a little offended. "Not all of it."

El Capitan laughed. "All right. Down to business. First of all, any progress on getting your princess to commit to more public outreach?" *My princess?*

I sighed. "It'll take time. She still isn't comfortable with me being Coyote, yet."

"Okay. If we can get both her and King on board, then we will be in a position to maybe actually change things for once, though we are putting a lot of faith in her."

"Trust me, she won't let us down." *I hope.* "How is the coding for Operation Blackout coming along?"

"Slowly. Their systems are a tough nut to crack, but the tech guys have reassured me they will figure it out in due time."

"Okay. Well, hopefully things like tonight will make people more aware of those cameras and the UPF's spying at least."

"Hopefully."

Delaware stepped up. "You ready to go? We need to be quick about this."

"Of course. In and out with hopefully no one dead."

El Capitan scoffed. "Maybe you are getting soft on us."

The Secretary's manor was along the river in Minneapolis, near the University of Minnesota's campus. We drove one of the Militia's old beaters to a nearby lot and parked, approaching the manor from down the street and taking mental notes. Two Green UPF guards were posted out front, but the fence around the place was climbable and, from our observations, there was only one other guard on the premises, patrolling the inside of the house.

We snuck through the neighbor's backyard and I helped Delaware over the tall stone privacy wall between the lots before following behind. It felt good to be running a mission again. It was late October and the temperature had already taken a large southern turn. We could see our breaths as we surveyed the back of the manor, looking for the best way in.

A cold wind shook the trees through the yard with a *whoosh*, and I got goosebumps from excitement mixed with the cold air. We snuck behind the trees to get a closer view. There were a few windows on the second story, where Heller's bedroom would be, but breaking one would be loud. There was also the sliding back door, but that was likely to be locked, since Heller was out at some UPF gala. A camera overlooked the door as another scanned the yard.

I whispered to her across the yard. "I'll take out those cameras. You get the door. Got the lock picks?"

She dangled one from her fingers. "Let's roll."

I took a deep breath, pulled one of my knives, and turned from behind the tree, flinging my knife into the camera watching the yard. It fizzled out, and we slowly crept up towards the back door.

Delaware waited as I grabbed my knife from the first camera and slid along the wall towards the second, avoiding its range. I jumped and cut its cord. "Your turn, Del. We have to move quickly. It won't be long before they realize something is up."

Delaware nodded, and I kept watch as she went to work. It was a little loud, but the guard was on the second floor, so I hoped he wouldn't hear. After a few moments, the door popped open and Delaware looked up at me, a little too proud of herself.

"Good job. Let's move." We entered a sitting room at the back of the house, and I looked at the stairs off to the right. "Let me go first." I crept up the staircase as silently as I could, hoping to avoid a creak.

As I reached the top, I heard the beep of a radio. "All clear upstairs. I'll see if the noise came from the first floor. Over."

The radio crackled. "Roger that."

The guard was was walking towards me, and I had just a moment to dive quickly into the open room on the left. As he passed the door I grabbed him around the throat from behind and executed a chokehold that knocked him out as he struggled to break free. *Clean and quiet. That's how I like it.* I whispered down the stairs, "Del, Del, we're clear."

After a moment, she peaked her head out and met me at the top of the stairs.

I motioned towards the guard. "They're going to be waiting on a report from him about the first floor. We need to hurry."

She looked at me like the answer was obvious. "Grab the radio and imitate him if they call in."

We found the safe behind a painting in his room. *Classic.* Delaware went to work trying to crack it while I searched the room for some hints. I shuffled through the desk, breaking open some locked drawers but not finding anything that could be the six-digit code. As I searched, I grabbed an old photo on the desk of Heller with what looked like his dad on some golf trip. It came from one of those old cameras that had the date printed in the corner. I whispered, "Hey, Del. Try 0-7-1-5-9-5."

I heard her spinning the dials and then a *click.* "Holy cow, that actually worked. Nice job." She grabbed the journal. "Should we take anything else?"

"What else is in there?"

She checked the safe again. "Some money and a gun."

"Leave it, but..."

The radio interrupted me. "Is everything okay in there?"

I grabbed it and imitated the guard's deeper voice. "First floor is clear. Over."

We moved towards the stairs while waiting for a response through the radio. "I saw a light on in the boss's bedroom. What's going on in there?"

I looked at Delaware. "Run."

We booked it through the back door and over the fence just as the guards entered the front door to look around. By the time they noticed the guard's unconscious body, we were long gone.

Chapter 26

We had scanned the journal at Aaron's for re-publishing and were heading back to the Enclave. I let Delaware keep the original as a souvenir. *Her intel, her reward.* The journal copies would be distributed throughout the night by various Militia members and the St. Paul Free Press; people would be able to read the source themselves. It provided the juicy details that we needed to expose the UPF's privacy invasions in their entirety. Publishing the full version meant the government couldn't claim that we had manipulated the journal by picking bits and pieces. It was a genius plan on our part and amazingly stupid for a UPF leader to leave his secrets in a journal, thinking a simple safe could keep it away from prying eyes. *No secret is safe nowadays.*

There would be an attempted coverup, but the damage would be done too quickly for them to respond. I looked forward to seeing what the public media would come up with to cover the scandal. The UPF could try to take away our light, but we thrived in the darkness.

We drove along in the old car as we approached the Enclave. A rattling noise constantly reminded us that it could break down at any second and the smell of way too many cigarettes gave me a solid headache. "How are you enjoying life as an acting lieutenant, Del?"

She was gazing out the window into the night. "It's fun to be a part of the big decisions, even if a lot of it is running things through you, but I don't know how I'd feel if we lost someone while I was in charge." *I hope you never have to learn.*

"Shitty."

She shook her head, confused. "What?"

I looked at her. "You'd feel shitty."

She was silent for a moment before responding quietly, "I missed you, Coyote."

I sighed before lightening the mood. "Missed you too, Del. Speaking of what I missed, did Snap ask you out yet?"

An excited grin came across her face and she bit her lip. "Maybe, what's it to ya?"

I laughed. "Glad he finally had the guts to follow through."

She punched my arm. "You knew he would ask?"

I laughed, proudly. "He was always talking about it, and I'd been trying to convince him to actually do it for months. Took him long enough."

Her mouth was open in a kind of faux shock. "And you didn't tell me? Screw you."

I smirked. "What's the fun in ruining the surprise? Did it go well, or did he decide you were too short for him?"

She rolled her eyes. "Ooh a short joke, real creative."

I just looked at her.

She sighed. "It went fine. I don't know. He's cute."

I chuckled. "That's always a plus."

"Shut up."

"Oh come on. I can't be happy that my little recruit is growing up?"

"Alright, *bro.*"

"Seriously though, Del. You've come a long way in the past four years since I pulled you out of... you know."

"Thanks. It feels like it has been longer than that, though. It honestly is weird to remember life before the Enclave."

"Same."

She looked surprised. "I thought you'd been here your whole life."

"Most of it. I was a kid in the public orphanage out in River Falls until Poseidon dragged me out of there when I was eight."

Her eyes narrowed. "You never told me that."

"That I pulled you out of the exact same hell hole that I came from? Yeah, it was always hard to get into those places to rescue the kids that wanted out. River Falls was one of the toughest ever since they started the check points after the operation that got me out. Damn, it was tough. It took a lot of persuasion on my part to convince Hades to let me bring a team."

Hades, Poseidon and Zeus's oldest brother, was the Militia captain until a few years ago. He died during the water poisoning caused by the government's mismanagement of a water treatment plant that just happened to mainly impact the majority Red and Orange Enclave and Eastern St. Paul areas. A ton of people got sick and hundreds died, including Hades. A lot of Oranges who were affected started reaching out to help in the aftermath. In a way, the tragedy had woken up a lot of people to the evils of the UPF.

"You saved ten of us that night. Why did you end up taking me under your wing?"

I sighed. "I saw a lot of me in you: young, ambitious, no family, ready to stab anyone who dared to tell us what to do, and desperately in need of someone to prevent us from doing exactly that. You were alone, and I knew how that felt: a Black Tag lost in the world before passing through the Prism." I chuckled. "And now you're stealing my job."

Her face shifted back to a devious smile. "El Capitan better watch out."

I laughed.

We drove in silence for a bit. As I turned onto the bridge, Delaware broke the silence again. "So, you got to ask me about *my* relationship..." *Please don't go there.* "Anything happening between you and your princess?" *She went there.*

"*My* princess? Ha. She's about to be in an arranged marriage, Del. And besides, I'm a Red, she's a White. Not exactly possible."

She raised an eyebrow. "That's all fine, but you didn't answer my question."

"Alright, Detective Delaware." I sighed and looked out into the night for an answer to that question. "No... maybe... I don't know."

She laughed. "Solid."

"I mean, there's definitely something between us, but there are a million barriers in the way of that even being a possibility. I don't even have a last name..."

She grinned. "So, you like her."

"Stop."

"I've known you too long, Coyote, and you set me up with Snapback, so you owe me this much."

I laughed. *She's right you know.* "Fine. I do. Happy?" It felt weird to admit that to her, and myself.

She giggled. "Very. This is sounding like the start of some fairytale."

"A frustrating one."

"Maybe you're just overthinking it?"

"What?"

"Do you think she feels the same way?"

"I... I don't know. Maybe? She said I was one of the only people she could trust, but does that mean she is interested? She keeps acting all weird whenever we make any type of physical contact, making sure no one is around. She's also uncomfortable with the whole Coyote thing."

"Well, she's probably worried about perception. She *is* a princess after all, and she'll come around on you being Coyote. Still, maybe you should tell her how you feel? What's the worst that could happen?"

"I could lose my job, get kicked out of the palace, never see her again, and never have the opportunity to convince the King to help us."

"Shit."

"Yup. Besides, I think she has enough on her mind with Isaac."

She shrugged. "But maybe she needs something to give her hope that it'll work out okay?"

"Dang, it's like you're a girl or something. I'll have to think about it. It's all too much at once."

Chapter 27

The reaction to our mission was immediate on social media, even with the government censoring as much as they could. We needed the Yellows and Oranges behind us if we were going to further fracture the Prism, and they did not appreciate being spied on. Heck, even some Greens were outraged. Most were quiet about their frustrations, though, as the worst thing possible was being knocked down a color or more post-Prism. There was no way back up. The average person just cared about keeping themselves and their family alive. We needed to give them a big enough reason to stand up against the UPF.

My op-ed in response to the journal's release had been published in the St. Paul Free Press. The media was plastering Coyote everywhere as the terrorist who broke into Secretary Heller's house and created fraudulent evidence of the spying program. It was a pretty weak response, but I was quickly becoming the UPF's favorite Militia poster boy. Everything I'd done was annoying the hell out of them, and I loved it.

Anti-spying posters were also scattered throughout St. Paul the next day, calling for reforms. The UPF responded in force and arrests were made among those who were the perceived heads of the movement while protestors were beaten down or shot in the streets. We had gotten their attention, and the propaganda machine was in full force to try to quell the outrage.

I was waiting outside Julia's room, thinking about how I wanted to handle her discomfort with Coyote. She'd been quiet that morning, and I could tell last night's mission had brought back her concerns. We needed to talk, and I wasn't looking forward to the potential confrontation, but anything would be better than the tense silence.

Eventually she opened the door and smiled to her handmaidens before silently leading the way to the garage. We were heading towards her visit to one of the Minneapolis elementary schools, where she would be reading to a class of students. I knew it was a PR stunt planned by her dad, but for her it was more genuine than that. She actually cared about seeing and talking to the kids.

We didn't speak for most of the car ride there until I decided to cut through the silence. "I was wondering if you wanted to see the Enclave sometime. We could disguise you and go at night, if you're interested."

She shook her head and looked out the window, sounding dismissive. "Why?"

"I don't know… just… I've seen your world. I thought you might want to see mine. It might help me explain why I've done the things I've done."

She bit her cheek, thinking.

"It's okay if you don't…"

"No, I… I'd like that." Her eyes studied me as if trying to figure out some type of puzzle. "I've got time tonight, but we can't be gone too long."

I smiled softly. "Great. I'll… um… I'll grab some spare clothes for you, so you don't stick out like a sore thumb."

She half-smiled in response as her eyes gazed out the window, lost in thought.

We pulled into the school and I opened her door before following her into the building. I knew she was still uncomfortable with Coyote, but I hoped that visiting the Enclave could put things perspective and give her a chance to talk. *Why is nothing easy?*

At least my actual job was easy that day. The little kids posed no threat to her, unless their star struck eyes could summon lasers. They were a sea of Black Tags gawking at her as we passed through the halls, guided by a secretary who showed us to the classroom. Along the way, I took in the atmosphere. The walls were coated in propaganda flyers thinly guised as educational encouragement. *So, this is what a real school looks like...* If the child of a Red received any education at all, it was from their parents or a mentor in the Militia; keeping us uneducated was part of the UPF's plan.

Julia thanked the secretary as we reached the classroom, and I smiled, standing in the back, as she charismatically met the teacher and hugged the kids. She was in pure princess mode and the kids adored her. She talked to each one of them, genuinely listening to every child.

As she began to read to them in the front of the classroom, the Yellow teacher approached and stood beside me, looking towards the kids. "So, are they letting just anybody become bodyguards nowadays?"

I continued standing formally, facing forward. "No, ma'am, they do not."

"Hmph. Well, I hope you do your job well. She's one of the good ones."

"Yes, ma'am, I believe she is." I noticed one of the textbooks on a nearby desk, open to a page about the Prism. I hesitated before gesturing towards the book. "If you don't mind me asking, do you really agree with everything they make you teach?"

She furrowed her brow and whispered harshly, "Do you want to get me fired?" She shook her head before storming off towards her desk. *Guess she minds.*

Eventually, the bell rang, and we met up before heading towards the offices so that Julia could shake hands with the administrators. I smiled at her. "You're a natural."

She smiled softly back. "Thanks. This is the part of being a princess that I love."

We started walking. "You know, they're going to remember this for the rest of their lives."

She looked down before back returning her gaze to me. "If I can do something for them, it's worth it."

"Any of them say anything interesting?"

Her face became more solemn. "One little boy said his older sister was about to go through the Prism. His family is Yellow, but he is worried about her because she 'doesn't believe the textbooks.'"

"Well, at least there's one independent thinker. What'd you tell him?"

She smiled softly. "I pointed to you while you were talking to the teacher and told him, 'My bodyguard is a Red, but he went out of his way to save my life. You sister sounds brave, like him. She can be a hero too, no matter what color the Prism gives her.'"

I bit my cheek, not knowing how to respond. "I... I don't know what to say."

He eyes met mine. "You don't have to say anything. I meant it, Ivan. You were a hero that night."

We reached the office and the principal plus a few other administrators were waiting for her. I stood to the side and planned our trip to the Enclave while she schmoozed with them.

Chapter 28

Julia looked adorable in an old black hoodie and a baggy pair of ripped jeans. Luckily, she was only slightly shorter than me, so my spare clothes could loosely fit her and work well enough as a disguise. I was happy to get her to laugh while trying the clothes on, totally out of her comfort zone but willing to come anyway.

We parked the car in St. Paul and walked towards the Enclave. She was tense as we approached the bridge. I didn't know what she imagined the Enclave to be like, but either the idea of it or our impending conversation scared her. The latter scared me, too.

The cool fall air howled under the bridge as we began to cross it, and I couldn't help but smile. "The old High Bridge. Hello old friend." Julia didn't respond but looked in awe to the east, towards the lights of downtown St. Paul. I stood next to her. "Isn't it amazing?"

She smiled softly and looked off back towards the west and the forest. "It's beautiful."

I held out my arms and gestured to the sky. "We may be the poorest part of town, but the best view is all ours. Welcome to my favorite place in the world." I gestured for her to follow me as I moved towards the western side and sat along the bridge's edge where it had lost its railing.

She stayed back, reluctant. "I'd rather not fall to my death."

I bent over forward, looking into the water below and bracing my left arm on the railing next to me. I looked back at her and smiled jokingly. "Oh, it's only fifty meters. That can't kill you, right? C'mon, I promise you won't fall. It's my job to protect you."

She giggled, "Fine," and sat next to me, gripping tightly onto the railing to her right. We sat for a while, looking over the water. It was so peaceful, and I was happy to be able to share it with her. I smiled at her as the moonlight reflected off the little hair not covered by her hood. She raised an eyebrow. "What?" *Caught.*

Looking forward, I responded, "Thank you for coming. I wasn't sure you'd be willing to with Coyote and everything."

"I... I'm not okay with it all, but I want to see your world." She looked at the view and smiled. "I'm glad to see there's at least one beautiful thing in it."

I smiled softly. *There's two now.* Standing up, I looked towards the Enclave. "If you think this is beautiful, you should see El Capitan's beard. C'mon, I'll show you my house." I reached down and helped her up from the ledge. She stumbled for a second, falling into me with a yelp. Our eyes met for a second and she smiled for a moment before backing up and brushing herself off as I laughed.

We continued across the bridge. As the first buildings came into view through the darkness, she covered her mouth with her hands in shock. From across the bridge, it was hard to see the damage that had been done from the bombings, but now Julia could see it up close. Through the years, I'd become numb to it, but for her, it was the same shock that I had when I saw the palace.

Her voice was shaky as she searched for words. "Oh my… People live here?"

I kicked some of the dirt along the path. "Now you're starting to see why nobody comes to the Enclave unless they're a Red."

We were silent for a while. Julia's tear-filled eyes scanned the wreckages of the buildings and the poorly dressed Reds scuttling around the side trails as we slowly walked down the street. "It's worse than I imagined. Everything you said… it's all true. They're lying to us, and we were too blind to bother looking across the river to see the suffering we created."

I could only nod. What she saw meant more than anything I could say.

We reached a dark, deserted intersection, and I signaled for Julia to stay back as voices came from around the corner. Three Reds wearing leather jackets were walking down the next street. One of them called out when he noticed me, "Hey! What you doing walking around alone this late? Don't you know better?" As he approached, he noticed Julia and winked. "Oh, not alone I see." *Back off, asshole.*

With only the dim moonlight, I couldn't tell if there were any gang markings on their leather jackets. While the Militia tried to maintain a bit of order in the Enclave, there were a few gangs that would catch people out at night. "Heading home. My friend is in a bad spot and needs a place to stay for the night."

The leader approached, his unshaven rugged face appearing in the moonlight once he was close enough. I finally got a closer look at his jacket. *Shit. Timberwolves.* "How about you and your 'friend' spare some rations, or maybe she could stay with us for the night? What color she even?" He walked slowly towards her.

I grabbed his arm, stopping him in his tracks and looked him dead in the eye. "She's a Red, just like you and me, man. We don't have any extra rations. Besides, I don't think your boss would appreciate you messing with a Militia lieutenant. What's your name? I'm sure El Capitan would love to hear it."

Realization crossed over his face. "Shit. Wait. Which lieutenant?"

I cocked my head and showed the knife up my sleeve. "That's none of your business."

The leader looked at his two goons before turning back towards me and spitting at my feet. "Fine, but you Militia bastards better watch your backs." He motioned to them. "Let's go." *Thank God.*

As he turned, he reached into his jacket and everything after that turned into a blur. I realized what he was doing and dove towards him while he pulled his gun. *Please be the only one with a gun.* Knocking the gun from his hands before he could shoot, I swept his legs, throwing him to the ground. The smaller one of the goons charged Julia with a knife and the bigger approached me, unarmed.

I quickly kicked the leader's head, knocking him out before running to intercept the first goon, hoping that the bigger guy couldn't keep up. The smaller one slid around my tackle attempt and knocked me to the ground as I charged in recklessly. I smacked into the dirt painfully and rolled to see him standing over me with the second goon straight behind him. Looking around, I was desperate for options that didn't involve butchering another person in front of Julia.

Julia backed away slowly and screamed as the second goon moved towards her. *Don't you dare!* I rolled to my right and threw myself at the legs of the goon in front of me, knocking him off balance as I pulled my knife and stabbed his thigh. *Not lethal, but necessary.* He yelled and fell as I scrambled to my feet and kicked him for the knockout. My heart sunk as Julia turned to flee from the goon, who was in hot pursuit. *He's going to catch her.*

Running faster than I felt I ever had before, I chased after him. *Please be slow, please be slow…* He wasn't, and he tackled her before I could close in. She struggled against him as I reached them, and her hood fell, revealing her tag-less ear. Confusion washed over his face and he hesitated long enough for her to break away as I grabbed him, threw him to the ground, and started punching his face repeatedly in anger.

Fueled by rage, I couldn't stop the punches as Julia struggled to her feet and pleaded with me. "Ivan! Stop! He's done!" *Finish him…*

She broke the spell, and I paused, looking down at his unconscious body and bloodied face before releasing him. I struggled to my feet. "Are you okay?"

Her eyes were wild as she looked around at the three men in fear. "What? How?"

I moved slowly towards her and spoke intently, "We need to get out of here. My house is nearby, come on."

She followed reluctantly as her mind tried to grasp the situation. We reached my house and I sat on the edge of my old bed as she paced around, panicked and oblivious to her surroundings. "I thought you said the Militia controls the Enclave?"

Stressfully, I ran my hands through my hair. "We do, but there are still the gangs that run around at night. We're not the police. We can't control everything, especially when everyone is so desperate." I sighed. "I'm sorry. We shouldn't have come so late at night."

She was not happy. "Did you know this would happen? How often do you get attacked?"

I stood quickly and tried to calm her down, but she moved away from me. "They must be getting desperate if they're willing to attack a lieutenant. I didn't know they would be out. Attacks are pretty rare, but this isn't the first time I've had to deal with them over the years." I sighed and looked down before back at her. "First time I had to protect someone else, though."

She scowled at me.

Emotionally, I paced and spoke forcefully, "Ugh! I didn't mean it like that, Julia. I'm just glad you're alright. Now you see, though, the shi... crap we have to deal with every day. If it's not some goons, it's the UPF or everyday people spitting at us because of our earrings. We live on nothing, we have nothing. Look at this damn place!" I gestured angrily at the single room that was my home for so many years, and tears started flooding my eyes. "The Militia, fighting for something. That's all I had for most of my life. There's so much I regret, and I'm sorry you had to get a taste of it. It was unfair to you."

Her eyes met mine in a duel as we faced each other. She spoke, harsh, "They could have killed me... killed us, Ivan! Don't you see?

You're supposed to be my bodyguard, but all of this with Coyote, it puts me more at risk." She paced around the apartment, taking deeper breaths and calming down slightly. "This place, it's awful. I understand, but you can't just go around killing people. That won't change things."

I looked towards the crack in the wall where my gun was stored. *Is she right?* "Someone needs to fight back. We can't sit back and passively wait for change, Julia. We are trying to change people's minds, not to start a war, but we have to defend ourselves when they come for us."

She held her hands close to her and sat on the edge of the bed. I could see the gears turning in her head, and she looked down. "All the people you've killed. Did you have a choice?"

I crossed my arms and looked at the ceiling. "There's always a choice." Meeting her eyes, I continued, "Sometimes that choice is they die, or I die. That's the worst one to make."

She furrowed her brow. "But you didn't kill those three thugs tonight."

I sighed, frustrated. "I told you, I don't kill someone unless it really is life or death." I knelt on both knees in front of her, taking her hands as emotion flooded my voice and tears ran down my face. "I would rather do anything else but fight if I knew it could make a difference, Julia. Anything. But for the average Red, there's not many options besides fighting or laying down, getting beaten, and letting the system remain as is. You've given me another route, and I want to take it, but the world still needs Coyote for a little bit longer. Please, believe me that I hate this, I hate so many of the things I've done, but I've always tried to do what's right."

She looked away, pursing her lips and thinking. Eventually, she looked down at her hands before up at me, her eyes full of tears of her own as she spoke softly, "If I'm going to help you, then you need to promise me something."

"Anything."

She sighed, and her voice shook with emotion. "I believe you, Ivan, but I need all of you, not half, if you're going to be my bodyguard." She sniffled as a tear ran down her cheek. "I forgive you for what you've done, but you have a choice to step out of the darkness. We can change things together, but you need to promise me that all of this is going to stop, that you'll give up Coyote. I can't have my bodyguard and my... friend as a leader in the Militia, killing people. If you actually want another way, let's fight the system from within. Promise me this, and I'll help you shatter the Prism."

Give up Coyote? I looked down at our hands and then back up at her. *Why is it so hard to let him go?* "You're asking me to give up everything I've had for the last thirteen years of my life. I... I don't know if I can do that."

Silence fell over the room for a moment as she looked at me with pain in her eyes. I didn't know what to do and closed my eyes, trying to hold back the tears. *Step into the light, or keep fighting in the dark?* Taking a deep breath, I opened my eyes. "You're right. The Militia is needed, but I've got a chance to help you change things from inside. They need me for now, though, at least until Operation Blackout is done. After that, I promise." I knew it wasn't what she wanted, but I needed time to wrap up as much as I could.

She bit her cheek and looked down. "Thank you, Ivan. That means a lot to me. And... I'm sorry, I don't want to be controlling, but we have to be careful. Everyone is watching you, waiting for you to slip up so they can get rid of you." She gripped my hands tighter and looked at me, her eyes full of concern. "I don't want that to happen."

I smiled softly. "I'm not going anywhere. Who's going to protect you from the small children and scary paparazzies if I'm gone?"

My joke managed to lighten the mood as she gave a reluctant smile. *Thank God, she doesn't hate me.* She looked down at our hands and thought for a second before slowly letting go and standing as she looked around the room. "So, this is where you lived before?"

I stood as well and looked into the night through the cracked window. "Ironically, it's larger than my room at the palace, but, yes, this is my old home. It's not much, but it's mine."

She touched some of the off-white paint peeling from the walls. "How can they let so many people live like this?"

Leaning back against the windowsill, I crossed my arms and looked towards her. "We are excess, disposable. At best, we're nearly free labor, at worst we're rebels. All they need to do is keep us strong enough to work while ensuring we are weak and repressed enough to not actually revolt. Even with the Militia, they don't consider us a real threat, and, without help, we aren't. We don't have the weapons or resources to fight a war."

Julia turned towards me, a look of pity on her face. "I'm sorry,

Ivan."

I shook my head. "Don't. I wanted you to see it, that's all. This isn't your fault, it's theirs, and we're going to make them pay..." I gave her a half-smile. "... and, with your help, have as few deaths as possible."

She softly smiled back and looked at her feet before checking her phone. "We've been gone too long..."

"No problem. Let's get you back." I headed towards the door.

She softly grabbed my arm as I was about to open the door, and I looked back at her as she spoke, "Thank you for showing me your world, Ivan. This... this helped."

I smiled softly at her and stepped forward, into the darkness.

Chapter 29

Back at the palace, Julia had requested a self-defense training session in case I couldn't get to her in time. After our scare in the Enclave a few days before, it made sense, and I was happy to help her. Things were still a little uneasy between us when it came to Coyote and the Militia, but our talk had helped us vent and get on the same page. We both were willing to compromise to make things work, and she obviously cared about my safety.

We were in the Royal Household's gym, which was fully outfitted with everything you could ever want to work out with and more. We had the place to ourselves besides the noisy oversized fan on the ceiling. I was showing Julia how to respond if someone grabbed her from different angles, using pressure points or kicks to a sensitive area. I had expected her to be cautious or nervous, but she seemed determined to learn. She was a pretty good student, though, she seemed to enjoy getting to beat me up a little too much.

"Let's review. How do you escape from this hold?" I had her in a simulated choke-hold from behind, as if someone had snuck up on her like I had done to the guard at Heller's place. Her hair was flung in my face. *Wintergreen.*

She concentrated and responded intently, "Chin down, step forward, and then groin kick with that same foot."

"Good, now do it. Nicely please."

 She tried to execute the move, and I turned sharply, keeping the hold in place to counter her. She was offended. "That was cheating."

"No, that is something you might have to deal with. Do it again, faster."

This time she clenched her jaw, moved quickly, and actually surprised me when she went left instead of right. I was thrown off balance, and the ugly scar on my abdomen was revealed as I fell to the floor. She noticed, and I self-consciously pulled down my shirt as I threw myself to my feet. "Nice addition of the fake to the left. Any way you can throw your attacker off balance is something you can use to your advantage."

She pointed softly to my side. "Was that..."

I rubbed the back of my neck uncomfortably. "From the knife? Yeah."

Her eyes were full of concern. "Ivan. That's..."

I responded sternly, "No big deal. I've got worse." *As if that's comforting at all.*

She looked at me skeptically before dropping the topic. She jokingly put her fists up and danced around in a fighting stance, losing the princess front with nobody around. "So, when do I actually get to hit you?"

"Well, not that you've actually learned how to pull your punches." I looked at the bruise marks on my arms. "But, never."

She looked disappointed. "Come on. I can spar you."

I counted on my hand. "One, you'd lose quickly. Two, I'd rather not hurt you. Three, your parents would brutally murder me for what we're doing now, but they would torture me first if they found out we were sparring."

She shrugged. "Okay, true."

I clapped my hands like I was a coach. "Now. Side hold." I walked up beside her and put my arm around her waist. "I have you like this, plus an arm free to counter you, though it could also be a knife or a gun, as well. How do you escape?"

She just looked at me for a second and giggled, checking around shyly to make sure no one had come in.

Confused, I shook my head. "What?"

She was cautious. "You just put your arm around me and are teaching me how to get out of it."

Rather awkwardly removing my arm, I stepped back. "Sorry, I was just..."

She laughed. "Apparently that's how you get out of it."

I blushed and stumbled over any real reply... *dang it.*

She was trying to read me, her eyes narrow and analytical. "You okay, Ivan?"

I rubbed my hand along the back of my head. "Yeah, I'm fine. Sorry. Did you still want to do this last hold?"

She looked at me skeptically but let it go. "Yeah, just making sure."

Why is this so different now? I put my arm around her again. "This one is pretty easy. You'll want to drive your heel down into their instep, which is a pressure point at the top of their foot. That should cause them to release their grip and give you enough space to throw a quick punch, knocking them off balance."

"Can I use this on Isaac?" *That explains it.*

I responded sharply and released her. "Wait, is that why you asked me to do this? I thought it was because of the gang."

She looked down. "I... I just want to be able to protect myself."

Spinning around in front of her, I probably pushed too hard with my response. "Is he threatening you?"

Her expression hardened, and she stepped away, shaking her head and packing up her things hastily. "I...I need to get ready for the TV interview. Thanks for the training, Ivan. If you can meet me outside my room in about 45 minutes, that'd be great. Wear whatever."

She picked up her bag and walked out swiftly as I just stood there and watched her go, only getting out a "Julia, wait..."

I turned and kicked a nearby bag angrily, knocking it off its base. *Idiot.* Out of the corner of my eye I saw her look back at me as she heard it fall. *What now?*

Chapter 30

After wailing on a punching bag for about fifteen minutes, I went back to my room and showered quickly. Afterwards, I stood, bent over the sink, looking into my reflection in the mirror. My deep blue eyes scanned my pale face. *What do I do: push, and risk her getting mad, or let it go and risk her getting hurt? I know what Delaware would say...*

I changed into a dark blue shirt with a navy suit before waiting outside Julia's room for a few minutes. That, unfortunately, gave me more time to think. *Why is she so uncomfortable talking to me about this? Was it me just being awkward? Is she just worried about the interview? Did I do something wrong? Ugh, women.* I rested the back of my head against the cool stone wall.

Eventually, she emerged with Anne and Rachel in tow and I quickly stood at attention. The handmaidens were coming along to help ensure she looked perfect on her first solo TV interview. She was looking professional with a navy blazer over her ice-blue button down and khakis. She avoided eye contact at first as she spoke, determined through veiled nervousness. "Let's get going. They want me there a little early to go over what we'll be talking about."

Silence filled the sedan on the ride to the studio as Julia said nothing, besides whispering something to Anne and Rachel in the back for a few seconds. I parked the car, and we took the elevator up to the third floor. When we arrived, Julia was taken to the make-up room and prepped by some Greens for the extra lights. I stood back, letting her have her space.

Propaganda posters were hung everywhere, saying things like "Work Today For A Better Tomorrow" and "In the Prism We Trust." I wondered if the people who created the propaganda actually believed their own messaging or if they did so out of fear. *Fear is a powerful weapon.* Typing filled the air along with some producers calling over the speakers for people to move into positions.

Jasmine Emerson, a Blue, was the host of the show, "Real Talk," and from what I'd seen from her, I was actually impressed. I was biased, though, as she was the only public TV host that didn't display Coyote as a straight-up terrorist. That being said, she was restricted in what she could say by the government, and it was quite obvious when she was told to switch gears while on air. Still, it was good that Julia would be on the air with a friendlier face.

When Julia was done in make-up, she sat next to Jasmine at the table on the set. Jasmine ran her through the questions that would likely be asked ahead of time, mostly nothing interesting: what it was like being a princess, how the family was, some small things about current events among the royalty, etc. There was also surprisingly going to be one question about privacy and the government, and when Jasmine brought it up Julia's eyes flicked over to me before dropping quickly. Her normal confident demeanor was replaced by a mortal one, but I was sure she would do great. She was a natural.

Once the interview began, it went smoothly, and Julia got comfortable quickly. Her charisma shone, even beyond what you would expect with such easy questions. She came across as relatable, likeable, and down to earth.

When the privacy question finally came up, she took a deep breath, changed her facial expressions and tone to convey a more serious message, and made me proud. "I think I can relate to many people out there when I say that I was shocked by the information released from the Secretary of Intelligence's journal. To not only have been lied to by the government officials that we trust to run our country, but also to lack the basic sense of privacy in our homes, on our computers, and on our phones is unacceptable. Northern Mississippians deserve to feel safe and secure in their homes, away from the prying eyes of the government."

Jasmine nodded. "So, it would be safe to say you believe in the authenticity of the journal, despite the United People's Front's claims of fraud, and you believe that government policy needs to change?"

Julia nodded and gestured softly to emphasize certain points. "I do, and I will do what I can to make sure that it does change. In fact, I have already reached out to my father, the King, as well as leaders within the United People's Front's government, insisting on behalf of the people that these policies must end, and that we, the people of Northern Mississippi, will not sit back and allow our basic privacy rights to continue to be violated."

If I didn't have a crush on her before, I definitely did after that. Rachel nudged me and showed me her social media feeds, which were already filling up with support. The discontent had been there before, but she had shone a light on the issues and gave the new movement a prominent voice against the propaganda. Her arguments weren't inherently anti-Prism, but they would bring with them more doubt about the government's honesty. *Snowball effect.*

I was unaware that she had reached out to the UPF, though I knew she had spoken to the King on the topic now that she had agreed to work with me. There was no way that either would be happy with what she just said, and on live TV, unedited. The socialists were going to have themselves another headache.

She walked over to us after the interview, beaming, and her handmaidens each gave her a hug. I congratulated her. "That was amazing! How come you didn't tell me that you were talking with the UPF?"

She looked around, avoiding eye contact. "We all have our surprises." *What is up with her?* I nodded, but the handmaidens jumped in before I could respond, pulling her away.

During the drive back, the girls were in full flowing discussion on how social media was fawning over her and her performance. The message had begun to resonate among some of the people watching. It wasn't much, but it was a promising start. Julia was quickly finding out how powerful her voice really was, and it shocked her. Shining a light on one important issue had led to attacks on the whole system already. The quiet and powerless third princess had taken a big step towards becoming a force to be reckoned with. *Watch out.*

Chapter 31

The calm lake shimmered in the moonlight that night. Julia had asked me to come with her, and we walked along the lake front. A cold front had moved in and it was nearly freezing. The trees had surrendered most of their leaves and each step ended in a satisfying *crunch* under our feet. Luckily, Julia had provided me with a new peacoat and gloves, so I wasn't as cold as I would have been otherwise.

She had said little up to this point. It was obvious she wanted to be away from anyone else, where there was no chance of being disrupted or eavesdropped on. She held one arm across her body, grasping her other arm shyly. She wore the ice-blue peacoat with the wrap neckline that she had worn when we first met, which felt like an eternity ago now. *Two months have changed everything.*

I left the initiative with her. Part of me wanted to take the lead and say so many things, but this was her time to talk and mine to listen. A million thoughts were running through my head wondering what she would say, but I couldn't get over how beautiful she looked casually strolling in the moonlight, her hair shining like a halo. *So out of my league.*

We reached a wooden park bench and she gestured for me to sit next to her. We just sat for a moment, looking over the lake and the trees along the coast. It was dark, but the reflection of the full moon on the lake was a wonderful sight.

Eventually, she spoke, her voice shaky. "I'm sorry for acting all weird today. It's just, everything is so crazy right now, and I don't know what to make of all of it."

I nodded, letting her continue.

She kept looking forward, picking each word with care. "Everything with Isaac, trying to put myself out there in the political scene, and you; it's a lot. I wasn't mad at you at the gym. I... I just panicked." She was beginning to tear up. "I am worried that if he, or someone else, attacked me that I'd be defenseless like I was with that gang. Every time I'm with Isaac I'm scared for my life. He is creepy, and he has tried to do things..." *That bastard.* She sniffled.

I put my hand on her shoulder for support. "I'm so sorry, Julia. Why won't your parents stop this?"

She looked up at me and our eyes met for a moment before she looked down nervously. "It's not your fault. Don't be sorry. And my parents don't care. They think I'm exaggerating or lying to them just to end the relationship."

I held my hands in my lap and shook my head. "Some parents."

Her eyes dropped to the ground in front of her, her face full of exhaustion. "And now, with the stuff I said on TV today, they are angry with me and don't want to hear anything I have to say." She sighed, then sniffled, her brow furrowed and her eyes searching. "What am I doing, Ivan? If I'm doomed to marriage with Isaac and a duct taped mouth, what's the point?"

I considered that for a second before responding, speaking softly, "Because people need you... I need you. You know, I asked myself that question, I mean, generally, every day for years. What is the point if everything I do is supporting a broken and corrupt system I don't believe in, and if nothing I can do will really change that? But then… then I met you, and it just made sense. I kept going with those questions for so long because the Militia needed me, Delaware needed me, then Razor needed me, but now, I don't even ask the question, because I know what I'm doing, Julia, and that's because of you."

She looked at me, her mouth open slightly, trying to find words. "That… Ivan… that means so much to me. I…" She thought for a moment and shifted uncomfortably. "I don't know how I'd be able to deal with this if it wasn't for you. At the hotel…" She smiled for a moment. "…and with everything after. You've been there for me. You've cared for me when no one else has, truly. You've trusted me. I can't thank you enough, Ivan…" She hesitated. "But what am I going to do? I've tried to go along with my parents' wishes, but I… I just can't do it. Every day that goes by feels like Isaac is tearing a hole in my chest." *Mine, too…*

I grabbed her hands softly and looked her in her eyes. "You are not alone." My voice shook with emotion and my heart raced. "No matter what your parents say or what Isaac wants, you are in charge of your life. They cannot make you do this."

"But…"

"Julia, listen to me. Whatever the punishment from your parents, it is less than spending the rest of your life with someone you don't love."

She looked to the sky and back to me, her voice shaking constantly. "I'll be all but disowned. It'll be shameful for my family, and my parents will never forgive me.”

“You are their daughter. They will love you regardless, even if it takes time for them to get over it. Plus, the public will support you if it gets out. Nobody will think that your parents are on the right side on this. We just need to find the right time, and I’ll do anything to take as much of the hit from your parents as possible. Blame me.”

She looked down at our hands, pondering. Eventually, she pulled back softly and pursed her thin lips. “I don’t know what’s right.” She took a deep breath, looked forward and then looked back at me. “Why do you care so much about this, Ivan? We’ve only known each other for two months, and you’ve already sacrificed so much for me.”

Now. I took a deep breath, trying to remain calm but emotion cracked through my voice as I spoke, “Because I care about you, Julia, a lot. And I... I have feelings for you. I can’t stand to see you in this much pain. It has ripped my heart out the last few weeks trying to figure out how I can help you and how all I wanted to do was hold you and stop Isaac. And I know I’m a Red and you’re a White and that nothing can probably happen between us, but I just want you to be happy.”

She was crying again. *Oh crap.*

I looked down. “I’m sorry, I shouldn’t have...”

She put one of her hands on my cheek before pulling her hand back, hesitant. “No. I’m glad you told me. You mean the world to me, Ivan, and I... I have feelings for you, too. It’s just...” She bit her lip and looked over the lake.

I bit my cheek and softly followed her gaze. *Did she just?* "I understand if we can't..."

She retook my hands softly, thinking carefully about what to say next. "No, Ivan. I... just... We haven't known each other that long and with everything going on and with the Militia." She sighed. "It's hard... I don't know, but when we're together, things just make sense, you know?"

"Exactly..." *What is happening?* "It is easy with you. I mean, I don't need to pretend to be someone I'm not or be ashamed of a stupid earring around you. You see me for who I am and have tried to understand me when everyone else just sees a tag."

She giggled, moving her hand to my tag, spinning it through her fingers. "It's cute on you." She dropped her gaze again, nervous, before instinctively checking to see if anyone was around.

"Glad you think that, because I doubt it's going anywhere soon." I hesitated for a second. "And neither am I." I put my hand on her cheek and our eyes met again. She pulled back before letting my hand rest, and I tucked her hair behind her ear and leaned in. She hesitated before meeting me halfway and I kissed her slowly, just for a moment, but I felt the rest of the world disappear. It was just us, the bench, and the night sky.

We pulled back slowly, and I whispered. "I just put a couple thousand suitors to shame I'd say."

She giggled and bit her lip. "That's what you have to say after our first kiss?"

I smiled and shrugged. "What can I say? I'm a romantic."

She smiled, still nervous but breaking through her shell. "Well, you somehow managed to make this day even better, so I'll give you a pass on that one."

"Give me a second chance, and I swear I'll do better."

She giggled, hesitated, and then kissed me.

I met her gaze. "I am the happiest guy in the world right now: a lost Red Tag who just kissed the most beautiful girl in the world, inside and out."

She smiled ridiculously and giggled. "Okay, maybe you can be romantic."

"We all have our surprises."

She shifted closer next to me and put her head on my shoulder. We sat like that for a good while, perfectly happy in silence, the world was ours for once. Eventually, she pursed her lips for a moment before breaking the silence. "And I was wondering what I was going to do *before*. Now I'm kissing a Red Tag boy on a park bench in the middle of the night."

I responded sarcastically. "You make some weird life choices. See, I'm making great choices. I'm kissing a princess on a park bench in the middle of the night."

She just laughed and then sniffled, still recovering from her tears. She spoke softly, but sternly, "Nobody can know about us for now, though, unless I say otherwise. You know that, right?"

I sighed. "Yes, I understand, but what do you mean 'unless I say otherwise.'"

She giggled a little. "Well, Rachel and Anne know I like you already," *explains the giggling*, "and I assume Delaware might know something, but we need to be careful, Ivan."

I smiled. "She does, and okay, you're right. No one else will know."

"Good." She sighed softly, and we enjoyed a few more minutes just being together.

Eventually, she checked her phone and sighed. "I have to get back. People are going to wonder where I am. Plus, I need to prepare for the party I'm hosting with all my friends on Saturday."

"Sounds dangerous. I think you need a bodyguard for that."

She looked at me, bit her lip and smiled. "Very. Luckily I have you." She kissed my cheek and popped up off the bench. I followed.

I put my arm around her waist as we started to head back. "Remember how to get out of this hold?"

"Make you feel embarrassed?" She smiled.

I chuckled. "What were you thinking when I did that?"

"That you were a guy near a cute girl and that you would act awkward at the smallest little thing. Also, I thought you were adorable and respecting my space."

"Dang, you read me like a book.... But seriously, do you remember how to get out of this hold?"

She replied in a voice that told me to behave, "Ivan."

"Trick question, I'm not letting go."

Chapter 32

We strolled through the woods together back towards the palace, walking on a cloud of fallen leaves. I felt at peace for the first time in a long time. It just seemed so easy with her, natural. I looked at her and smiled. Her cheeks and ears red from the cold air. She looked back at me, her eyes matching the soft blue-tint of the moon. She giggled. "What?"

I smiled with the right side of my mouth. "I'm just really happy right now, for the first time in a long time."

She smiled. "You're cute, Ivan. I really didn't expect tonight to go like this, but I'm really happy it did. I was wondering, though, you haven't told me much about your life before, besides being in the Militia and living in the Enclave. Where are your parents, your family?"

I looked at my feet as we walked. "I don't know, to be honest. I assume they were Reds, though, because when I was little, I was in one of those child labor orphanages in River Falls until Poseidon, one of our lieutenants, saved me and a bunch of other kids with his team. I don't know if my parents died or what, but I don't remember anything about them and no one ever told me. My first memory is of little me helping assemble munitions in a hot factory. Poseidon saved my life. Kids die in those places all the time..." I trailed off.

She looked concerned. "Why didn't you tell me?"

I looked into the sky. "Because that's just where I came from, not who I am. It was out of my control, so it doesn't define me."

She pulled on the chest pocket of my jacket to get me to look at her again, and I complied. Her eyes were full of concern and care. "Ivan, I want to know about you, about your life, the good and the bad. It's all part of who you are, and I care about that. You opening up in the Enclave meant the world to me. We need to be honest with each other, even when it's hard."

I sighed. "You're right. I'm sorry. I... I'm just not used to talking about it. I despise those orphanages with everything I have now, but they are off the official record and heavily guarded. I just think about the little kids trapped in there..." I paused. "I led the second mission to the River Falls Orphanage almost ten years after that first one. Others were resistant to it, because of the risk, but I couldn't accept that we could do nothing about it. That's how I met Delaware. Rescued nine years after me from the same hell hole."

She smiled softly. "You are her Poseidon."

I sighed. "Not really. Poseidon and others in the Militia basically raised me. Delaware was fourteen when we got her out, and she had time with her parents before ending up there. Still, we could relate to each other a lot. I mentored her, like Poseidon mentored me."

She looked proud. "That's amazing!"

I shook my head. "I just did what I thought was right. She needed someone, and I was there. I'm proud to see what she has become since. It's not really amazing, it's just what happened. Besides, you've inspired countless people, even before today."

She looked at the ground and kicked some leaves. "I try. I just wish there was more I could do to reach out to people and help them. Like a charity or something."

"Sounds like a fantastic idea."

She shook her head. "How would I even do that?"

I laughed. "No idea, but you have all the staff in the country to help you."

She smiled. "I just want to use what I have for some good, you know? I'll have to see about a charity."

As we approached the public areas behind the palace, I took my arm from around her and we walked side by side. It would suck to keep us a secret, but it was worth it.

We walked through the gardens and she admired the flowers in the moonlight while I looked up at the stars. "So, who all is coming to this party of yours?"

She bent down and smelled one of the flowers, before looking around to make sure we were alone and gestured for me to smell. "This is one of the few ones where I can choose all the guests, so it is just my actual friends. A few friends from college, you met two of them, Karen and Alice, at that restaurant..."

I crouched next to her and smelled... *warm and inviting.* "It's, uh, nice. And, ah, yeah... of course I remember their names..."

She jokingly rolled her eyes. "Also, some of my royal friends that I've known since I was little. There will be about ten of us. A few of us often meet up, but it is rare that the whole friend group can get together, so I'm really excited about it." She looked at me, the moonlight reflecting off her iced eyes.

I smiled. "Good! I'm glad you have the opportunity to see all of them. You've had a rough few weeks."

We reached the palace and entered through the main back entrance. It felt so surreal re-entering the royal world in a completely different position than we had left it just over an hour ago. I no longer cared about the glares and slight mockery I received from the Whites and Blues. They didn't matter to me anymore. They were just names on my list.

We both hoped not to run into her parents as I walked her back to her room. Luckily, we didn't, though we did run into Alexandria, who looked distracted. "Ivan, can you give us a moment?"

I looked to Julia as she nodded. "Alex, let's head to the small parlor. Ivan, if you can wait outside."

I shrugged. "Of course."

They walked into the parlor as I waited. *Wonder what that was about.* Julia and Alex were close, so it wasn't abnormal for them to be talking, but the secrecy was new, at least since I had become Julia's bodyguard. Of the other sisters, Alex seemed to trust me the most, though she also seemed willing to talk about most things, even things that probably should be private, with just about anybody. *It's gotta be something important.*

It was at least half an hour before they emerged, both looking serious. Julia quickly gave me a look that said, "not now," and hugged her sister. She whispered softly, "Love you, Alex," looked at her sister, almost reassuringly, and then continued the journey towards her room as I followed behind. I figured Julia would tell me if it was important or when the time was right.

When we reached her room, she walked over to her desk, threw her coat over the chair, grabbed a notepad and pen, and slumped into one of the couches. She seemed deep in thought, completely different than before entering the parlor. *Something's wrong.*

I hung up my peacoat and gloves and joined her on the couch, putting my hand on her back softly as she wrote. "Everything okay?"

She ignored me for a moment before throwing down her pen and looking straight forward, speaking cautiously. "I'm not sure."

How do I respond to that?

She huffed. "Why do people hurt each other?" She sounded almost wounded.

I thought for a second before responding, "Because some people are cruel, though sometimes it's on accident... What happened?"

Her bottom lip quivered and her voice cracked. "I... I... You can't tell anyone, Ivan."

"I promise."

Her face became serious. "Alex was attacked at a party downtown last night."

I responded intently, "Is she okay?"

She hesitated before responding, "Apparently someone, a Purple in the army, dropped something in her drink and..." *Shit.*

Rage started to fill inside me, and I bit my cheek. "You don't have to say it. I'm so sorry Julia. Is... is there anything we can do?"

"If it is who she says it is, no. The UPF will protect him, claim she is lying, and cover up the evidence. He's a Purple. Even my parents can't do anything." *Do they ever do anything helpful?*

We sat there for a second, my hand softly resting on her back as I tried to think of some way to fix things. "Is there anything Coyote can do?"

She was sharp. "Ivan, no. We talked about this."

I shifted and took her hands intently. "Someone needs to put the piece of crap in his place, Julia. If you can't do it through legal means, let me do it through less legal ones, give the system a push. Alexandria didn't deserve this. He can't just get away with it. I'm not saying I can fix it, but maybe I can put a little justice back into the world."

She was crying, so I just hugged her and stopped talking. My rage was replaced with sadness as I thought about Alexandria, too. She didn't really have anyone for support besides her hand-maidens and Julia. To be alone and dealing with that; I wouldn't have wished that on anyone.

Julia tried to talk through the tears. "It just isn't fair."

I whispered, "No, it isn't."

She turned and looked at me, responding sternly, "You can't just kill him."

I shook my head softly. "Who said anything about killing him?" She raised her eyebrow. "Then… what are you going to do?"

I sighed. "Break into his home, trash the place, and put a knife to his throat. Tell him that if he doesn't turn himself in he'll be found in the Mississippi."

"You said you wouldn't kill him."

"I won't, but I need the threat to make sure he follows through."

She shook her head. "I don't… I don't know. You said it would just be the one last mission…"

"I told you I don't like killing, because I don't, but I'll enjoy scaring this bastard and bringing some justice. If I don't do this, he gets away with it and could target someone else."

She looked down. "Promise you won't go all Coyote on every problem I have with someone. I understand why you do it, Ivan, but I like you for you, and I don't want you to lose yourself as some vigilante. This is a one-time thing."

I thought for a second. I didn't think I was losing myself. Coyote was just part of me. It would be hard to get rid of him. "I promise. Violence is not my solution for everything, but someone has to teach this guy a lesson."

She looked at me, reading my face. There was a vengeful look in her eyes now. "Fine. When can you do it?"

I sighed. "I'll need some time to get my gear from the Enclave and prepare, so tomorrow night. That's Thursday, right?"

"It is. You don't need to do recon or something?"

"Just give me his name, and I'll find where he lives. Most UPF elites actually live in pretty unguarded houses."

She looked down for a moment, before flicking her eyes up. They were like daggers. "Lt. General Jonathan Gilvan."

I nodded. "I know the name. Justice will be dealt."

She hugged me. "Thank you, Ivan."

I hugged her back. "Alexandria cannot know."

"But..."

"No. Coyote is my secret, and it needs to remain that way. This isn't about me anyway. I'm sorry. Go, spend some time with her. We will have our time. She needs you now."

Chapter 33

Snow fluttered through the air and I caught a flake on my tongue like a kid enjoying the first snow of the year. *Welcome to old Minnesota.* I shivered a bit and looked down; the wind whistled through the buildings, and I tried not to think about how far down it was to the street below. Perched on the corner of the apartment building across from Lt. General Gilvan's, I could see the whole city of Minneapolis. I was the king of the night, overseeing my domain as the few remaining lights shimmered through the darkness. *I could stay here forever, but I have work to do.*

Gilvan had the entire top floor of the building to himself and, from what I could see, there were no guards beyond the lobby of the building. *Too easy.* He wouldn't know what hit him. I was looking forward to placing the fear of God into the scumbag. Sometimes I didn't know if I was doing the right thing, tonight was not one of those nights.

Stepping out onto the wire running between the two buildings, I carefully moved across it. Even with the snow, the cable was not icy yet, making my life much easier. Cable walking was one of the more advanced skills that few of us knew in the Militia, but it allowed those of us that could do it to have more creative entrances to certain missions. Going through the lobby would be too loud and would draw attention, but the cheap lock on the roof's door would be no problem for me if I could reach it. Breathing slowly, I paced across the cable.

The key to the balancing act was always moving forward, keeping the momentum along the cable. Slowing down, or worse, stopping, was a good way to die as your weight would shift left or right instead of forward, dooming you to a long fall. *Don't look down, don't look down.*

As I reached the other side, I took a deep breath and jumped onto the roof, creeping along it and avoiding the first camera along the edge before sliding behind a short generator. Peaking around the corner I noticed the poorly positioned second camera just watching the door and missing the rest of the roof. One quick throw of my knife and it was out. I grabbed the knife and picked the lock on the door, which took a few minutes. Delaware was better at it, but I wasn't completely incompetent. Eventually, it clicked open, and I slid into the stairwell.

Walking down the staircase, I checked for cameras around the corner. Unfortunately, Gilvan had one covering his front door, but luckily, like the one outside, it didn't cover much more than the door itself and a quick knock put it out of commission. The UPF thought they were clever putting cameras everywhere, but they often seemed to forget that the coverage of the cameras meant more than where they were located. I knew Gilvan was asleep already from watching his lights go out across the street, so I didn't worry too much about the noise from picking his lock.

The door opened with a *crack*, and I snuck in. *Now I can break some stuff.* I had to be careful. Waking him up was okay but him calling for help was not. I stopped for a second, looking at myself in the bathroom mirror just off the hallway on the way in. I looked scary as hell with my black and crimson coyote bandana and black jacket. *He's going to shit himself.* I slid back into the hall and crept through his kitchen, throwing anything that looked fragile and valuable on the floor. The shattering echoed throughout the apartment.

He stumbled awake from the nearby bedroom and grumbled. "What... what the hell?"

I strode towards the bedroom, smashing a lamp and throwing a knife through his TV along the way. He opened the door to find me waiting for him and yelped as I threw him back onto his bed. I growled, disguising my voice. "Where the hell do you think you're going?" I pulled my knife from my sleeve and put it to his throat. *I could kill him right now...* Then I remembered Julia, her blue eyes pleading me to promise that I wouldn't take his life.

His voice became shaky and pitched. "Please... stop, I'll give you anything... My money is in the safe."

I pressed the knife tighter against his pudgy chin, almost drawing blood. "I don't want your damn money, you bastard."

His almond eyes looked at me in fear. "Wha... what do you want? Who are you?"

"My name is..." *No.* "...my name doesn't matter. This isn't about me."

I saw his eyes studying me, and his fear turned into rage as he saw my tag underneath my hood. He spat at me. "You Red piece of shit."

I upped the intensity. "Better than being a low-life rapist. That purple tag doesn't mean you can attack women."

His upturned eyes widened in shock. "I didn't…"

"Don't mess with me, Jonathan. I know everything. So, listen closely. You're going to turn yourself in to the royal guard and admit your crime on the record by noon tomorrow or you'll be found in the Mississippi by your friends in the UPF. Understand?"

He whimpered. "I… I can't… I'll lose everything…" *Good.*

"Exactly what you deserve. You're going to do it… or are we going to have a date tomorrow?" I cocked my head and glared.

"I… I… damn it. Fine, I'll do it."

"Tell me you'll go to the royal guard."

He cried, "I'll go to the royal guard and confess!"

I pulled the knife from his throat. "And I'll know if you tell anyone about this. So, don't get any ideas."

He waved his hands in defense. "No, I won't…"

I punched him in the face a few times, knocking him out. I couldn't kill him, but I could at least give him a black eye without feeling bad. Looking down at his large unconscious body, I couldn't help but feel a bit of pride for putting him behind bars, where he belonged.

It felt good to avenge Alexandria. She had never wronged me, and even if she liked to party, she didn't deserve what he did to her. While she would never know what I did for her, that wasn't the point. If I could use one of my last missions as Coyote to make things better, then it was worth it, even though I knew nothing could really fix what happened. At the very least, I could deliver a sliver of justice to the cruel unjust world that we lived in. Not just for Alexandria, but for all the women who felt helpless and abandoned after attacks like that. The law had failed. I gave it a push.

Just as I was about to leave the apartment, I heard a door creak open and I slid against the wall. *Is someone else home?* I heard shuffling from around the corner, on the other side of the apartment. Creeping along the wall, I prepared for a guard that I hadn't noticed before.

The shuffling got closer, and I heard the person reach down and grab a piece of a broken vase. A small, shivering voiced whimpered out, "Dad?"

In an instant, Coyote was gone. Instead, I was Ivan, hiding against the wall in an apartment that I just trashed while a little girl stood confused at why her dad was slumped over in his bedroom and everything was broken. I was no longer triumphant. He had a daughter who wouldn't understand why her dad would be taken away in handcuffs and ridiculed for years to come. I had stolen her dad. *No, Ivan. He is responsible for his own actions.* But I was also responsible for mine, and I stood there as the room spun in my mind.

The small child began to cry. She would end up like me, lost and alone in the unforgiving world we called home, the daughter of a rapist. My heart was broken, and I couldn't move. She wandered around the apartment before looking down the hall where I, a scary guy in a black bandana and hood, stood, looking at her.

Tears filled my eyes as she looked at me, fear flooding her face. I wished I could give her a hug and tell her it would be okay, but I couldn't, and I knew it wouldn't be. All I could do was weakly whisper, "I'm so sorry," and leave quietly. I heard her cries as I left. *I am a terrible person.*

Chapter 34

It was late as I pulled back into the palace. Julia was still working on convincing her dad to let me have a phone, so I needed to check in with her in person. I knocked on her door, no answer. It was past midnight... *She's probably asleep.* I stood there for a minute, trying to decide what to do since I didn't want to intrude. I placed my forehead against the cold stone wall next to her door. One part of me wanted to wail in victory over Jonathan Gilvan being brought to justice and another part wanted to curl up in a corner and cry for his daughter and Alexandria. *Why is nothing simple?*

Eventually the door cracked open and Julia smiled softly. "Oh, hey Ivan! Come on in." She opened the door for me.

Obviously dressed for bed, she was in shorts and a T-shirt, the most casual I'd ever seen her. It felt like a kind gesture letting me in when she had completely let down her princess guard, even with the beginnings of our relationship. That was my favorite Julia. She looked gorgeous as a princess, but she was her beautiful self when she didn't have to try.

She sat on one of the couches and gestured for me to join her. She looked at me in anticipation. "How did it go?"

I started talking as I dragged myself over to the couch, "Easy as you could imagine. No guards, weak security cameras. I broke some of his fragile decorations and plates, and he was scared out of his mind. He said he would turn himself into the royal guard by noon tomorrow."

She smiled and hugged me. "You don't know how much this means to me, Ivan. Alex might not know what you did, but…"

I didn't return the hug. "It doesn't matter to me if she knows. I just want her to know that that bastard is going to be behind bars. His life is ruined for what he did to her, and it is entirely deserved. It doesn't fix what happened, but at least she can have some kind of closure."

She smiled softly and ran her fingers softly down my cheek, studying my face. "My dad didn't know he was inviting a guardian angel into the palace."

I scoffed and looked at my feet, whispering, "More like a guardian devil."

She cocked her head, concerned. "Don't think about yourself like that."

I continued quietly. "Everyone else does. And besides, I didn't tell you everything that happened."

Her eyes narrowed. "What?"

My chest felt like a ton of bricks had been dropped on it. "He… he has a daughter." I sniffled as a tear ran down my cheek. "She came out after I was done and was sad and confused. She saw me, just standing there."

"Oh, Ivan…" She put her hand on my back as I rested my elbows on my knees, rubbing my hands across the back of my head.

"I saw her eyes, Julia. She had just seen her home destroyed and her father knocked out on his bed, and then she sees me, a monster, standing in the middle of it all. I ruined that child's life.

I will be in her nightmares as she wonders why her dad is gone and why he left her alone."

She rested her head against mine, and we just sat there, connected for a moment by the crowns of our heads. Tears streamed down both of our faces as we sat in silence. There was nothing for her to say, nothing she could say. Everyone was in pain and when I tried to fix a bit of it, I made myself a monster to a child, a child that would no longer feel safe at night because of me. I tried to bring justice, but I broke a home in the process.

Eventually I moved my head away. "I... I don't deserve you, or any of this. I'm a monster."

She grabbed my hands as I tried to pull away. "Ivan, no, you were trying to help."

Frustration filled my voice with intensity. "No... I know exactly what it feels like to grow up with no one in your life, abandoned. I ruined her father's life as revenge, and I took hers right along with it."

She responded softly, trying to calm me as she stroked the back of my hands, "Ivan, a monster wouldn't care about her. The fact you're sitting here, mourning the rest of her life, which could turn out fine, shows that you're not. Her dad ruined his daughter's life, not you. You're getting her away from an actual monster."

I sniffled, and the tears wouldn't stop. "This is just how things go with me, Julia. This girl, Southpaw, Bobcat, others I've lost on missions. People are destroyed because of me, while I get to keep going." I hesitated. "And... there's something I haven't told you about me."

She looked at me with concern and sorrow, weeping with me.

"What is it?"

I looked down and let loose. "A few years ago, before I was a lieutenant, we were working on destroying a UPF rifle production line. A few well-placed explosives would bury the factory. We went at night when we thought no one would be around, to avoid killing any of the workers. I... I was to set up the bomb in the southeastern most corner of the main production floor. I can still smell the gunpowder from the factory. We were each supposed to set a bomb, get clear, check that no one was inside within our view, and report back to the guy with the trigger. I didn't see anything and radioed in that it was clear. Then, I saw a guy carrying a bag and coat, looking like he was packing up late and heading home for the day. An orange tag hung from his ear and a slight smile was on his face, like he was happy to finally be going home. I scrambled for my radio and started yelling, 'Wait! Wait! There's someone...'"

I hesitated. My chest was on fire and it was hard to breathe. "And... and then it went off." I broke and put my head in my hands, breathing heavily. After a few moments I looked forward. "All I could do was watch as fear filled his eyes and the building fell on him. I killed him."

She was speechless. I could tell she was trying to say something but didn't know what. Her face switched between shock and worry.

"I... I did everything I could to find out who he was. If he had a family, and if so, what I could do to make things better for them. Well... he did. His wife had died a year before that, and he had a teenage daughter. Since she came from an Orange family and was without a parent, she would be placed into a work orphanage and be destined to pass through the Prism as a Red."

She gasped with realization before cocking her head and whispering, "Delaware. Oh... Does she know?"

I could only look at the floor. "No. I killed her father, and she thinks he died in an accident. That's what the UPF told her. That's why I was so determined to get her out. That's why I did everything I could to help her afterwards. I owe her everything."

She spoke intently, "You need to tell her. You've done everything you could to help her, but she needs to know, Ivan."

I took a deep breath. "I know. You're right. I just don't want to lose my best friend."

She nodded. "I hope that she will find it in her heart to forgive you, but she needs to know in order for that to happen. And if you need someone to forgive you for everything you think you've done wrong Ivan, I forgive you."

I winced. "Please, don't. These are my burdens to bear and mine alone."

She put her hand on my cheek as I avoided eye contact. "A wise man once told me, 'Everyone has their struggles,' and that comparing ours to someone else's is not productive. Ivan, you don't have to do this alone. We're in this together now. Nothing you just told me makes you a bad person, even if you have regrets."

I still couldn't look at her. "Thank you. I... I just need time to comprehend everything."

She looked at me with a sad smile. "And you know what? We can do everything possible to make sure that Gilvan's daughter ends up in the best home possible, okay? Though she might get knocked down, she was born to a Purple, she will be okay. We can't fix things for her, but we can make the best out of a bad situation for her. Maybe that should be my charity, an orphanage where the children are actually cared for."

My voice cracked. "I don't deserve you."

"Look at me, Ivan." She softly pulled me to look at her. I didn't comply, and she spoke with intent, "You feel for the most broken people. Stop telling yourself you're a terrible person, and realize that you're trying to make the broken world in which we live a little better. When you rattle a world of glass, some of it cracks and breaks, but you, you try to put the pieces back together, and that is amazing."

I could only muster a tiny smile. "Thanks, I guess I just don't see it that way right now."

"Look at me, Ivan. Please." I mustered the energy and looked at her, tears in her eyes. I'd never seen someone look at me with such care. *Why does she want this burden?* "You brought a rapist to justice. You prevented his daughter from living her childhood looking up to a terrible person. You gave Delaware a new life by putting your own at risk, and you're going to tell her the truth, so she can finally come to terms with what really happened. You took a knife to the gut to save me, a random stranger, and I fell for you because beyond your brash exterior and stupid red tag, you have the kindest heart I've ever seen, and you were honest and open with me. I'm not going to let you believe the lies that everyone has been telling you. You understand?"

I responded shakily. "Thank you, Julia... I... I've never told anyone about what happened at that factory. I couldn't bring myself to do it."

"And now you will. She will appreciate it in the long run. Believe me."

I sighed. "You're right. She deserves to know regardless." I softly gave her hand a squeeze. "I should let you rest. Thank you for listening." I started to stand.

"Wait." She caught my arm and locked eyes with me.

I kissed her softly. "Better?"

She smiled, "Maybe a little," and walked me to the door. She checked the hall and whispered, "Goodnight. And thank you for telling me everything. We will work through this, together, I promise."

I sighed and checked again that no one was in the hall. "You're right. Sleep well, beautiful."

Chapter 35

Sleep was not kind to me that evening. I spent most of the night staring at the stone wall in my room. Julia had reassured me, and I was glad she did, but doubt was an ugly beast that fought for control of my mind. I told her the worst things I had done, and she didn't hate me. Either that meant I wasn't the demon I thought, or she was crazy.

My world felt like a blob of grey and for once I wanted things to be black and white. Everything felt like one step forward and two steps back, except Julia. With her, I had accidentally stumbled upon my favorite person in the world. Everything else felt shaky, though, like that glass world she spoke about had a crack that was spreading and threatening its structure. *How do you put back together something that large when it shatters?*

Eventually, I gave up on sleep and went to take a shower. I let the water run down my neck, back, and shoulders. It felt like a ten-ton weight had been added to me, though it really had been there, ignored, for years. I needed to talk to Delaware. I'd carried this secret too long, and she deserved to know the truth. *It's fine. The world hates me, and now she will too.*

I changed and headed to the garage, nodding to Jonah along the way. He stopped and looked back at me as I passed. "Do you ever sleep?"

With a smirk, I shrugged. "The red tag grants me unlimited energy, Jonah. It's a secret the Prism doesn't tell you Blues."

He just laughed, shook his head, and continued on his patrol.

I reached the garage, pulled out the cheaper sedan, and radioed to Delaware. "Del, you up?" I waited for a second. "Delaware, you there?"

Her voice crackled over the radio, confused. "Coyote? It's like 3 a.m. What do you want?"

"We need to talk."

She sighed. "Now? Really?"

"Yes. It has waited for too long. I'll be there in half an hour."

She yawned. "Okay. This better be important."

I drove through the night with the lights of the car piercing through the foggy veil that hung over the Earth. The guards gave me a weird look as I drove through the gates but didn't ask any questions. Being Julia's bodyguard had a few perks. The guards didn't like it, but they couldn't really question what I was doing.

The moon hung high in the sky and I stopped for a second as I crossed the bridge. That time of night was surreal. The city was almost completely quiet, and it was the only time that nature was louder than humanity. The water splashing underneath the bridge always made me feel at home.

When I reached our rendezvous point, Delaware was in her pajamas, her hair a mess. "Everything okay?"

I pointed to one of the chairs and spoke firmly, "Sit. I have a lot to explain."

She looked concerned but did as I said. "What'd you do this time?"

I sat in the other chair. "This is about something I did a long time ago..." I told her everything, crying through half of it. She just looked stunned, occasionally nodding but showing no other real reactions. "I... I'm so sorry Del. I should have told you before. It has been eating away at me for years and I couldn't hold it in anymore. You deserved to know years ago. There is no excuse."

She stood and paced a little bit, still showing no reaction until she spoke, and her voice cracked a little, "You... you did all of this, everything, because of that?"

I looked down. "I knew I could never make it right, but I couldn't leave you there knowing that it was my fault you were there in the first place." I stood and walked over to her. "I'm so sorry. I know this doesn't fix anything."

She looked up at me, and her face flooded with emotion all at once: rage and sadness combined. She started punching me. My side still hurt a bit from where I'd been stabbed, but I just stood and took it. *I deserve it.* She stopped, breathing heavily. "I can't believe you didn't tell me. I trusted you. You were the only family I had left, and you couldn't tell me why I didn't have any real family. I... I don't blame you for his death. That was an accident. I blame the UPF for overworking him in the first place, but letting me live a lie the last few years?"

I just hung my head in guilt.

"So, taking me under your wing, making me acting lieutenant... this has all been a mirage to make you feel better about yourself?"

"No..."

Her thick eyebrows formed a ridge. "I thought you actually cared about me. That you were my friend."

"Del, I rescued you because I couldn't forgive myself, but I took you under my wing for all the reasons I told you before. You're strong, independent, and quick on your feet. You were always my best friend. None of that was because of this. I don't feel better about myself. I just wanted to get you out of the hell hole I accidentally put you in."

She glared at me. "Fine." She sighed. "Anything else?"

"Unless you have anything. No."

She stomped towards the door, before stopping, sighing, and looking back, her eyes cold. "I forgive you, just... just give me time to think. This is a lot. And don't *ever* lie to me again."

I responded softly, "Thank you, Del, and I promise, I won't."

"Good... I can't afford to lose my big brother too." She opened the door and stepped into the night.

I felt like a weight had been lifted. I understood why she would be upset for a while, but I was glad that she finally knew the truth.

Chapter 36

The first light had not appeared by the time I had returned to the palace. I parked the car in the garage. I needed to get to the gym and hit something that wouldn't cause someone pain.

The palace was nearly empty that early in the morning, with no one around except a few guards patrolling the maze of hallways. It was eerie, with little light available beyond the dull glow emitted by the ceiling lights and chandeliers in the hallways. The moonlight crept in through the few available windows, casting soft shadows across the floor from the few pieces of furniture near the walls.

As I walked, I felt abnormally skittish and behind my racing adrenaline I felt an unexplainable feeling that someone was watching me. I checked over my shoulder often but saw no one. *The tired mind plays tricks in the night.*

The feeling, combined with the thick fall air, sent a shiver down my spine as I exited out the back door of the palace and headed north towards the royal gym. *What is going on?* I scanned the windows of the palace and my surroundings in the garden... *Nobody. I'm losing it.* I shook my head and hurried towards the gym, winding through the garden on my way. The wind rustled the bushes, throwing leaves past my feet.

As I turned past the towering marble statue of Timothy Hughes

II, a shadow slid through my peripherals. I was thrown to the ground with a *thud*. With my eyes in a panic and the lack of light, I couldn't identify my attacker at first. They jabbed their forearm into my throat on the ground and I pushed, trying to force them back with a shout. "Who are you?!"

The assailant's voice was as chill as the night, and I met his wide green eyes. "You think you're funny, don't you?" *Isaac.*

I struggled against the force placed on my throat, and my voice came out weak, "Typically, yes... ack... but I don't know what you're talking about."

He spat at me and drove the fist of his free hand into my side. His ring struck where the knife had stabbed me. I cried out. *This piece of crap really wants it, but how does he know where the wound was?* His brow furrowed with intensity. "Shut up! It was you... It was you..." I attempted to roll him over and gain a better position, but he held me down. "You sent that shit to my room! You ruined everything!"

How did he find out? "What... ack... what do you think I ruined?"

He delivered a quick punch to my cheek, *shit!* My ears rang from the impact and I looked up at Isaac's reddening face. "Julia. She... she thinks I'm a fool and a drunkard because of you Red Tag piece of shit."

In his emotion he left a space for just a second, and I jabbed him quickly in the jaw before flipping him off me. I rolled against the cool stone path and stumbled to my feet, setting up in a defensive fighting stance. "What then? You come here to kill me?" *You picked the wrong night asshole.*

Isaac threw his arms forward bluntly. This was not the well put together Isaac that I had seen before. He was uncaged, his voice like venom. "You are going to regret getting in my way." He leaned forward and wildly pointed to himself. "She is mine! You hear me? Mine!"

Good old-fashioned fighting over a girl. I let my guard down for a second, taunting him with my arms. "Is she really? Or are you just some White snake who thinks he gets everything he wants?"

With that, he threw himself at me with a brutal yell. He wasn't very quick, but he was bigger than me and could pack some heat in his punches; I felt them even through my blocks. He kept trying to go for my stab wound again but I swatted away his attempts and jabbed at his body, dancing around him in my stance to keep him off balance.

He ducked in close to me, grabbing my arm and delivering a tough upper cut to my jaw, making me taste warm blood. From the hold I stuck my lead leg behind his left ankle, sweeping his leg and throwing my weight into him as he fell to the ground. I spat out the blood in my mouth and tried to get on top of him, but he managed to scramble to his feet. *This is way better than a punching bag.* I was filled with emotion and adrenaline from everything that had happened with Julia, Alexandria, the Lt. General, Delaware, and now Isaac, and it was all coming out in a hell-bent rage. *I could kill him and end this...*

He leaned in for an overhand cross but was slow, leaving his lead hand too low to protect his head. I exploited that gap with a roundhouse kick, knocking him back and to the ground near the bushes. He was dazed and confused. I towered over him. *...but I shouldn't.* "Stay down and stay away."

He shook his head, regaining focus and gritting his teeth. He yelled and threw himself to his feet, trying to attack, but I kneed him in the gut and threw him back down. *Just stop. For both of our sakes.*

Isaac looked ready to stumble back to his feet when I heard a loud "Ivan!" from across the garden and turned my head to see who called my name. It was dark, and I couldn't see the person calling for me as I scanned the nearby paths. Suddenly, I remembered the fight, and I turned my head back to Isaac too late as he smashed the side of my head with one of the rocks that lined the flower bed, knocking me onto my back. The world spun, and my vision began to slip. The last thing I saw was him over me, raising his arm for the second blow.

Chapter 37

I awoke to the familiar overwhelming smell of antiseptic and... *Is that wintergreen?* Laying on my back, my eyes fluttered as I tried to comprehend what was happening. Squinting, I looked into the bright lights, still disoriented and light-headed. I groaned and held my head, grasping the situation. *Isaac knocked me out. I'm in the royal hospital. I guess that means I survived.*

The machine hooked up to me started making some weird beeping noises and I mumbled, agitated, and swung my arm at it. "Shut up... shut up! Piece of crap..." I sighed, beyond my head, the rest of me hurt from the fight as well. *I had him.*

A yawn came from my left and I cocked my head slowly to see Julia stretching, laid out on the padded bench along the wall. *She waited for me. Aw.* Her ice-blue eyes flickered to life as she looked around and yawned again. She caught my eyes and the drowsiness flowed from her face as she flew to my side. "You're awake! Oh, thank God." She was shaking, and tears filled her eyes. "I've been so worried."

I smiled at her weakly and grabbed her hand, rubbing my thumb across the back of it to calm her. "How long was I out?"

"It's Saturday morning," she checked her phone, "around six." *It's been a day?* "The doctors said you might be out for a while and I... I just couldn't leave you alone, not after what Isaac did to you."

A tear slid down her face and onto my arm. "Sorry."

I laughed softly. "You slept here for me? What about your parents? The other royals?"

She smiled without actually lifting the corners of her mouth and nodded shakily, sharply dropping her head before looking back at me, her bottom lip quivering. *She is hurting more than I am.* "You could have died, Ivan."

I squeezed her hand softly. "It's going to be alright, I promise." We shared a moment, eyes locked.

She was about to speak but was interrupted by the door opening. A Green Tag nurse entered. We quickly let go of each other's hands, though it was pretty obvious what was going on.

Julia ran her hand through her hair uncomfortably. She was always concerned about perception, understandably, and we had already been noticed when she let her guard down. The nurse pretended to ignore it, though, as Julia returned to the bench, her cheeks flushed with slight embarrassment.

The nurse approached me with a flashlight and shone it in both of my eyes as my dull headache throbbed. Her dark brown eyes were analyzing something. "How are you feeling?"

I sat back and sighed. "Terrible. I'm light-headed and have a massive headache too."

She nodded. "That is to be expected. You received a serious concussion, though you're lucky it wasn't worse than what it was. You're likely going to have some light and sound sensitivities for a day or two and probably a pretty bad headache along with some serious bruising. If you feel nauseous, irritable, or have trouble concentrating, that is normal as long as the symptoms don't last beyond the next few days. If they do, tell us, because that could mean something more serious is going on. Do you understand?"

I tried to crack my neck, which was stiff as hell. "Yeah. Ack. I think."

She sighed. "We're going to keep you for a few tests now that you're awake to make sure everything looks normal. Hopefully we can get you out of here soon. Take it easy, you're going to feel off for a while."

I nodded. "Thanks, doc."

She shook her head. "The actual doctor will be by to take you for a PET scan of your brain before you go."

Julia smiled at the nurse sweetly. "Thank you for everything Josie."

"Your highness." The nursed bowed before shuffling out the door.

The door shut behind her and I turned my head towards Julia, who had her arms wrapped around her knees on the bench, looking out the window. I chuckled. "You are a princess, through and through."

She raised her eyebrows and looked at me. "Would a goody two-shoes princess fall for you?"

I mockingly raised my eyebrows in response. "Who said you don't just like bad boys?"

She giggled again and shook her head, looking back out the window. "If you really think you're a bad boy, you don't know yourself Ivan."

I laid my head back on the pillow and shut my strained eyes. "How is Alexandria?"

"She seems lost, honestly. He took a piece of her that she is figuring out how to live without. The Lt. General turning himself in helped, I think, but revenge doesn't fill the hole. I just can't help wondering how easily it could have been me at some party, you know?"

The bed squeaked as I repositioned. "I won't let that happen." I sighed. "I wish I could do more for her."

She hesitated, and the machine's slow, annoying beeping filled the gap. "Just… give her a smile and ask how she is. I think it would mean something to her. She actually respects you and would probably appreciate it."

I smiled softly. "That's the least I can do. Consider it done." I groaned from my headache and held my head in my hands. *Did they really give me no painkillers?* "What happened after he knocked me out?"

She didn't respond for a moment and pursed her lips, thinking. "Jonah saw you rushing around while he was finishing his patrol and was worried. He said he saw you two fighting in the gardens and called out before you got knocked out. Isaac saw him and ran. Jonah called an ambulance and then me. I rode with you and have been here since."

I looked over at her again. "You didn't need to do that. What is everyone going to think?"

She stood and glided over to the side of the bed. "I couldn't just leave you, Ivan. As you're my bodyguard, my parents understand my concern. Other royals…" She shrugged. "The ones who hate us will despise that I'm worried about a Red Tag. The others will understand. They all might mock you on the surface, but they're just trying to maintain a perception. I mean, we all are, but this was a sacrifice I was willing to make after what you did.”

I was confused. “I thought you wouldn’t want me to fight him.”

She held my hand, her eyes full of concern. “Did you have a choice? Jonah didn’t see how it started.”

I looked forward, thinking before returning my eyes to hers. “He jumped me, had me pinned down for a while, but he was sloppy and emotional. Once I could get to my feet, I had him on the ground pretty quick. I was trying to convince Isaac to stop fighting until Jonah distracted me.” I chuckled. “It’s actually ironic. He was trying to help. Isaac got the jump on me with the rock when I was distracted. Cheap shot.”

She sighed and paced over to the window, looking out into the flurries beyond. “This looks really bad for him. I hate that he did this to you, but maybe something good can come of it at least. He showed his true nature, the snake.”

She almost spat out that last bit. I was surprised to see her fired up now, passion flowing through her slender frame. In no way was she a fighter, but I would not want to get in her way when she was angry. “If I bring this concern to my parents now, they won’t have a choice, and I’m sure they’re doubting it already themselves.” She spun towards me, a hand covering her mouth in realization. “Ivan, you may have freed me.”

“Well I’m glad to have killed that bird with one stone. Ha!”

She didn’t laugh as she excitedly sat along the side of the bed. “Ivan... there’s no more Isaac. It’s you and me. It may have been an accident, but I think you did it...”

I smiled softly. “Even if it’s just in private. I couldn’t hope for more."

She leaned over and kissed me. "Get some rest. Hopefully, we can get you home soon." *Home.* It was the first time I had ever related the palace mentally to home. I still felt like an alien there, but maybe that could change with her. I closed my eyes and dozed off. *God, I'm lucky.*

Chapter 38

A few hours later, the doctors cleared me for release, and I rode along with Julia back to the palace. Our hands barely touched in the middle of the back seat, out of sight of the chauffeur and his rear-view mirror. We enjoyed our little rebellion. A little touch was enough to ignite the fire within me and I yearned for the future we were working towards where a stupid earring didn't matter. *For us, for everyone.*

She gazed out the window as we drove. I admired her bravery. She was risking everything by being with me, and unlike me, she had the world to lose, even if it was a glass one.

The chauffeur had the radio on, and something caught my attention. "Sir, could you turn that up a bit?"

He was a bit surprised at the request but complied. The anchor's smooth voice crackled through the speakers, "...the terrorist threat. Therefore, the General Secretary announced this morning in a speech at the People's Assembly that the United People's Front will be instituting a, quote, 'bold and new security strategy to ensure the safety and success of all people in Northern Mississippi.'" I looked nervously across the back seat at Julia before concentrating on the broadcast again. *They're pulling themselves together.* "We will now play a clip from our leader's speech."

There was a rustling as they roughly switched over the recording. The General Secretary's rough and fervent voice flooded through the speakers. "This three-year plan is essential as we shake off the rust that has accumulated around our ankles; we have been infiltrated by forces seeking to destroy our glorious system. The Planning Committee has approved three crucial changes that are needed to shield ourselves and protect our enlightened nation. First, we must shift away from importing international goods produced by enemies of our people. I have instructed the Ministry of Trade to institute an extensive and comprehensive round of embargos and tariffs on offender nations, including, but not limited to, the United Kingdom, the Republic of Dakota, the Republic of Texas, and the Scandinavian Union." It sounded like he almost spat in disgust after speaking the country's names.

The inspiration for the embargos was definitely the Anglo-Nordic Coalition's consistent pressure on the Fifth International's western and northern Europe allies. This would only further increase tensions. *Royals won't like that. Can't get fancy clothes from the collective. Meanwhile, the rest of us will starve reliant on the socialists' useless farms. Great plan.*

After a round of applause, he collected himself and continued. "Second, to accommodate this shift, there will be a reallocation of the Red population from within the service and entertainment-based sectors into industrial and agricultural output. All Red Tags not under special arrangements will also be provided housing for the first time in our new production cities: Aitkin, Willmar, and New Ulm in Minnesota, Harshaw in Wisconsin, and Clarion in Iowa."

He paused as this was met by applause again from the UPF puppets in the parliament. "We will no longer allow large swathes of our people to live in squalor in places such as 'the Enclave.' They will produce for the collective and will be provided for."

Camps. They are recreating the camps. The Enclave is done. They're going to kill them... I gripped Julia's hand nervously and bit my cheek. She looked nervous, but there was no way she could understand what his true plans were.

"Finally, we must address the security concerns stemming from a conspiracy against our people and the collective. We have uncovered a plot, financed by capitalist scum within the so-called Free State of Dakota, who seek to undermine everything we hold dear. These foreigners have secretly been funneling money and weapons to the terrorists. They are attempting to weaken and divide us from the inside while they prepare for war."

Fear is a powerful weapon. Dakota had been one of the few areas in the former Kingdom of America that didn't fall to the socialists. Instead, they instituted a fairly freedom-oriented republic, and over the last century, thousands of Northern Mississippians had attempted to flee across the border. The country was the constant target of socialist rhetoric and, while their system had its own problems, they didn't enslave a significant portion of the population. Dakota also had nothing to do with the Militia as far as I was aware.

"They seek to sow doubt in our minds about our way of life

through lies and deceit. This conspiracy, led by the terrorist Coyote, has led to rumors about government surveillance." *I'm famous. Why does that scare me?* He coughed and spoke sternly, enunciating every word clearly. "The United People's Front will not tolerate foreign actors undermining our system, and we will take the necessary actions to prevent the perpetuation of such deceit by terrorists." *He can't even deny the spying.* "As a result, we will be redoubling our efforts to punish those who commit crimes against the collective, in action, written word, or speech. Our cherished Prism and way of life must be protected against these threats, no matter the cost."

The tape ended, and the anchor's smooth voice returned, "That was our glorious leader, the General Secretary Lawrence Bachton..."

Julia and I's eyes met across the backseat. *This is bad.*

Chapter 39

We have awoken the beast. Social media was flooded with reports of raids and arrests against some of the more vocal anti-government leaders following the General Secretary's speech. Julia was rightly nervous, but she had the protection of the monarchy, even if her parents had their disagreements. *The rest of us aren't so lucky.* So many others were at risk, though, and it appeared that the UPF's complacency was gone as the streets once again were full of their goons. *If they can't convince us to be loyal, they'll beat us until we change our minds or die, whichever comes first.*

Upon our return to the palace, we were met by Michael and his usual nose-held-high demeanor. "The King requests both of your presences in the throne room."

Julia softly nodded, the princess had returned. "Of course. Thank you, Michael."

He didn't leave. "I have been asked to escort you."

They don't trust us? She nodded and softly raised an arm horizontally, palm up. "Of course. After you." She collected herself, regaining her regal demeanor and preparing for the impending confrontation.

As we walked, a few of the guards and servants who we passed gave me sorrowful looks, the only ones I'd ever received from them since my arrival. By then they must have known what had happened. *And they actually feel bad? Maybe they do have some humanity left.*

The throne room doors creaked open as we entered, and I surveyed the large, stone room with its ice-blue decorations. It was amazing how two months ago I had walked into this room, alone and a stranger to the mysteries the palace held within. Today, I was far from alone and all too familiar with the secrets of the royals.

We were met by a wintery aroma which flowed from the candles scattered throughout the throne room. The watchful eyes of the King's council studied our approach from their herd to the King's right. *Be careful.*

Isaac knelt to the left of the King, his head down and his parents standing at his flanks. A bruise graced the left side of his face where I'd kicked him. It felt good to have given his annoyingly perfect face a solid blemish. Wilhelm Preus's glare met mine and sent a shiver down my spine. *What is it like to watch your only son kneel in defeat for attacking someone like me?*

Julia held her head high and glided down the aisle towards the throne as I slid behind her, still light headed. The King looked fondly upon his daughter and furrowed his brow upon me. *Glare all you want. This is your fault.*

We approached, and I dropped to one knee. "Your highness."

Julia gave a slight, respectful bow, remaining standing. "Father."

He nodded, acknowledging us and rubbing his large stubbled chin, pondering. His icy eyes showed sorrow and exhaustion. With everything that had happened with Alexandria and now this, it had been a long week for the family. Despite my disagreements with the King, I pitied him as a father, helpless to stop all of it.

The King spoke flatly, his powerful voice under leash as he considered his words. "I do not believe that it requires explanation why you are all here today." He surveyed us all. "The events of Friday morning were shameful and completely disrespectful to the royal family. Isaac, you attacked one of my servants in *my* house." He slammed his fist onto his arm rest and Isaac flinched. "Instead of bringing your concerns to me directly, you believed it acceptable to beat him over the head with a stone, like a barbarian." His eyes fell bluntly upon Isaac, who did not raise his head. "You have brought shame upon both your house and mine."

Isaac's voice came, short and raspy. "Yes, your highness."

The King turned his attention slowly to me and sighed. "And you, Ivan. You felt that it was acceptable to order, what was it, five bottles of $5,000 champagne under his name?" I nodded as he continued. "You intervened in my affairs, violating my family's arrangement with the Preus family with your immaturity and rashness." *Fine, but I didn't hit anyone with a rock or force my daughter into a marriage.*

I lowered my head before meeting his eyes. "Yes, your highness."

He rubbed his hands restlessly along the throne's arm rests and looked to the sky for a moment, taking a breath and searching for inspiration. He looked back and forth between Isaac and me. "After consulting with the council, I have settled upon what I believe to be appropriate punishments for you both."

He sighed again, looking at me before speaking to Isaac. "As a result of your actions, the Queen and I are no longer comfortable with your betrothal to my daughter and our agreement is terminated."

Wilhelm scowled and raged. "This is unacceptable! My son was attacked by the Red boy and forced to defend himself."

"After hearing a guard's account of the incident, I have no choice but to say that the opposite seems to be the case, Wilhelm. With the evidence before me, I find Isaac Preus guilty of aggravated assault." He upped his intensity. "By the power vested in me as King of Northern Mississippi, I strip you, Isaac Preus, of your royal status and ban you from royal property indefinitely." *That's it? He'll be forced through the Prism but will be given a cushy spot with his connections to the UPF.*

Isaac did not seem to believe the punishment was light and snapped. "You can't do this!" He struggled to his feet, eyes wild.

Wilhelm hissed and joined in. "My son shall not be expelled from my property by an arbitrary decision of a biased King! You refuse to honor our agreements and deny my son his birthright? What kind of King are you?"

The King raised his voice. "You would do well to remember to whom you are speaking. The decision was reached by unanimous agreement of the council, unless you would like to challenge our system of laws?"

Isaac scowled and returned to his knee, shaking his head while his father stood, arms crossed. "You will regret this, Timothy."

The King shook his head and gestured to the guards. They held Isaac's arms, forced him to his feet, and walked him outside the room, followed by his parents. Isaac scowled at me as he passed. "You'll pay for this."

I just cocked my head to the side and glared at him. He had won the battle, but I had won the war, and dang it felt good.

The King returned his attention to me, studying me for a second. He spoke, softer and more understanding than with Isaac, "You crossed the line, Ivan." He sighed. "You are to repay your debt to the Preus family, $25,000. Beyond that, I believe you received a more than adequate punishment from Isaac yesterday." *$25,000?*

I tried to find words, stumbling over them. "I... I don't have that kind of money, your highness."

Julia stepped forward without hesitation. "I will pay my servant's debts father."

The King nodded. "Very well." There actually seemed to be a hint of pride on his face. *This isn't a punishment for me. He is testing her honor.*

She wouldn't be able to use the family's money for such a payment, so she would have to use her personal funds. They were extensive, but $25,000 was no chump change, even for a princess. *How can I possibly repay her?*

The King gestured to the door. "That is all. Isaac, the guards will see you out. Everyone else is dismissed, except for my daughter. We have much to discuss."

I rose and bowed. "Your highness." I looked at Julia, checking that she would be alright. She gave a slight smile and rocked her head to the side, letting me know it was okay to go. I nodded and followed the council members out of the throne room and into the hall.

Waiting outside in the hallway for Julia, I leaned my head back against the cold marble wall, my fingers rubbing my temple. The chill from the wall was the only thing tying me to reality as my pounding post-concussion headache had my vision spinning again. *He didn't kill me, but this might.*

One of the guards noticed my struggle. "You okay, Red Tag?"

I held my eyes shut in pain. "I'm fine." *I'm not fine.*

It felt like an eternity before Julia emerged from her discussions with the King. "Ready to go, Ivan?" I hadn't noticed her approach and lost my balance in surprise. She looked concerned. "Everything alright?"

I massaged the front of my head. "Yeah… just… ack… my head is spinning."

She spoke calmly, "C'mon, let's get you some rest."

We headed towards her room. Julia glided down the halls, smiling and nodding to people who we passed as I shuffled behind, trying to avoid embarrassing her but looking like an absolute wreck in the process. *I am doing wonders for her reputation.*

A cool pine aroma met us as we arrived in her room, adding another unnecessary input to my brain. *I forget. Is irritability a side-effect of the concussion or am I just in a mood?*

Julia shut the door and pulled me to the couch. "Lie down for a while. I have some letters to write and the girls won't be coming to the party for a few hours."

I sat and squinted. "What did your dad want to talk about? And how can I repay you?"

"We had a nice father-daughter chat, that's all, and consider that repayment for saving my life." *Why do I feel like she is hiding something?* I didn't have the energy to question her, though. "Now, sleep."

"Are you sure? What if someone comes in?"

She leaned over in front of me and gave a wry smile. "That's why you're on the couch…" She kissed my forehead. "I'll wake you up in a bit."

I groaned in protest but lied across the couch and quickly faded to sleep as she drifted towards the desk.

Chapter 40

My dreams were rarely pleasant, but the nap brought with is a particularly disturbing image. I stood, wearing my white blazer, in an open prairie, the wind howling and the grasses rustling against my legs. Thunder rolled in the distance and a chill ran down my spine. I scanned the field. *Empty. I need to find cover.*

Pushing my way through the field, I headed towards the tree line for protection from the oncoming storm. As I neared, a piercing scream came from the hill to my right. I looked at the tree line one last time, abandoning safety under the rustling trees and instead sprinted towards the hill, desperate to find the source of the scream. My heart pounded as a second scream followed as I neared the summit. *Where is it coming from?*

The sky darkened as I reached the top of the hill, and thunder cracked nearby, the lightning providing but a few flashes of light. Rain poured from the sky as I scanned ahead, searching for the voice and yelling, "Hello? Where are you?"

Lightning flashed, and another scream followed just ahead. My heart was racing, and adrenaline pumped through my veins as my body entered fight mode. *What is happening?* I followed it into a second field that stretched endlessly into the distance.

I couldn't see anyone until a crack of lightning illuminated two figures a dozen or so meters in front of me: a woman and a figure in black. *Careful.* I approached, slowly, my hands raised to protect my face from the driving rain. I called out, "Who are you?"

The woman struggled against the figure, who had a knife to her jugular from behind. She screamed, panicked, "Ivan!"

Julia. No. I continued my approach, cautiously, and tried to calm her down. "Julia... Julia, it's going to be alright."

She was breathing heavily, her icy eyes wide in fear. "I... I don't remember how to get out of this... not when he has a knife."

Another flash of lightning cracked nearby, allowing me to get a better view of the attacker. His deep blue eyes dared me to approach as his red tag flapped in the wind. He did not speak.

I looked at him, at most three meters away. "Who... who are you? What do you want with her?"

His upturned eyes narrowed, challenging me. *I know those eyes.* Suddenly I realized, *the bandana.* A shiver went down my spine as the freezing rain smacked against my face.

Coyote tightened the knife to her throat; a drop of blood slid down her long pale neck. *You know who I am.*

Why? I raised my hands in surrender. "If you're me... you love her as much as I do. Let... let her go."

He slowly shook his head. *Love?*

I stuttered, "But... why?"

His brow furrowed. *You know why.*

I shook my head. "She is different. The Whites... she is different."

He shook his head again. *They're all the same.*

"No. Her blood doesn't make her who she is."

He gripped the blade tighter. *She makes you weak.*

Tears ran down my cheeks as I inched nearer, pleading with him. "No. Let... let her go. If you kill her..."

His eyes narrowed. *You killed her, not me.*

"No!" I dove forward, yelling and grabbing at his arm, but he was too fast. Julia's eyes rolled back into her head as he released her body. She fell into my arms and the crimson blood flowed over me, staining my white sleeves. I shook as tears streamed down my face. "Julia! No, no, no... Julia!" I pulled her in, cradling her corpse in my arms. *What have I done?* I knelt there for what felt like forever, wishing for a miracle. My chest was an empty hole.

Rage filled me, and I looked up at Coyote, who stood, staring down upon me. I yelled in pain, "You killed her! Why?! Why?!"

You know why.

I screamed and lunged at him, but he used my momentum, throwing me into the ground. I whimpered, tears flowing down my cheeks. "Why?"

He looked across the field and pointed with his finger, silent.

I slowly returned to my feet and stood next to him, my gaze following his finger across the field. Bodies lay strewn across it, crimson staining the grasses as small fissures spread from them. "You killed them..."

His cold eyes bored into me. *No, we killed them. There's no Coyote without Ivan.* He turned his head back towards the field. *How many?*

Looking across the field, I didn't need to count the number, I knew how many. I sighed, looked down, and whispered softly, defeated, "Seventeen."

Coyote looked at me, his eyes unrelenting, before looking back at Julia's body. *Eighteen.*

Chapter 41

I awoke in a panic, breathing heavily and mumbling frantically.

Julia had my head in her lap, her hand softly stroking my hair. She spoke softly, "It's okay, Ivan. You're safe."

I looked up at her. My heart felt ready to explode out of my chest. My mind was split, still trying to grasp my return to reality. "Wha…"

She ran her hand through my hair, trying to avoid the bruised area. "Shhh. It was just a nightmare."

Nightmare. Right. I was still in shock. "You're… you're alive."

She gave me a wry smile. "Dreaming about me?"

Not in the way you think. I took a deep breath. "Not like that… It was awful."

She smiled softly and kept rubbing my head, trying to calm me. "Tell me about it."

Hey, so I killed you. Well, technically it was Coyote, but he is me, so… I was a great boyfriend. I deflected. "It was just a nightmare."

She looked concerned. "You sure? You look like you just saw a ghost."

I groaned and closed my eyes. "Yeah, it's fine." *It's not fine.*

She wasn't convinced. Her lips pursed, and she looked around the room, thinking as we sat in silence for a few minutes. I felt better physically, but emotionally I had been hit by a truck. *I just saw the woman I love die at my hand. Love? Is that it?*

Someone knocked at the door and Julia jumped a bit. I reluctantly sat up and swung my legs back to the floor as she answered the door. "Already? Okay. Thank you, Michael."

She glided back over to the couch. "I need to put together the final preparations before my guests arrive." She looked at me reassuringly, her eyes understanding. "Do you need some time?"

I looked down at my hands and took a deep breath. "No, a walk would do me some good." I put on a fake smile, so she wouldn't worry. "Besides, who else would protect you from the boiling hot tea?"

Her eyes narrowed, understanding what I was trying to do, but she let it go. "Okay. Can you wait outside for a minute while I get ready?"

"Of course."

With some effort, I rose and slid into the hall. Her handmaidens were waiting. Anne gave me a slight smile and entered the room, while Rachel gave a look of concern. "How are you, Ivan? I heard about what happened…"

I gave a small smile and responded calmly. "Don't worry about it, Rachel. I'll be alright. Thank you, though. I appreciate the concern."

She still looked concerned but nodded and followed Anne into the room.

I leaned against the hallway wall and shut my eyes, thinking. My headache was better, but I couldn't get past the image of Coyote, *me*, slicing Julia's throat, his cold eyes boring into my soul. *What was it trying to tell me? That I'm going to kill her?*

It had been a long time since I had thought about my seventeen kills. I considered myself lucky that the number wasn't higher, as I tried as hard as possible to avoid it, but each was still another weight on my shoulders: one that no words or attempted good deeds could remove. The last thing I wanted was to put Julia in danger. She meant too much to me for me to be responsible for something terrible happening to her. *There's no Coyote without Ivan. Is there Ivan without Coyote?*

That didn't even take into consideration what was about to happen to the Enclave and my friends while I was worried about my petty issues in the palace. Red Tags would be herded like cattle into camps to work until they starved or were shot for dissent. The Militia had thrived during the recent period of UPF complacency, but it appeared that those days were over. The UPF army itself would be raiding the Enclave soon, and a fire fight would not end well for us. They would take serious losses, but we were not prepared for all-out war. We were lucky they had left us mostly alone up until that point, seeing us as nothing more than a slight nuisance. With the flash drive and the publishing of the journal, though, we were now becoming a problem that had to be stomped out before we actually threatened their power. I was useless to help in my current state, right when they needed me the most. *I need to radio Delaware.*

Julia emerged, wearing a white cable knit sweater and jeans, followed by her handmaidens. She smiled at me softly. "Ready."

I followed behind the girls and looked ahead at her, her ponytail bouncing behind her as she glided through the halls. It had been a rough couple of days, but in princess mode she held herself with poise and determination. *She won't die... not on my watch.*

The party was to be held in the homier living room upstairs, near the royal family's bedrooms. Here, carpeting covered the stone floor and a modern aesthetic contrasted with the more public and formal first floor of the palace. Julia spent a lot of time here reading or watching TV when not in her room or outside the royal grounds. She found it a good space to relax while not being cooped up alone in her room or the small parlor downstairs.

The space was a beautiful one for a gathering, with large ornate paned doors opening out onto a balcony at the rear of the palace. It was a fairly warm afternoon, so the doors were open, flooding the space with natural light and the scents of the Fall air. The small stone fireplace was lit as well, providing extra warmth and hominess to the room.

Julia ran her hand smoothly along the top of the light grey couch across from the fire as she glided through the room towards the maids, who were preparing for the guests' arrival. Maria, a Green, began walking her through the drink and food options that were prepared for the evening. They chose a playlist of music, and the soft chords began to flow through the room.

It felt weird but satisfying to just sit back and watch Julia dance happily across the room in her socks, preparing for her friends. *She deserves a fun evening.* The living room and her bedroom were the only places she could be herself away from the other royals and guests, who were not permitted upstairs unless given explicit permission. There, she somehow managed to look like a stunning princess while at the same time being a joyous and approachable girl. With her sweater hugging her frame softly and the comforting feel of the room, I just wanted to wrap her in my arms and sleep next to the fire. Seeing her happy made me forget the problems of the world for just a few seconds, and that was enough. *Happy thoughts, Ivan.*

She caught my staring from across the room and bit her lip in a bit of embarrassment. I just smiled, checked both directions to see no one was looking, and did a quick spin, landing with my arms extended like I was finishing a routine. With my concussion, though, I was more wobbly than expected, and I promptly lost my balance, flopping onto the floor. She giggled and held her hand softly to her face. *Sometimes it's the little things in life.*

One by one, the guests arrived, and I tried and failed to catch and remember all their names as Julia met each one with a hug. They mingled throughout the room and grabbed drinks and hors d'oeuvres.

I felt like an intruder on their "girl time," so I took my leave onto the empty balcony, out of earshot and radioed to Delaware. Her voice came over the radio, hesitant. "Hey, Coyote."

It felt weird checking in now that she knew my secret. "Hey, Delaware. I heard the news…"

She waited a moment before responding. "Yeah… People are really worried. El Capitan is trying to figure out how we're going to get through this. They've already started trying to grab people. It's bad, Coyote."

I was solemn. "Does he have a plan? Because I do, though, it is risky."

"He wants to blow all the bridges between the Enclave and St. Paul except for the Smith Avenue High Bridge."

He wants to fight. Stupid. "He doesn't think going underground is a better idea? Try to remain undetected. We don't have the fire-power to take on their entire army and blowing the bridges won't stop their air force from bombing the shit out of us."

There was a delay. "I'm with him now. He says you might be right, but where would we hide? We don't have enough safe houses to protect everyone."

I paced along the balcony, looking over the garden and the lake beyond. "A full-on war isn't an option without the support of the royal military. We all know that. We will use the safehouses and hide in friendly non-Red homes. It doesn't matter how much space there is. We *have* to make it work or we all die. We need to execute Operation Blackout or everything we've done has been for nothing, and starting a war ends any possibility of pulling it off."

Another delay. "He says that *we* all die while you get to sit in your palace." That stung. I didn't have a response for that brutal of a jab. "Coyote?"

I lowered the radio and thought for a second, fiddling with my royal servant pin before raising the radio to my mouth again. "If he wants to question my loyalty, he can say it to my face. Until then, I'm going to see what I can do to get as many of *our* people protection as possible instead of getting them killed in a failed last stand."

She cut in. "Coyote, I agree with you. Just... give me time. I'll try to convince him."

"Thank you, Del. Coyote out."

Pocketing the radio and leaning my arms against the stone railing along the edge of the balcony, I looked down onto the path below. *El Capitan is going to get everyone killed.*

After a few minutes, I turned and leaned back on the rail, looking back into the living room. Julia was sitting, legs crossed on the couch, laughing with her friends, more relaxed than I'd ever seen her in two months since we had met. *That's the girl I fell for.*

Chapter 42

For the rest of the party I stayed out of their way. I highly doubted any of these increasingly tipsy girls were a threat to Julia's life. *Apparently, I'm more of the threat anyway.* The image of Coyote's black knife pressed against her neck flashed before my eyes and I flinched, holding my palm to my forehead. *What is happening?*

When I recovered, I stood against the wall near the stairs, watching curiously as the girls played some type of game that mainly involved a lot of laughing and giggling. Eventually, one of the Whites, whose name I believe was Mariana, called over to me drunkenly, "Hey, *bodyguard*. Come over here."

I looked at Julia, questioning what was going on. She just giggled and called over, "It's okay, Ivan."

I tentatively shuffled over to them and stood at attention, hands behind my back, in front of the fireplace. "What can I do for you, m'lady?" *Why is this scarier than most of my missions? Man, Ivan is a wimp...*

The girls sat on the couches in a semi-circle in front of me. Mariana cocked her head and looked at me quizzingly. "What's it like being the only Red Tag in the Royal Household?"

I squinted, confused, but responded flatly and formally. "It is an honor to serve the royal family and Princess Julia, m'lady."

She wasn't satisfied, and she continued her slurred persistence. "Oh, come on. It's just us here. Nobody will tell the King and Queen."

I appealed for intervention from Julia with my eyes, but she seemed interested in where this was going. I sighed. "It is an honor to serve. That wasn't a lie. But it is always difficult to be an outlier, especially in a place like this. It is far better than the work I did before, but it has its own unique struggles."

Mariana nodded, appeased, and I turned to return to my position before Julia interjected, "Stay, Ivan. We're not done yet."

I rolled my eyes but returned to the fireplace at attention. *What is this? Did she tell them, and this is a relationship interrogation? Or is this another test?*

Another of the royal friends, Vivian, bit her cheek before she spoke, "What do you think about us?"

"Us?"

She moved her arms in a sweeping motion around her. "The royals... in general?"

I looked at the ceiling and pondered for a second before looking at Julia and smiling. "There are some great people in royalty..." I hesitated and then returned my attention to Vivian. "...and there are some snakes in royalty."

She seemed impressed and looked at Julia. "I thought he was a bodyguard, not a politician." Julia giggled and gave me a sharp look. *She's challenging me. Wow. Is she seeing how I hold up against her friends? I could use the distraction...*

I added a bit of sarcasm. "Sometimes we are more than we appear to be... Any other questions?"

They seemed entertained. *Glad I can entertain some drunk royals while my friends try to survive. Hey, at least Julia will owe me after this and can help find people to host the Reds.*

Another royal, Elena, took her turn eagerly. "What was your first impression of Julia?"

I bit my cheek to hold back a grin and looked at Julia, who had her eyebrows raised curiously. "She was someone who needed help, and I was there to help."

She pushed. "Your actual first impression."

I sighed reluctantly. "I thought she was brave... and cute," smiling a little at the end.

That was met by sarcastic *oohs* and Julia biting her lip.

Elena quickly jumped in again, eager. "Do you have a girlfriend?"

I scoffed. "My job is my girlfriend. I'm here on a Saturday night, so I think that says enough." *I won't lose this battle of wits.*

Alice, the Yellow college friend, jumped in. She was one of the few other under-Greens who had been in the palace, both of us because of Julia. "And you were the one that stopped Isaac Preus, right?"

I held my hand tentatively to my head. "That's a nice way to put getting beat over the head with a rock."

She smirked. "So, you're single *and* fought with the guy Julia was betrothed to."

"Well he jumped me, so..." *I can't tell if they know and are messing with me or what?*

Olivia kept on the pressure. "Sounds like you were willing to sacrifice a lot for her."

246

"That is my job." *Don't you dare…*

She raised her eyebrows. "Seems like more than a job."

I didn't hold back the sarcasm and narrowed my eyes. "Perhaps."

Mariana jumped back in. "So, you don't have any feelings for her?"

I bit my cheek and looked down, *dang it.* "I don't know if…"

Vivian insisted. "Answer the question."

I cocked my head and looked at Julia with my eyebrows furrowed. *Apparently, this falls under the category of "unless I say so."* "What is this?"

She smiled reassuringly, looking like she was trying to avoid laughing. "You can trust them Ivan."

I sighed, and my mouth betrayed me. "Yes, I do."

The girls erupted in excitement, and I decided that this was the point of this charade, but why? *Girls are confusing. Royals are confusing. Drunk royal girls are really confusing.*

They pulled Julia off the couch and pushed her towards me while I looked at her inquisitively, asking her non-verbally if they knew about us. She stood in front of me giggling and gripping my blazer, her bright blue eyes gazing into mine, alight with passion. She whispered, "They knew. I wanted to see how long it would take for you to give in."

Shaking my head, half-annoyed half-entertained, I whispered in her ear, "You're lucky I like you, a lot."

I was suddenly extremely conscious of the fact we were basically surrounded by a sea of eager eyes. *This is worse than the UPF.* Someone yelled at me to kiss her, and I was too stunned to react at first.

Eventually, I came to my senses, wrapped my arms around her waist and kissed her, slower and longer this time. It was weirdly freeing to be a little less in the dark, her closest friends aware of, and apparently supportive of, us. This was met with a few *awws* followed by a sudden deathly silence.

We pulled back and noticed the girls staring towards the stairs. We followed their eyes and my heart sank. *Oh come on...*

Chapter 43

Apparently, the girls had made quite the ruckus, and Alexandria had come to investigate. She stood between the hall to the girls' bedrooms and the staircase, gawking like a child looking at the tree on Christmas morning. The world seemed to freeze for a moment. Julia and I stood holding each other and looking at her sister before coming to terms with the situation and stepped back from each other awkwardly. In ten minutes, I went from thinking three other people knew about our relationship to fourteen. *At this rate, the whole palace will know by Monday.*

If any of her family was going to know, though, Alexandria would do the least damage. Anyway, Natasha had gone along with her parents on a diplomatic trip to California earlier in the afternoon and would be gone until late Sunday, so it wasn't like the risk of being caught had been very high. Alex had enough of her own controversial relationships, and right now, she probably needed something to smile about anyway after the week's events.

The sisters stood looking at each other in shock for a moment before Alexandria let out an excited squeal and hug tackled Julia, almost knocking them both to the ground. "Why didn't you tell me?!" *Okay. Well, that could have gone worse.*

Julia was beaming and hugged her sister back, half-screaming herself. "We are trying to be careful. I'm sorry!"

I stood there and rubbed the back of my neck. *Is this normal?*

The two sisters held each other's hands excitedly jumping up and down before Julia became more serious. "Alex, nobody else can know. We're already taking a risk with this many people."

"I get it. I'm just so happy for you two and, even though I'm mad you didn't tell me, I forgive you." She smiled at me before looking around excitedly. "Now, where's the alcohol? This just became a celebration!" She ran to grab herself a drink.

Oh, boy. I took a deep breath and met Julia's alive eyes as she laughed in relief herself. In that moment I pledged to myself that I would do whatever it takes to ensure we could last and be free to live our lives. She had given me something to lose.

She grabbed my hand and pulled me over to the drink table. "Anything with Alex is a real party. C'mon, you have some catching up to do."

As I looked at the options, I felt a little out of place. I'd had more than a few beers in the Militia, but the spread of expensive liquors in front of me was a bit overwhelming.

While I was pondering my options, Alex turned up the music, danced over, poured me a mix of either bourbon or whiskey and some foreign soda, and handed it to me in one fluid motion while I stood still in shock. She whispered in my ear, "If you're going to date my sister, we need to teach you how to party, Red."

Looking down at the brown liquid in my glass, I just shook my head before looking up at Julia. I met her gaze and took a sip of the sharp liquid, giving her a wry smile as the alcohol burned its way across my tongue and down my throat. She glided through her friends and grabbed my free hand, pulling me to dance with her. I pulled back with a bit of resistance and spoke over the music, "I can't dance."

She insistently pulled me closer and bit her lip, her eyes alight. "Well, it's time to learn."

Well, here we go... I downed the rest of my drink and quickly realized how little experience I had with hard liquor as my mouth caught fire. Julia laughed at my reaction and took my empty glass, placing it on an end table and starting to dance, leading me along with the bass-heavy pop music. Part of me wanted to fight and stay on guard, but I let her lead me through the dance.

Eventually, the party ended after some casual conversation, and the girls went on their way, leaving me alone with Alex and Julia, who were still busy giggling and laughing together on one of the couches. I slumped down on the one across from them and rubbed my head. "I don't know if it's the concussion or the alcohol, but my head is spinning."

Alexandria laughed and raised what had to be her seventh or eighth drink and slurred a response. "You haven't seen a *real* royal party, Ivan."

She is way drunker than me. "You scared the shit out of me when you walked up."

Julia laughed. She was obviously less drunk than her sister. "You don't know Alex well enough."

Alex gave her sister a sloppy hug. "I'm just so happy for you two. You may be a Red, Ivan, but I see how you make her happy, even if she tries to hide it around us."

Julia and I's eyes met, and she blushed as we both grinned like maniacs. We were out of our minds: a White princess and a Red slave fracturing the Prism from both ends.

Alex finished her drink and stood, shakily. "All right. I need to sleep. I'll leave you two love-birds." We laughed, and she stumbled off towards her room.

At the last second, I stood, turning towards her and smiled. "And Alex." She looked back at us, supporting herself with one arm against the wall. "Thank you for a fun evening. I'm glad you came by. Next time we do heavy metal instead of pop."

She looked down, solemnly for a moment, before looking back at me and almost whispering, "Glad to be a part of it, Red."

I gave her a soft smile, and she shuffled towards her room. I looked back towards Julia as a wide, proud smile stretched across her face. Shaking my head, I chuckled. "What?"

"Thank you for caring about her. I don't think you realize how much tonight meant to her, Ivan."

I slumped onto the couch and put my arm around her. "I just did what you told me to."

She snuggled into my side and leaned her head softly against mine. "But you cared enough to listen and remember things. That means a lot to her, and me."

We were quiet for a few minutes, just enjoying the evening breeze and each other's presence until I laughed. "So, was this a plan to embarrass me or what? I thought we weren't going to tell anybody."

She giggled. "We were playing truth or dare. One of the truths they asked me was if anything was going on between us..." "Was it obvious?"

She bit her lip. "They said I looked at you way more often than most people look at their bodyguards"

"Ah, so it was your fault."

"Hey, stop looking cute in the clothes I got you and we won't have a problem. And later for a dare they said that I had to let them interrogate you."

"That was probably the weirdest experience of my life."

She giggled and played with one of the buttons on my shirt. "Well you passed the test. In case you couldn't tell, they love you, and that's important for girls."

"Glad to make a good first perception with the friends. So, when do I get to take you to the Enclave and have my team interrogate you."

She smirked. "Right when we fix the world."

"I don't feel like that's fair, we'll probably break it first."

She laughed. "All's fair in love and war."

"I love you too, Julia."

She looked up at me quickly in a bit of shock, her cheeks red. "I didn't mean…I…"

I laughed. "Don't worry, it was a joke."

She stuttered through the shock. "I know… but… I love you too."

Oh. I stared into her eyes and grinned. "That was payback for the interrogation."

She was offended and punched me softly. "That's not funny!"

I smiled and responded softly, "I meant it, though. I love you, Julia. I know we haven't known each other for that long, but it feels like it's been years and I can't imagine life without you."

She bit her lip. "You know how to talk your way out of trouble."

I shifted and kissed her softly. "When you get yourself in trouble a lot, it is an important skill to learn."

Chapter 44

I woke up holding Julia in her bed. The aroma of pine wafted through the air from her candles and mixed with her wintergreen perfume. We had half-drunkenly fallen asleep after we left the living room out of fear of a guard walking past on a post-party patrol. She had asked me to stay, and I remembered falling asleep lying next to her, my arm around her waist. It was weirdly natural to be holding her, not worrying about the world for a few hours.

She wasn't awake yet, so I just laid there, staring at the back of her head, thinking about the dream from yesterday and what I was going to do about the impending fall of the Enclave. El Capitan needed to keep his head on straight or a lot of people would die unnecessarily. *Hopefully Delaware and Poseidon can talk some sense into him.* It was a bad situation, but, for now, we needed to focus on the plan. I wasn't going to let all of my work to maintain peace go to waste. Besides, I was slowly gaining the royal family's trust. I just hoped I wouldn't have to choose between my two loyalties. If the plan worked, I wouldn't have to, but there were a million moving parts, and the imminent UPF threat was growing ever stronger.

Eventually, Julia woke up slowly and shifted back into me mumbling. "It's cold."

I laughed. "Good morning, princess."

She coughed. "What time is it?"

I looked at the large platinum analog clock on the wall. "Eight-thirty." She groaned. "Hangover?"

She sighed and mumbled, "No, I was just enjoying that sleep."

I kissed the back of her shoulder. "Same. First time I haven't had a nightmare in years."

She rolled over to look at me, yawning. "Aww. So that nightmare you had yesterday… that was normal?"

"Yesterday's was… worse… than normal. But, yes, dreams don't really like me. That tends to happen when you've lived your entire life in fear," *and killed seventeen people.*

She smiled softly. "I'm glad I could scare them away." She ran her hand softly through my hair. "Though this can't be a normal thing. Understand?"

I chuckled. "Understood, though I was surprised by how rebellious you were. Was that the alcohol?"

She smirked. "No, it was just refreshing to just have fun with my closest friends, my boyfriend, and my rebel sister all in one night. I didn't have to be what anyone else wanted me to be." I smiled, and she giggled. "What?"

I ran my fingers along her cheek. "You're beautiful, and I loved seeing you like that… like this. It's rare I get to really see you without the princess guard up, not that there's anything wrong with *Princess* Julia."

"We both have two kind of separate lives, don't we?"

"I mean, I wouldn't quite equate our situations, but I guess you have a point. Though, the jewelry you got at birth is way better than mine." I held her hand and fiddled with her ring.

She furrowed her eyebrows, insistent. "You know what I mean. We each have another side that very few people have seen."

"That's true, and I'm glad we can trust each other with them."

She smiled softly and felt my side. "Can I see the scar?"

Which one? I responded, reluctant. "If you insist."

She slowly lifted up my shirt, revealing the scar from the knife wound as well as a few other scars from years ago. Her hand trembled as she ran her hands across them, her eyes full of worry.

I sighed. "My life... my old life. It came with a cost. Coyote survived, so Ivan could live."

Our eyes met. "But that's going to change, right? We're going to fix things, together."

Tucking her hair back, I thought for a second. "Things will change, and together we will." *I hope...*

She smiled softly and laid her hand along mine on her cheek. "Speaking of fixing things, I wish we could just spend the day here, but Princess Julia is needed in the world, and that won't change. I've got that Sunday roundtable this afternoon on TV."

I wrapped my arms around her, pulling her tight to me. "So, you're telling me we have a few more hours."

She giggled, her eyes studying my face. "I need to make an appearance soon or people around the palace will start asking questions."

I kissed her. "Let them ask."

She was stern. "Ivan, you know this is important to me."

"Yes, m'lady."

She smiled wryly. "Fine, a few more minutes," and she kissed me for more than a few minutes.

Chapter 45

The Sunday roundtable was a weekly session on the "Collective Chat" show, consisting of a few different well-known faces or at least, debatably, somewhat interesting people who would discuss a bunch of topics that didn't matter. Occasionally, though, someone would have some guts to bring up a challenging idea and a real discussion could occur. This week, Julia would be joined by Simon Tillman, the show's Blue host, as well as General Demetrius Johnson of the UPF, a Purple, pop singer Olivia Bowman, a Green, and University of Minnesota running back Xavier Morgan, a Yellow.

The handmaidens had Julia looking stellar compared to the rest of the group, her sapphire necklace shining against her pale skin and white open collared blouse. She was determined to challenge the Purple General on the UPF's recent decisions to oust the Reds and restrict trade with even somewhat capitalist nations. She knew she had to be careful, though, with the fragile state of political affairs. The international situation with the Anglo-Nordic Coalition was still tense, and the calls within Northern Mississippi for privacy reforms were causing a massive headache for the UPF. The government was responding with increasing levels of force.

Her last interview had made waves, but if she could put the General on the spot, there would be an uproar, especially if he got tough on the cute, innocent-looking princess who seemed to care about people. *The two things I love the most: watching Julia be her amazing self and embarrassing the UPF.*

As expected, the majority of the show consisted of talk about wishy-washy entertainment news, yesterday's football game, how the collective is advancing, etc., but then Julia got her chance. The General mentioned the "new strategies" in his statements about why people should feel more secure about the future than ever before.

Julia calmly, but firmly, intervened. "But General Johnson, are these strategies actually anything new or simply a repeat of the camps and failed plans we saw thirty years ago that led to massive starvation among the Red and Orange Tag populations?"

The General raised an eyebrow, surprised by the sudden challenge, and responded, his voice deep and condescending. "On the contrary, *princess*. This plan allows the Red Tag population access to housing and a more effective and consolidated rationing system than the variable ones of recent memory. These production centers will allow for greater security as well as efficiency for production and oversight of the Reds."

Julia pushed harder. "But isn't it true that we have consistently failed to produce enough food internally to account for demand, particularly in the winter? How do you expect to feed the everyday people of Northern Mississippi without access to these foreign markets? Are we going to just prioritize people on the color of an earring to decide who lives and who starves?"

He was stern. "These are questions to be handled by the planning committee of the United People's Front, not the monarchy, and I struggle to believe that you have a better grasp on the concerns of the people than the collective's governing body, *princess*."

Surprisingly, Xavier, the running back, stepped in. "I don't know anything about this plan, but the princess was at Minnesota and in more than one class with me. She knows her stuff. She's seen what we see."

Olivia, the singer, nodded, remaining silent but in agreement on camera, trying to be careful as a Green. *Three on one.*

Julia smiled. "Thank you, Xavier. I *have* seen the concerns of the average person, and I've felt the pain of the people impacted by government policy, but this is not about me or what I think." She turned her attention to the General again and was dead serious, her eyes like daggers. "This is about preventing our already fragile economy from crumbling by repeating the failures of the past and cutting us off from the world while at the same time arresting people who dare to ask a simple question of 'why?' We sit at a crossroads, in which the government can continue to increasingly violate people's privacy and control their lives no matter who they are, or we can prevent the repetition of our parents' and grandparents' failures and work together towards a better future through openness and dialogue instead of fear."

Simon, the host, stepped in eagerly, obviously being instructed to do so by the producers, and changed the topic. It didn't matter, though, as Julia had brought the General to a personal attack and got in the last word while getting back-up from a popular football player of all people. It couldn't have gone much better. She looked bold and determined while maintaining her innocent appearance for the majority the discussion. Meanwhile a general in a military uniform attempted to condescend her and pretend he was more connected to the people than her. Julia, with the help of Xavier, proved that she was speaking for the average person and managed to point out the failed policies of the past.

It was risky, and the UPF's crackdowns on the growing reform movements would bring them into increased conflict with the monarchy now. This slyly worked into my plan, though, as increased pressure from the UPF could potentially be enough to convince the King that it was finally time to fight back. We were not there yet. Operation Blackout was needed before we could even consider a real political fight, no matter how popular Julia was becoming.

Social media had lost its mind, with videos of the debate going viral, and polls, before they were taken down by censors, showed overwhelming agreement with her. Various reformers had banded together in recent days to create a group named "The Fracture," inspired by the metaphorical fracture in the Prism that allowed the Whites to remain unfiltered. Popular accounts within this new group had begun hinting that Julia needed to enter the political sphere in some form: be it as the future queen, in the assembly, or some other leadership position. The movement was growing, now we just needed a catalyst to escalate its spread.

Chapter 46

Weeks passed as we plunged headfirst into winter, and Julia turned her public focus towards shifting the opinion of the average people, the Yellows and Oranges, through the occasional TV and radio appearances on top of Q&A's and live videos via social media. She had to be careful supporting the protestors, but she did everything she could indirectly. While minds were not overly difficult to sway, people lived in fear of being arrested or moved down a color if they spoke up against the UPF. They were people with families, homes, and jobs. Despite their struggles, not everyone was willing to risk everything they had to change things.

In private, as well, Julia whispered about the movement among the Whites, especially with her father. Some among the royalty were surprisingly receptive, though more because they wanted the monarchy's power restored than because they cared about destroying the Prism. Regardless of their motivations, though, we needed the power of the royals if we wanted to make progress.

The UPF was watching Julia with interest. She had quickly become a sharp thorn in their side as the informal face of the reform movement but had her family's immunities. The UPF would be taking a major political risk if they acted against her. The monarchy was the Prism's weak point, and we intended to exploit it as much as possible. Even my plan didn't account for the massive following she had obtained among the Reds and Oranges.

Her more public status changed how she could move throughout the Twin Cities. In addition to the usual little girls, she now had political supporters carrying homemade Fracture flyers with her face on them and chasing her down for a picture and an autograph. Julia had risen from the cute, quiet third-born princess to a political idol, and it was rough for her at first. While she was outgoing and charismatic, she enjoyed her space at times and struggled to adapt to the constant attention and pressure. More than once I had to push people away as she became overwhelmed.

Not everyone was supportive, though, and the negative pressure had begun to creep into her head. Many of her friends beyond her closest ones had become more distant in the recent weeks. Many Whites, Purples, and Blues felt calls for reform were an attack on their way of life and that there was a reason the Oranges and Reds were the colors that they were. She couldn't please everyone, despite the fact she took a more moderate position than the Militia and acted diplomatically. Sometimes we even had to bring a couple of royal guards along with us as extra protection from the occasional heckler or someone trying to get in her face. She was brave, but it was a dangerous position for her to be in, and I felt responsible for it.

While busy with this political outreach, Julia also used her connections throughout the city along with her new, yet to be opened, orphanage to assist in the relocation of Reds. Our system for shuttling Reds around the city undetected had been effective, and because of her, we had successfully hidden thousands throughout the Twin Cities: both Militia and not. It was an accomplishment, but it was temporary, and we needed to move quickly; it would only be a matter of time before the secret police discovered many of them.

During this period, I decided that more frequent trips to the Enclave were worth the risk. We were in the final stage of preparation for Operation Blackout, and El Capitan had called one final meeting ahead of the operation itself.

The Twin Cities based lieutenants and agents gathered with El Capitan around the pool table in the war room, and our out-of-town lieutenants listened in over our radio system. In front of us were the blueprints for the four UPF security stations. There was one for each target city: St. Paul, Minneapolis, Milwaukee, and Des Moines.

El Capitan ran his hand through his red beard and pointed at each blueprint, giving each squad its tactical instructions. We had gone over them a dozen times, but the plan needed to be executed to perfection. In two days, it would be all or nothing.

When he finished with the squad-specific instructions, he stood up straighter and spoke to us all, "It is crucial that we deliver the virus into each security station. If we don't, they'll keep their cameras and systems up in that district, and all of this will have been for nothing. Zeus and I have everything in position for alpha squad in St. Paul." He looked towards one of the radios. "Husky, how are beta squad's preparations in Des Moines?"

Husky's voice crackled through the radio. "UPF activity has increased in the area recently, but we will be ready. The rifles and flash drives arrived yesterday."

El Capitan nodded. "Good. Caesar?"

"Charlie squad is finalizing preparations in Milwaukee. We had some difficulties finding a van but have an exchange scheduled for tonight. We'll make sure it's ready in time."

El Capitan examined the Milwaukee blueprint for a moment. "Make sure that thing gets reinforced. The last thing we need is y'all getting shot up in the van."

"Affirmative, captain."

I took a deep breath as El Capitan paced to the Minneapolis blueprint and looked up at me. "Coyote, how's delta squad?"

I crossed my arms. "Preparations have been slow, with the effort to relocate people taking priority, but we are almost there, thanks to Poseidon and Delaware." I smiled at my mentor and my mentee, both to my right. He nodded, and she grinned. "Aaron is holding the ammunition for me to transport to the Longfellow safehouse. I'll have that finished tonight."

El Capitan sighed. "Make sure it gets done, Coyote. Minneapolis is the heart of their power. We can't afford to cut corners." I nodded, and he continued, speaking to everyone as he walked around the room, "If each squad executes the plan, in two days, we will have dealt a massive blow to the UPF's power, blinding them. This will be our biggest step yet towards freeing ourselves from the Prism, and it will be because of the work of all of you."

Silence hung over the room as he finished, standing in front of the table. A looked of pride crept over his face as he looked each of us in the eye. He paused when his eyes met mine. I nodded to him. "The eye goes blind."

He nodded. "You're all dismissed. Good luck to you all."

Poseidon put a hand on my shoulder. "Let's take a walk."

I followed him out of HQ and down a side route near the entrance. I kicked some of the rocks along the path. "Am I doing the right thing, Poseidon?"

My mentor stuck his hands in his pocket and sighed. "Many of the more aggressive agents have questioned your actions. They think you're too close with the monarchy."

I looked into the night and thought for a moment. "And what do you think?"

He gazed at the stars. "I think that you've found another way to fix things, and they're too blind to see that there's more than one way to skin a cat. It's impossible to know whether it's the *right* thing, but if there's one thing I've learned in my years, Coyote, it's that in a place like this, opportunities to do something meaningful don't come every day. You've been given a position where you might be able to change things without guns and bombs. You'd be an idiot to not at least try."

I took a deep breath. "But what if I have to choose between the Militia and the allies I've made among the royals?"

He smiled. "I don't think it's that simple. Princess Julia has had an impact because of you. Don't let a mask come between you and what you think is right. The Militia needs Coyote, but soon, the world may need Ivan."

I stopped walking and thought about that for a moment. *I've missed these talks.* "I think it might be time, soon, for Delaware to take over my position. She's ready."

Poseidon chuckled and pulled out a half-finished cigarette, lighting it as he thought. "That girl is tougher than you and me combined. She's ready. Hell, she'll be our best lieutenant if Snapback doesn't distract her too much." He took a puff and blew out the smoke. "You've done well with her, son."

"Thanks, Poseidon. I appreciate it." I looked around at the buildings. "So much has changed so quickly. It's crazy to think this place will be abandoned soon."

He took another puff of his cigarette. "They've tried to kill us time and time again, yet here we are. If this is finally our time, at least we're going out with a *bang*."

I shook my head. "I'm not going to let that happen."

He blew out a puff of smoke. "Sometimes, you don't have a choice."

Chapter 47

Julia and I watched the news coverage of her most recent statements in her room, and, of course, the state-run media was spinning the story to claim she was an out-of-touch monarchist who wanted to "reverse the last century of progress." We knew that we could never control the traditional media, but her appearances had been crucial to making the arguments, allowing people to draw their own conclusions, even if she was so often drowned out by the propaganda. Unfortunately, the UPF had quietly banned her from appearing on television anymore in an attempt to quell the outrage.

Julia laid across the couch in her room, her legs over my lap as she watched, scowling at the TV. "It's all lies, and so many people don't see any of it. I didn't know about the reality of it until I met you. There's so much ignorance, reinforced by the media."

I shook my head. "It's disgusting, but they haven't censored you enough." I raised up my newly acquired cell phone. "This is the most powerful tool in the world, and they still can't handle it, no matter how many people they try to arrest. Even the new social media bans haven't worked."

The UPF had finally had enough of the reformers' messages spreading across social media and, following Julia's verbal showdown with the General, attempted to cut off the country from social media. Within hours of the cutoffs, though, hackers had found a way around the block, and newer, underground and uncensored networks had begun to gain prominence. People were angry at how they'd been lied to and lost the privacies they believed that they had in addition to the base discontent around the Prism itself. For the first time, a significant number of the Yellows and most Oranges finally were beginning to see why the Reds were fighting so hard for change.

She looked down. "I hate seeing so many people in jail because of what I started."

I rubbed her legs in reassurance. "You didn't start this, but you gave the people a voice. The arrests are only making your arguments stronger, and besides, when they arrest and kill people, they lose even more support. We have them on the hook. The only way to prevent more deaths and arrests is to move forward with the plan. Operation Blackout is tonight, so now we have the catalyst and the pressure; it's time to execute."

She groaned. "Do you think it'll actually work?"

I bit my cheek. "Yes. It has to."

"And if it doesn't?"

"Then I'll be dead, so I won't have anything to worry about."

She curled in her legs and held them defensively, her eyes drooped and lost. Without her saying anything, I knew what she was thinking. *That was too much.* I wished I could reassure her, but at the moment, I couldn't even convince myself that everything would be fine. It was unfair to her. She had enough to worry about without me reminding her that I could die. She'd seen the scars: she knew the risk.

I lowered my head solemnly. "I'm sorry. It's just... facing death is too normal of an occurrence to me. I forget this is still new to you." Dread sunk into me. These missions were normal for me, so why was I worried about this one all of a sudden? We had trained and prepared for this for over a year, yet all I could think about was the risk of it, heading into the heavily guarded snake pit.

She looked up at me, wounded. Her hands shook, and she pursed her lips. When she spoke, it was cold and direct, "You don't get to just run into my life, take my heart, and then die, Ivan. Do you know what it felt like for me when you were gone to get that journal or climbing between buildings attacking rapists, or when I saw you barely alive with your skull beaten in?"

A chill went down my spine as I searched for a response, but I had nothing. She was right, of course. I acted too often without much regard for the consequences or what the risk meant for my life, or hers. It was unnatural for me to have someone outside of the Militia worried about me. In all my realizations about how much I needed her and how I couldn't lose her, I selfishly missed an important part of love: *She needs me too.* My death would tear a hole in her heart.

I struggled to meet her eyes. She continued. "I don't know what I would do if something happened to you while I sat here in this marble prison. Sometimes, it seems like I value your life more than you do."

I bit my lip, ashamed that I had unknowingly hurt her and that she had waited so long to tell me. "You... you're right." I looked at her softly. "I never thought what it would be like for you. My whole life, I've never had anyone to come back home to, until now. I'm so sorry, Julia. I didn't realize... Please forgive me."

Her eyes met mine as she analyzed my face sorrowfully. "Tell me it is going to be okay."

I slid behind her, wrapping my arms around her. Our breaths fell in sync as she calmed slowly. "It will be okay. I will be safe, I promise. We have planned for every possible scenario, and none of those involve me leaving the bravest and most amazing woman I know alone in the world."

She whispered, "Promise?"

I pulled her tight to me and kissed the back of her head. "I promise. I love you more than anything or anyone in this world, and I will come back to you every time, no matter what."

There was a soft series of knocks at the door. *Don't make me get up.* I comfortably held Julia on the couch, feeling her long breaths and calm heartbeat through my chest. It was the best feeling in the world, a rare moment of intimate privacy with the woman I loved. I did not appreciate it being interrupted. I sighed and kissed her on the cheek as I rose. "I'll get it."

She smiled softly. "Thanks, Ivan."

I assumed the visitor to be either Michael or a guard. My assumption was wrong. Instead, Princess Helena stood at the door, her face questioning why I was there and not her sister. Helena's oblong face showed her English genes from her father more than her older sisters, who resembled their mother. She was only fifteen, but she liked to shadow her older sisters, learning every step of the way. Despite her age, she let her opinion be known, though, she knew her place as the youngest princess. On a "properness" scale from Natasha to Alexandria, she was close to the former, having studied her oldest sister's perfectionism. Her wide eyes narrowed. "Is Julia in?"

I nodded and opened the door wide, stepping back for her to enter. "She is, m'lady."

Helena smiled softly at her older sister and straightened her knee-length coral dress before sitting properly across from her. Julia sat up, returning the warmness. "Good morning, Helena. How are you?"

Aware of Helena's dedication to the rules, I stood near the door at attention. Julia looked at me before turning her attention back to her youngest sister, whose eyes looked upon Julia with admiration. She really did look up to her older sisters... except Alex. Julia was really the only one in the family who got along with the rebel sister. Julia took that respect seriously and tried to be an example, though Helena didn't approve of her little rebellions. It was tough to be the youngest. She wanted to do her best and, well, matter. With her sixteenth birthday rapidly approaching, she was nervous about her non-royal friends, who were about to pass through the Prism. *It's not an easy time.*

Even if passing through the Prism was more of a celebration than a test for the Purples and Blues, there was always the occasional failure, followed by a lonely life as a stain on their family's spotless reputations. For many, that was too much to bear, and suicide rates were tragically high among those whose color was lower than their parents'. There was no support for those struggling post-Prism, except in groups like the Militia where the entire idea of the Prism was rejected. When you lived your entire life groomed for one thing, only to fail, it was hard to find purpose. *So many lives lost because of a stupid test.*

Helena's voice was proper, even when talking to her sister, though it lacked Michael's condescending tone. "I am well. Though, mother and I are worried about you."

Julia fiddled with her family ring and stuck her tongue in her cheek. We both knew why Helena was there already. "I appreciate the concern, but I am fine. The protestors have been annoying, but what I'm doing is important, Hel. Anyways, if *mother* is concerned with things, she can tell me herself." *She can sting with that wit.*

Helena clicked her tongue, thinking intently as her sister exposed their mother's ruse. "Mother believes you're raising popular support to challenge Natasha."

Julia crossed her legs and ran her hands along her dark jeans, her eyes studying her sister. "What do you think?"

She hesitated. "I don't know."

"You shouldn't listen to mom all the time. She's using you as part of her game."

"You have yet to answer the question."

Julia laughed sarcastically. "No, sometimes there is more to life than the throne, Helena. Is Natasha worried? If she bothered to talk to me, she would realize that I respect her and dad's wishes, and, unless something changes, I have no plan to actively pursue the throne and am unaware of any support among the electors."

She's wrong about that last part. Natasha was seen as the passive and safe choice, but unlike many of the presumed heirs of the past, she really hadn't established herself outside of her father's shadow; she was a proper princess but not a leader in many royals' eyes. As the oldest, though, she likely still had the backing of most of the electors, but some were looking for another option. Julia's independence and diplomatic demeanor had resulted in some whispers in support of her.

The royal electors, consisting of the adult members of all royal houses, met following the death of a ruler. Any royal could be nominated to be the next King or Queen, but traditionally the first nomination was always the oldest child of the previous ruler, if they had one. The winner only needed a simple majority of the vote, with more rounds of voting taking place, if required, as the lowest ranking nominee was eliminated. There hadn't been a contested election since the foundation of Northern Mississippi, though, as Timothy Hughes II and III were elected unanimously. Ironically, this system made the monarchy the most republican part of our government, even if only the royals could vote.

Helena's eyes softened. "I am glad to hear it. The last thing we need is more divide in this family with Duke Bilgram becoming more aggressive and the Preus family seeking revenge."

Bilgram had been set back slightly with my discoveries at the opening of *The Cherry Orchard.* I felt my temple where his ring had struck my skull. The physical mark had faded, but mentally, that bastard slave trader had bruised me and was on the top of my list, right next to the General Secretary. The Preus family, on the other hand, was a wild card. They were like snakes in the grass, pouncing when you least expected it.

Julia's eyes narrowed. The Queen obviously had sent Helena to press Julia harder about the throne, but this seemed like the more important topic. "They have been more openly hostile recently. Why do you bring them up?" *She knows.*

Helena ran her hands along her pleated dress, thinking, before giving her sister a slight smile. "Mother believes your... outspoken... statements are drawing too much attention. Those opposed to reform are aligning themselves with Bilgram, and your resistance to Isaac has Wilhelm enraged." *There it is.*

Julia bit her cheek and shook her head. She coughed and sarcastically smiled at her younger sister. "And let me guess, *mother* wants her daughter who isn't in line for the throne to stop causing problems for the one that is."

"Mother wishes for you to refrain from speaking about politics for the time being."

Julia scoffed. "I thought you were on my side. You said that you wanted reforms."

"We all do, except Duke Bilgram's faction. Your ideas are too radical, though, and are a threat to the family. You know that our family is the most important thing, right?"

While the opposition to some of our more ambitious ideas was not welcome, hearing that the rest of the family did quietly support some reforms was a positive. *We can use that.* One step in the right direction was better than war, though it needed to be a big step.

Julia pursed her narrow lips, her eyes ice cold. "Is it? Is it really? Because I'm not happy or content sitting here in the palace as thousands of people starve while the incompetent UPF elites use the Prism to their advantage. Imagine if you didn't have that ring to protect you and instead were out there." She pointed into the distance, beyond the royal territory. "And if the family supports reforms, why haven't we talked about it instead of mom sending you as a veiled threat? If we are a family, aren't we supposed to support each other?"

"You may be right, Julia, and we should talk, all of us. Request that father call a family meeting on the topic. Though, anything they agree to may require you to be more reserved."

Julia nodded. "Thank you, Helena. I will consider it. Is that all?"

Her sister softly nodded her head and stood. "Yes. Thank you for listening. I hope you can see that mother simply wants the best for all of us."

Says the girl that hasn't been forced into a betrothal. She is too young and innocent to see the bigger picture.

She left, and Julia followed her to the door before looking at me, her voice soft but her eyes stern. "You better go get ready. Do this job, Ivan, so Coyote can be finished."

Finished. That word hung in my mind. "Are you going to be okay?"

She nodded. "Call me when you're safe. Don't worry about the gala tonight. It's in our ballroom. I will survive one night without your protection."

Chapter 48

The van lurched as we turned another corner. I gripped my rifle through my gloves, trying to focus as we bounced down the road. I shook my head. *Did they forget to install the suspension?* Taking a deep breath, I laid my head back and shut my eyes. *You're going to live. You promised you'd live. Just remember to tell that to the guys shooting at you.*

My earpiece buzzed as El Capitan's staticky voice came through. "Alpha squad is parked and in position. St. Paul ready. Status check."

Husky was next. "Beta squad is pulling in now. Coast is clear in Des Moines."

Then Caesar. "Charlie squad locked and loaded. Milwaukee is all quiet."

My turn. "Delta squad is behind schedule. We took a precautionary reroute around some patrol cars. E-T-A five minutes in Minneapolis."

El Capitan returned. "Roger that, Coyote. Keep us updated. We can't sit here forever. Out."

I looked at the other occupants of the van, half from Poseidon's team and half from mine. Each squad had a dozen members, all of us with the same flash drive containing the virus. *Only one has to survive.* Looking around the van, though, I decided that was not how this was going to work. The mission would be accomplished if only one of us got to the control room, but I would have failed if that happened.

Delaware met my gaze, her eyes full of worry above her bandana printed with the blue flag of Delaware. I was proud of her. She ran multiple missions while I was gone, all but one of them successful, and even with the failure there were no losses. My greatest mistake had become one of my greatest successes. Things were different between us now that she knew, but I did not regret telling her. She deserved to know the truth and could move forward now that she did.

"You good, Del?"

Her leg was shaking. "Yup." *Liar.*

"I've got your back. We've got this."

She took a deep breath. "I hope."

"We've worked years for this. It is all about to pay off. This is the start of something new. Believe it."

She unconvincingly nodded her head and looked down.

Razor sat to her left, his green eyes cold and focused. He had grown up a lot in the last few months, no longer the shaky kid who dislocated his shoulder flopping off a roof. There was something else I couldn't put my finger on.

I reached out my fist. "You ready?"

He bumped it softly. "Born ready."

I looked through the rest of the faces in the van. Each of us was ready to die for what we believed in so that this terrible world could change. Poseidon and I's eyes made contact, teacher and student. While he had seniority, Poseidon had decided that this was to be my squad; he was past his prime when it came to mission execution. As the van pulled into the alleyway, he nodded to me. *It's time. My turn.*

I sighed and stood, pacing through the van and looking at each individual on the squad. They were my responsibility, and I wanted to see each of them here afterwards. "Tonight, we show those UPF bastards that no chains are going to hold us down. This is our first step towards the destruction of the Prism and the UPF. We have worked years for this moment, this catalyst. Let's go show those Purple bastards what red looks like!" I radioed to El Capitan. "Delta squad is in position. The eye goes blind tonight."

"Roger that, Coyote. All teams roll out."

My heart pounded through my chest, and I hesitated before throwing open the van's sliding door. "Let's go, boys and girls." I pulled my bandana over my face and nodded to Delaware before stepping into the cold winter air.

The wind whistled through the buildings and a light flurry obscured our vision as we crept along the side of the white brick alleyway. The street was dark, the new moon providing little light. We had picked this night carefully; they wouldn't see us coming.

Across the street was the downtown Minneapolis UPF security station, its black glass exterior blending into the night. We had to reach the control room on the third floor, where they watched and analyzed the footage from the cameras.

Peaking my head around the corner, I checked the street for cars. "Hold." I raised my arm, signaling them to stop as a patrol car passed the alleyway, and I held my breath. *Please don't see us.*

The patrol car slowed, and my heart sunk as it began to turn. I readied my rifle and waited, but the car turned down the next street over. A puff of fog appeared in front of me as I let out my breath and lowered my rifle. "Clear. Let's move."

As we approached the front door, El Capitan came over the radio. "Alpha squad is ready for smoke. Status check."

"Beta squad ready."

"Charlie squad ready."

I looked around. *We've got this.* "Delta squad ready."

"Deploy smoke and breach. Good luck, everyone."

I nodded to Blitzkrieg and Pennsylvania, who each took a smoke grenade and prepared the toss while Atom and Wolf, both members of Poseidon's team, opened the doors. "Now!"

The world froze for a second as they popped the smoke and readied the throw. I breathed slowly, preparing myself for the chaos we were about to release, within the security station and beyond. *A silent night no more.* The Prism was fractured already. *Time to expand the crack.*

Smoke flew through the air and filled the lobby as a few of the guards called out. We burst forward, and a loud *crash* surrounded us as we broke through the doors and started firing, moving into positions behind columns and furniture.

Piercing through the smoke and sliding into the front desk, I peeked around the corner, unable to see effectively through the haze, though there was a sharp cough behind the desk. I aimed towards where the sound came from and fired three shots, the noise of the rifle joining the chorus of gunfire around me and making my ears ring. I heard a soft *thud* nearby. *Got him.*

As our fire died down, I called out. "Center is clear. Flanks?"

Snapback called from the left. "All clear."

Poseidon coughed before calling back. "Clear. Atom was grazed, but we will be alright." *Why are there so few guards?*

"Be careful, but be quick. We need to get to the back staircase. Let's move!"

I vaulted over the desk and scanned the area with my iron sights as a wide black hallway stretched in front of us with off-shoots in every direction. I led the way slowly and signaled for each of the halls to be checked for guards. An eerie quiet filled the hall as we advanced with only the scuffling of our boots echoing around us. A chain of *clears* came from each offshoot. *Something is wrong.* Raising my fist, I yelled, "Hold! Somethings off." I moved forward ahead of all but the last offshoot and towards the stairs at the end of the hall, my gun raised and prepared for anything. My stomach was doing flips. Something wasn't right, but I didn't know what to do about it. "Posei…"

Suddenly, in one swift series, around twenty guards appeared at the end of the hall followed by a wave of bullets, the noise of a harsh alarm, some screams behind me, and then a soft *ting*, as a cannister rolled in front of me. *No, no, no, no!* I shouted, "Flashba…" and a bright flash cut me off, blinding me.

Something you don't realize when your vision just goes like that is how the world instantly seems massive and small at the same time. I was a few feet from an offshoot to my left but diving towards it could have sent me into a wall or flopping in the middle of the open floor. I was claustrophobic in a large area. *Do something. You're a sitting duck.* "Get to cover!" I rolled towards where I thought the offshoot was and crawled, scrambling desperately for the wall as a stream of bullets whizzed over my head. *I'm going to die blind.*

The world was spinning in my head, but I couldn't see any of it as I rolled, disoriented. Suddenly, someone grabbed me, yelling and pulling. My senses were overwhelmed, and I couldn't understand who it was or what they were saying. *What a great leader I am, becoming useless right when the fight starts.* Someone screamed from somewhere to my right. *Was that one of us?* My heart was racing. I needed my vision back, or I was going to die. *Why was the first floor so clear until now? Were they waiting for us?*

Delaware's voice finally began to come through next to me as the drums of war echoed through the tight hall. "Coyote? Coyote! Look at me! Coyote! We need to move!"

My vision was slowly returning, blurry and inconsistent. The smell of gunpowder and death filled the air and my hearing was still damaged. *What have I done?* I responded shakily, trying to be confident but was completely disoriented. "Del... Del, I can't see. Give me a second." I shook my head and my vision cleared to see Delaware and Snapback standing over me. Struggling to my feet, I pointed. "Tell Poseidon to lay down covering fire as Snap and I move closer and flank them."

Delaware nodded and ran off, barking orders. Snapback looked me in the eye. "Indigo is down. Alive, but she can't move."

Shit. I surveyed the situation. Our squad was huddled around corners and some overturned furniture while the armored guards moved slowly down the hall. I had to reach the next off-shoot just across the hall so that we could hit them from every angle. "Tell Atom to stay behind with Indigo until we get back."

He nodded and ran off, relaying the information before returning to my side, breathing hard nervously.

Putting my arm on his shoulder, I looked him in the eye. "Ready, Snap?"

He took a shaky breath. "Ready."

"Let's do this." I signaled to Poseidon, and the bullets rained as I slid across the hall, firing a few shots of my own as Snapback crouched behind me. *Don't shoot me in the front... don't shoot me in the back...* A bullet whizzed past my ear as I arrived. *Missed by that much.*

We were outnumbered and outgunned, as the guards pinned us back with shotgun and submachine gun fire. The noise was deafening. At least a dozen of them remained, and they were advancing despite our better defensive positions.

A few seconds behind, Snapback reached my side, his eyes wild in fear. The kid was a rebel, not a soldier. You never got comfortable with that much gunfire, but this was completely new to him.

Guards yelled for a second, followed by a massive *bang*. My ears rang again as a blast knocked me backwards off my feet. A body flew into the opening next to me on the ground. Struggling to my feet, I cleared the debris from me eyes, trying to figure out who it was and what just happened.

When I got a clear view of the body my heart sunk. *Indigo. Shit. We couldn't save her.* Screams echoed from around the corner and as I stood, I saw the horror that the grenade had caused in such a small space. Two more from our squad were dead, as Atom and Pennsylvania's bodies laid as mangled crimson messes in the middle of the hall. *No, no, no, no...*

Turning back into the offshoot and closing my eyes, I took a shaky breath. *Stay focused. Mourn later. If they shake you, they win.* Closing my mind to the noises and smells, I spun, aimed around the corner and fired off a few shots, hitting at least two guards before returning behind cover. There was nothing I enjoyed about shooting these men who were just doing their jobs, even if it was a terrible job, but it was kill or be killed in this tight space. We weren't done with even the first floor and everything hurt, but I needed to lead on. "Forward! Let's move."

The squad moved slowly, exchanging fire with the remaining half-a-dozen guards. The smell of gunpowder and the endless noise of shots being fired was overwhelming, and my head throbbed. A yell came from my left as Blitzkrieg dropped to the floor, motionless, crimson flowing from his chest. *No! Damn it.* Snap cried out from around the corner, but we couldn't reach Blitzkrieg yet, his body sprawled out in the open.

I clenched my jaw. Four deaths on our side. *There is no going back now. We have to finish the job.*

Yelling, I turned the corner and picked off the guard across the aisle before creeping along the side and grabbing one more, throwing him to the ground, and knocking him out with a kick to his head. *Saved one life. Maybe I should count those instead.*

Snapback yelled and shot the last guard before running to Blitzkrieg's side, desperately trying to bring him back to life to no avail. He just lost his best friend. I couldn't imagine what I would

284

have done if that had been Delaware.

I looked back over the hall, the black floor and walls covered in crimson. The alarm the only sound as it eerily echoed through the death pit behind us. *We're doing this, so this never happens again. Keep going.* "Delaware, grab Snap, and let's go. There'll be time to mourn later."

We approached the stairwell and Caesar's voice came over the radio. "Package has been delivered. We're pinned down on our way out though, and I've lost seven. Someone tipped them off." *Something is wrong.*

Husky followed. "We're approaching the control room now. Agh! I've been hit, and we've lost five. They definitely knew we were coming."

I coughed through the overwhelming haze of gunpowder hanging in the air. "Delta squad is approaching the stairs now. They had us pinned down on the first floor. We've lost four."

We waited for El Capitan's response, but it didn't come. I put my finger to my ear. "Captain? Come in El Capitan."

A blast of static hit my ear. "We got it, but they know. They know. They're coming... Ah!" Silence. I closed my eyes, fighting back the emotion. *He's gone. Damn it. What do we do now?*

I looked around at my squad, their faces tired and worried. I hardened my face before radioing back. "We've got to finish the job. Make him proud."

Delaware came over. "Everything okay?"

"We need to keep moving. If they knew we were coming, then reinforcements will be here soon."

She looked skeptical, knowing that I wasn't telling her something. *It would crush them.*

Signaling Poseidon, I whispered to him what the situation was. He deserved to know; Zeus was with El Capitan, so things looked grim for his brother.

My mentor nodded, pondering for a second and running his hand through his wise beard. *How do you comfort someone after that without making a scene?* He cleared his throat and replaced the magazine in his rifle emphatically. He spoke with tears in his eyes, "They've taken everything... time to return the favor."

I nodded, understanding. "We'll make them pay, Poseidon."

The stairs and most of the third floor were eerily clear. It looked like a ghost town that was abandoned in the middle of a work day. Coffee cups sat on desks and screens flickered in the empty offices and cubicles around the floor. I raised my hand to stop everyone. "Stay focused. This could be a trap. The control room is ahead on the left. Wolf and Checkers, check the door."

As the rest of the squad continued scanning the other offices, we turned the corner and reached the thick steel security door blocking us from the control room. As the two moved to place the breaching charges I watched our surroundings but couldn't see any threats. My stomach lurched like it knew something that I didn't. *This is a trap.* They set the breaching charge as I reached out yelling, "Stop!" just as the door blew open.

Chapter 49

The explosion seared my skin. I had barely enough time to cover my face as I was blown backwards into the wall. The world was spinning as I clutched at my recovering head that felt like it was on fire. *How?* I wanted to vomit, and everything hurt. *I knew it, damn it. I knew it. Why did we keep going?* Tears filled my eyes as I tried to wipe away the debris. My ears rang, and the alarm sounded like a distant echo.

In front of me was a massive hole and the remains of Wolf and Checkers, their bodies charred beyond recognition. *Two more deaths on me. Why? Who sold us out?*

I closed my eyes and groaned; people were yelling, but I couldn't hear any of it through my ringing ears. *Let me go.* A few shots went off, followed by more shouting and someone shaking me. I looked up to see Razor's sharp green eyes looking down at me. "You've gotta get up, Coyote. We're almost there."

Coughing, I took his arm and struggled to my feet. I was definitely feeling the blast, and a rib was either broken or at least badly bruised, but I was alive. *Lucky me.* Poseidon, Delaware, Falcon, and Snapback had cleared the control room while I followed. Razor took the rear.

Screens were everywhere: peoples' homes, streets, computer screens, everything was on them. Rage filled me. These bastards had killed six of my friends in the last fifteen minutes and oppressed millions of people for a century. We were making the sacrifice for the greater good, or at least, I hoped we were. *It has to be for something.*

I stepped through the rubble from the bomb and approached the central terminal, passing Delaware's eager eyes and leaning my rifle against a nearby desk. Everything felt like shit, but we had done it. We were about to take down all the cameras and spying infrastructure in Minneapolis. *Blind them.* I radioed to the others. "Delta squad has arrived. The door was rigged to blow. We've lost six. You guys there?"

Husky came in, wheezing. "Only four of us made it out, but we got the flash drive in. Whoever ratted us out is going to get a bullet to the head."

Silence followed. I called in. "Caesar, you there? Caesar?" Nothing. *Shit. All of us did it, but whoever the rat was will pay.* "It's just the two of us, Husky. I'll let you know when we're out."

Husky was solemn. "Roger, Coyote."

Time slowed as I pulled the flash drive from my pocket and stepped up to the terminal. *So much power in such a little thing.* As I pressed it into the slot, the world exploded in gunfire as people screamed. Hitting the floor, I dropped the flash drive and failed to grab my pistol as it slid away. I scanned the room trying to figure out what was happening, but I couldn't see the attacker through my blurred vision. Delaware and Snapback were hidden behind a nearby desk, both bleeding. Poseidon's body was sprawled in the middle of the floor, unmoving. *No! Why?*

I scrambled for my gun, but it was kicked away at the last second. I looked up at Razor's cold green stare, his rifle aimed at my head. Anger boiled inside of me. *Traitor!* I glared at him. "Why'd you do it?"

He spat at me. "Isaac sends his regards, Ivan."

My mind was on fire, scattered between the deaths and Razor's betrayal. Why would he do this? Unless... *the eyes.* "You're a Preus?"

"Otto Preus." I knew Razor had been adopted, but never knew why. He was a spy, and the first we hadn't caught.

I looked up at the barrel of the gun. *I'm sorry, Julia. I know I promised.* "You're just as much of a snake as your bastard brother. You went through all of this work just to kill me? Do it."

"This wasn't about you, it was about all of this. Killing El Capitan, stopping Operation Blackout. That's why I passed the information to the UPF. They're raiding all the safehouses right now. After what you did to Isaac, though, killing you just became a beautiful side goal." *The safehouses... the UPF will kill everyone...*

"So what? You kill me, stop the operation, and destroy the Militia. What does your family get out of this?"

He laughed, a young but menacing one. "My brother and parents are seeing to that right now. You see, Ivan, when the Hughes family made their deal with the People's Front, they knocked us to an inferior position. Ever since, we've been a joke to them. All they worry about is the Bilgrams while we have plotted their demise in the shadows. This little deal with the UPF will earn us their good faith as we seize the throne; they won't protect the King or his family... and neither will you."

The gala. They're going to kill the royal family. Julia. How did I miss this? My mind scrambled for a way out of the situation. I had to get back to Julia before they killed her. Nothing else mattered, but that meant I needed to live. The thing about Razor was that he was a clumsy fighter. If I could get the gun out of his hands, I was home free. I looked over to Delaware and Snapback, who were struggling but still alive.

Razor followed my gaze and I took the chance, grabbing the barrel of the gun and throwing him off balance. I jumped to my feet, still holding the gun, now vertical between us. "Your mistake was going after her, you bastard."

He glared at me and struggled for the gun. "That's prince bastard to you."

I swept his leg, and he fell roughly onto the floor as the gun slid away. Stepping over him, I bent down, grabbed his fake black tag, and ripped it out of his ear before holding it in front of his face as he screamed in pain. "You don't deserve this." My anger took over as I reached for my pistol and held it to his head, my voice and hands shaking with emotion. "You killed Poseidon, El Capitan, Zeus, Blitzkrieg... you killed all of them, you piece of shit!"

His cold stare was unwavering. "It was worth it."

My hand shook. I took a breath as the two voices in my head screamed at me: Coyote told me to do it, and Ivan told me to bring him into custody so he could be used against Isaac.

Razor laughed mechanically. "Do it. Or are you too scared of what Julia will think?"

I took a deep breath and tightened my finger around the trigger, a million thoughts of rage filling my head. *He deserves it.* At the last second, I reactivated the safety, tossed the gun aside, and wailed on him in rage until he was knocked out. I turned to Delaware and Snapback, helping them both up. "You guys alright?"

Delaware looked up at me and groaned. "We'll live, but you need to get to the palace, now!"

I gripped the sides of my head in a panic. "What about the safehouses? They're going to kill everyone."

She shook her head. "There's nothing we can do. You need to save Julia! We'll watch the snake and figure out a way out of here. Don't worry about us."

I shook my head and reluctantly agreed. "Fine." I reached down and grabbed my flash drive off the floor. "But first things first." The screens flickered as I inserted the drive into the mainframe, and one by one, they made a *pop* noise and went blank. *It's done.*

I tried to call Julia, but it went to voicemail. *Damn it. I don't have time.*

"Coyote to HQ. Is anyone there?" No answer. "HQ?" *No, no, no.* "Husky, you there?"

"What's going on, Coyote? I'm not hearing anything from headquarters."

"One of ours, Razor, was the snake. He took out most of us, but the job is done, and he is unconscious, but he gave up the locations of our safehouses."

"No..."

"Razor let it slip when he thought he had me that he is a Preus, and they are attempting a coup of the royal family. I need to save them. I don't know if we can save any of the safehouses, but relay the message to whoever you can."

"Holy shit. Go. I'll do what I can."

"Thank you. Coyote out." I turned to Delaware. "You two going to be okay getting out of here?"

She looked at me in a panic. "Go Coyote. Save her. We'll get out of here alright."

I nodded to them and walked over to Poseidon's body for a second. He died, shot in the back by a traitor. *He deserved better, but he died a hero.* I shut his eyes and just knelt there by his side for a moment. Poseidon was the closest thing I had to a father, and now he was gone. My mind was a mix of panic, sorrow, and rage; I didn't know which emotion to pick.

I stood and surveyed the room before looking back down at him. My voice shook as I whispered to him, "Bye, dad. I'm sorry." Taking a deep breath, I grabbed my guns and ran back to the van. *Please be alive.*

Chapter 50

The golden palace gates were already open. The guardsmen were slumped over the booth, a bullet hole in both of
their heads. *Shit.* My heart was racing, and my hands
shook violently as I drove, skidding into the driveway. *If he kills
her...*

I flung open the main doors and my heart sunk. Bodies were
everywhere: blue uniformed royal guardsmen and black-clad
Preus mercenaries either dead or dying. I sighed, and searched
quickly through the halls, looking for Jonah. *Please be alive.* As I
was about to give up my search, I heard a gun cock behind me.
"Don't move."

Slowly, I turned around to see him and smiled, not that he
could see it through the bandana. "Jonah! Just the guard I was
looking for!"

He lowered his gun and raised his eyebrow. "Ivan?"

"Yeah, I'll explain the whole disguise thing later. We have to get
to the ballroom."

He grabbed my arm as I turned. "There's no way we can get in
there. The halls are patrolled, there's a couple mercenaries at the
ballroom door, and Isaac and Wilhelm have more in the room
with them."

"Then what do you think we should do?"

He looked down. "I don't know. That's why I was hiding and

hoping some of the other guards were alive, too. The only reason I'm alive is that they didn't come for the servants' wing, where I was stationed."

"You're a genius." He looked confused. "The servants. There are tons of guns laying around here. Arm anyone alive and willing, and then wait for me outside the ballroom. When you hear me yell, 'I am not alone,' storm the place."

"I don't know…"

"Got a better idea? No? Okay, just get them ready."

He nodded, and I turned, sprinting through the halls towards the ballroom, each step echoing like a chorus in the empty marble halls. The wounded guards still alive were shocked when they saw Coyote running by, not that they were in any state to stop me. I had no time to change, and my identity was the least of my concerns at the moment. There were too many bodies for my stomach to handle. I'd seen enough death already today.

As I neared the ballroom, I slid to the corner and looked around it. Two Preus mercenaries were stationed in front of the ballroom door, though not very attentively. I took a deep breath, *stay alive*, and turned the corner, taking out the first guard with two shots and the second with one to the head before either had the time to draw their weapon. The shots echoed through the halls. *So much for stealth.*

Slowly, I approached the ballroom doors. Taking a deep breath, I readied my gun and pushed open the door with my foot, entering the quiet ballroom. Whites stood huddled along the sides of the room, pressing themselves like pancakes against the windows and walls in fear as five mercenaries on each side waved guns at them, keeping them in place. The floor was covered in chandelier pieces, broken wine glasses, bullet shells, and more bodies. *They didn't come in peace. This has to end.*

At the head of the ballroom stood Isaac and his father, Wilhelm Preus. The royal family knelt in a line facing me, and my eyes met Julia's as she shook in fear. I tried to give her a reassuring look, but it was hard, given the gravity of the situation. *Stay strong.*

Isaac's sharp green eyes stared at me across the room, realizing what my presence meant. A purple tag had been added to his ear following his expulsion from the royalty. *What a downgrade.* He waved his pistol and spoke, his voice raspy and cold, "Look who it is everyone! The terrorist that just returned from killing my brother. How'd you do it, *Coyote*?"

Stepping towards him slowly as if on thin ice, I raised my rifle, pointing at his head. "Your brother betrayed my trust and killed my friends. He held a gun to my head. You know what? I let him live anyway. Not all of us are snakes like you."

His brow furrowed, and he pointed the gun wildly. "Liar! You killed him."

I pulled out my radio, still holding the gun in my other hand and inching closer. "You want to hear him? He is alive, Isaac. If he stays that way is up to you."

He spat with disgust. "You're not exactly in a position to negotiate."

"I pull this trigger, you die. You kill me, he dies. Your father becomes an heirless and hated king. Sounds like I have plenty to negotiate on."

All I wanted to do was check on Julia again, but I feared taking my gun away from his head for a moment would mean my death. I wondered what the rest of her family thought, seeing a renowned terrorist in the ballroom trying to protect them. *Oh, the irony.*

Isaac laughed manically and grabbed Julia, standing her up next to him. He put an arm around her waist, holding her and pointing the gun to her head. "Alright, *Coyote.* But how about you show everyone who you really are?"

Rage filled me, and I shook, my voice sharp as my knives. *She will not die, but he will.* "I will kill you."

Isaac shoved the gun into the side of her head as she winced. He was stern. "Take off the mask."

Time seemed to slow, and my heart stopped. *Coyote or Ivan. Only one can live. The dream. Damn it.* Tears filled me eyes as I aimed. *There's no Coyote without Ivan. Is there Ivan without Coyote? One shot...* Fear flooded Julia's face, and I knew I didn't have a choice. If I killed him, the mercenaries would kill all the royals anyway before I could do anything. "Don't you dare!"

He started counting. "Three...two..."

"Stop... stop! I'll do it." I reached with my off hand, ripping off my bandana and throwing it to the floor before quickly returning the hand to my gun. "My name is Ivan 181375, and I am the Coyote."

A slight gasp came over the crowd, and the King raged. "You bloody terrorist!"

I responded, not taking my aim away from Isaac as I inched forward, "I'm trying to save your life right now, your highness." *How long do I stall for? I didn't really plan this out.*

Isaac didn't remove the gun from her head. "Well done, Ivan. You've killed half of yourself trying to save the woman you love…" Another gasp came from the royals, followed by murmuring and incoherent yelling from the King and Queen. Isaac fired the pistol into the ceiling and marble dust rained down upon us. "Shut up! Shut up! All of you!" He pointed it at me, scowling and still holding onto Julia. "Stop moving closer."

I stopped moving. "Wilhelm, is this how you raised your son to behave, how you want to take the throne?"

He stepped forward, a pistol of his own in his hand, and pointed it at the King's head, flicking off the safety with a sharp *click*. His eyes and voice were sharp like his son's. "You have much to learn about the game that is royalty, my boy."

Now I was stuck. If I shot Wilhelm, Isaac would shoot me, and Isaac would live on to kill the rest of the Hughes family, not caring about his brother for an heir. If I shot Isaac, Wilhelm would kill the King and take the crown by force. *Do I have to choose the King or Julia?* "Shoot the King and both of your sons die. I don't like killing normally, but this will bring me great joy after everything your family has done."

He waved his hand. "Seize his weapon."

A mercenary approached me from behind. *Give in? Nope.* I spun around, pulling my sleeve's knife and stabbing his neck before he could raise the gun. Taking a deep breath and spinning back towards the front, I looked at Julia. "Remember what I taught you?"

She stuttered, failing to respond, but nodded.

Wilhelm raised his voice. "Drop the gun, or I shoot."

This better work. Please be ready, Jonah. Slowly, I lowered my rifle to the ground, and as I set it down, I looked up at Julia. "Now! I am not alone!"

Thankfully, she understood what I meant, and everything seemed to move in slow motion as she drove her heel into Isaac's instep, knocking him off balance before smoothly punching him and pulling his gun from his hands. With the distraction, I quickly pulled my pistol and took a deep breath before firing three times at Wilhelm. The shots sounded like a cannon in the marble room. His body whipped backwards onto the floor as one bullet struck him in the chest and another hit him in the side as the third whizzed by his head. *Thank God.*

Behind me, the doors burst open as Jonah led the armed servants into the ballroom, firing at the mercenaries, who turned just in time to see the bullets flying towards them. The room filled with gunfire as I turned back towards Julia, who shakily held Isaac at gunpoint, his eyes full of shock. She looked at me, lost. *She's never held a gun before.* I raised my gun. "It's over, Isa…"

BANG! A sharp shot to my right interrupted me and I turned to see where it came from. *No…* Wilhelm struggled to his feet, bleeding but alive, standing over the King's crumpled body. The Queen wailed and scrambled to hold his lifeless corpse in her arms as the daughters could only watch in horror. Wilhelm lifted his gun towards me, his arm shaking as his body fought against the two bullets within, his snake-ring finger wrapped around the trigger as his mercenaries slowly fell before his eyes. He spoke weakly, "Don't you get it, Ivan? You're helping the corrupt family that tagged your ancestors and threw mine to the gutter. You can't destroy the Prism by saving those who helped create it."

No. No. Damn it. Julia had been shaking, but this broke her courage, and the gun slipped from her hand. I watched, distraught, as the gun hovered between her hand and the ground. *This ends now... Isaac or Wilhelm?* I yelled, rage flowing through my body as I raised my pistol towards Isaac and pulled the trigger again and again until his body was slumped on the ground. He took their father, so I took his son. Julia screamed in shock, her hands covering her mouth, as his body fell in front of her. *I'm sorry.*

Wilhelm yelled and shot wildly towards me with his shaking hand, missing with all but one bullet, which struck me in the left arm.

I cried out and raised my gun towards him. "It's over Wilhelm."

Wilhelm looked at his son, the defeated mercenaries, and the dead King at his feet, his rage replaced by shock. He had killed the King, but he had also lost everything. *Kill him.* My arm shook as I aimed at his head. *Just one shot...*

Taking a deep breath and lowering my gun, I whispered to myself, "No." He deserved to die for what he had done but suffering through the rest of his life in prison, knowing that he was the reason his son was dead, that was a far greater punishment.

As Jonah and the servants finished freeing the trapped Whites and closed in around Wilhelm, the snake dropped his gun in defeat. The rest of the royal family joined the Queen at the fallen King's side, and I just stood, lost, as Julia's face filled with agony and tears streamed down her cheeks, her eyes fixed upon her dad's body. *I couldn't save him, but I could save her.*

Jonah hobbled towards me as one of the kitchen chefs shoved

Wilhelm to his knees. He looked at me in silence and gave me a brotherly hug. I returned it but couldn't figure out what to say. Words could not express what we had just done, and all I could muster out was a "thank you."

He released me from the hug, smiled, and patted my shoulders. "You did this, *Coyote*. We were just the back-up."

I looked at my bandana, sitting in the midst of death and carnage, before returning my gaze to Jonah's face and shaking my head. "Coyote is dead." I turned my head towards Julia. "I'm only Ivan now."

Jonah followed my gaze. "Is she..."

I knew what he was about to say. "Yes."

He nodded understandingly. "Go. She needs you."

As he headed towards Wilhelm, I stumbled over to Julia and knelt over her father's body. Her eyes flowed like a river as I wrapped her in my arms. My own tears began as I started to grasp what just happened. We just sat in silence, mourning the death of the King and so many others as the shocked royals gathered around us. She looked up at me for a second and our tear-filled eyes met before breaking back towards her fallen father.

Is this my fault? Isaac had become unhinged after he found out what I did, but his family obviously had larger plans of revenge. Everything had fallen apart so quickly. Operation Blackout didn't matter when I was watching a maniac put a gun to the head of the woman I loved. That was the first kill that I didn't feel bad about, and with Coyote gone, I hoped it to be my last. Coyote's death meant nothing if Julia could live. I couldn't save the King, but I could save his family and as many royals as possible. So many of them had spat at me and mocked me for the last few months, but none of it mattered in that moment. When it came to it, they were helpless as yet another tyrant decided he wanted to take something that wasn't his. It didn't matter who Wilhelm was, he would pay for what he did.

Everything was about to change. The UPF had lost almost all of its cameras and electronic surveillance systems, but that would just make them more ruthless; the real fight was still to come. We had so far avoided a war, but with the King dead and the monarchy on shaky footing, things looked bleak. There would be repercussions, and my name was public now. I would be a target, even more than before. Coyote may have been dead, but Ivan inherited his sins.

As I looked down at the King, I thought about what he had accidentally done for me. His last words were raging about my secret identity and relationship with Julia, but he had opened the door for me to be where I was, saving the rest of his family. With his death, there would need to be a new monarch, and after that night, nobody had a clue who it would be. The third most powerful royal family had almost conducted a successful coup through cooperation with the UPF, the Militia had lost its potential ally on the throne, and most, if not all, of the Hughs' guards were dead. Though the royal army was larger than that, it showed the Hughes family's weakness. Vultures would be circling, and Duke Bilgram's coalition remained a known threat. Unfortunately, the Preus family had remained an unknown one until the last second. Would there be others?

Miles away, another leader had fallen. We had lost El Capitan and so many others because of what Razor had done. We would make sure he paid for it. We were without a captain after our greatest mission yet. The Militia had lost so many in the UPF raids that night, and I didn't know how many of us were left. On top of that, we were now connected with the monarchy, further complicating the entangling alliances in Northern Mississippi. The few lieutenants still alive would want to stake their claim on the captaincy while our remaining forces scattered, fleeing from the safehouse raids.

As tonight had shown, everything was intertwined. The Prism was fractured but so was the world of glass in which we knelt, and I wondered how long we had until those fractures shattered everything around us.

Us. Julia laid her head on my shoulder, her tears running onto my jacket as we knelt. In one night, she had a gun put to her head, saw her boyfriend kill multiple people, and saw her father die. We had both lost our fathers, and a part of ourselves died with them. There was nothing I could say to change what happened, nothing to fix it. It felt like forever as I held her there, the cracks stretching beneath our feet.

END OF BOOK ONE

The Story Continues:

A Word From The Author

Thank you for taking the time to read my first book! I hope you have enjoyed reading it as much as I have enjoyed writing it. If you did, please consider giving it an honest review online.

To stay updated on my writing for the series, receive more insights into the world of The Prism Files, and have the chance to win free books, sign-up to receive my newsletter at: www.Brendan-Noble.com